MADNESS

A YOUNG DECAY NOVEL

Jack Whitney

Copyright © 2023 Jack Whitney, Jack Whitney Writer, LLC

Cover Artist: Pru Schuyler

Editor: Emily McClung @busybookreporter

Chapter Art: Jack Whitney (Images from Adobe Stock and Unsplash)

Band Logo: Rae - @waesmileart

All rights reserved.

All rights reserved. No part of this book may be reproduced, scanned, or distributed in any printed or electronic form without permission. Please do not participate in or encourage piracy of copyrighted materials in violation of the author's rights.

This is a work of fiction. Names, places, characters, events, and incidents are the product and depiction of the author's wild imagination, and are completely fictitious. Any resemblance to actual persons, living or dead, events or establishments is purely coincidental.

For everyone who **music saved**.

For everyone who was told it was **'just a phase.'**
For the ones who **hid their demons.**
For the kids who **'no one knew what to do with.'**
For those who screamed **in silence** because you didn't
want to be a bother to anyone else.

And for those now **befriending** those demons and giving
them the **understanding** they deserve.

This is for you.

WARNINGS

MADNESS is an adult, rockstar dark romance.
It is therefore not intended for persons under the legal age of 18.

The following are the **triggers** to be
made aware of in this book:

Graphic depictions of assault, domestic abuse, death, stories of childhood abuse, past trauma, suicide, self-harm, as well as explicit sex scenes including breath play, masks, and bondage.

No sexual acts within this book are in any way meant to be a guide to exploring sexual fantasies or give suggestion.

This is a work of fiction.
If you are curious about any acts, please do your own research, be safe, and remember aftercare.

MADNESS:
The Official Playlist

Welcome to the Black Parade My Chemical Romance

The Kill
Thirty Seconds to Mars

Fall
Pallisades

Jaws
Sleep Token

BREATHING UNDERWATER
Hot Milk

Just Pretend
Bad Omens

Perfect
Simple Plan

Be Somebody
Thousand Foot Krutch

Closer
Nine Inch Nails

Without You
Breaking Benjamin

Chokehold
Sleep Token

Popular Monster
Falling In Reverse

sTraNgeRs
Bring Me The Horizon

Bleed It Out
Linkin Park

Hold On Loosely
38 Special

*Maddox's Comfort Playlist & Concert Hype List
linked within pages*

*"I could conquer the world with one hand,
as long as you're holding the other."*

**- Jack Skellington,
Nightmare Before Christmas**

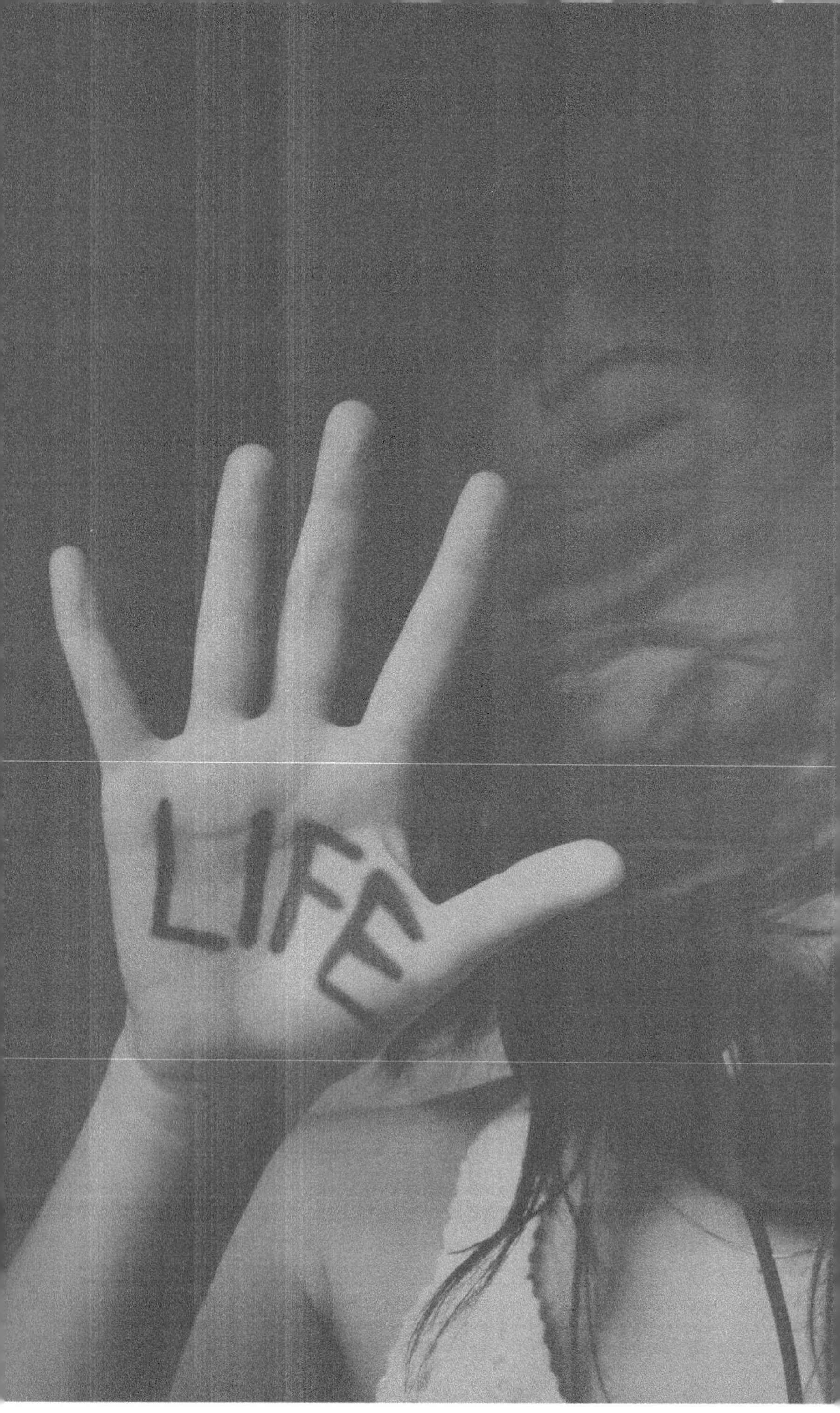
LIFE

CHAPTER ONE
ANDI

A guitarist is singing at the street crossing outside the high-rise building where I work.

I feel bad for him standing out there, singing his heart out in the hopes that one of the record execs might hear and think he deserves a shot at fame. What's even more is that he's actually pretty cute, and were he already famous on some social media site, one of these headhunters might have picked him up by now.

Despite the fact that I'm running late for my meeting with the big boss, I pause beside him.

"They hate this, you know," I say to him.

His smile widens, blue eyes seeming to gleam my way. "I know," he replies.

"So why are you doing it?" I ask.

He shrugs and plays louder, still smiling beneath his beard. "You never know when today might be different."

It's a cute sentiment. Nevertheless, as I look past his shoulder, I know someone upstairs doesn't feel the same way. "Tell the cops that."

"Shit." He throws his guitar around his back, snaps his open case shut, and then, with a grin at me, he bolts down the sidewalk through the throngs of people.

I start my music back up and let it play through the

headphones around my neck, just loud enough to hear it as the cops dart by after him.

I kind of hope he comes back tomorrow.

Inside the building is the lobby of Dead Tower Records. I have to smile as I pass through it. It's probably one of the only high-rise buildings with a lobby decorated for Halloween. It's the only holiday our CEO celebrates, and she tends to go all out.

She even has the elevators fashioned to look like old hotel lifts.

It'll all be wiped out overnight on November 1st, though, and we'll return to our everyday decor of signed records on the walls.

I wave to the security guard, Jessie, who's behind the front desk, smiling at me. He points to his hair, and I know he's referring to my freshly colored strands.

"New color?" Jessie asks.

"Thought I would try a violent plum for the holidays," I reply.

"I like it," he says. "Do you have plans?"

I scoff and point to the elevator. "I don't. All the same, something tells me Cynda has plans for me."

Jessie raises his brows, amusement in his eyes as if he knows something. With a look around us, he leans over the counter and jerks his chin to motion me closer.

"What's up?" I ask when I lean in.

"I hear your brother's band is sans photog for their homecoming run next weekend," he says, and I feel my expression sour.

God fucking dammit.

"Well, that makes perfect sense," I mutter.

Jessie chuckles. "I thought this would be good news," he says. "Thought you could sweep in and grab the gig. It's Young Decay, after all. Pretty big assignment."

I'm fully aware of just how popular my half-brother's band has gotten over the last five years. He and his friend, Maddox, started out in our old garage back in high school, only finding two others to join them during their freshman year in college. And since then…

"Thanks for the heads-up, Jessie," I say, tapping twice on the counter. "I'll let you know what Cynda says."

As I push through the security check toward the elevators, I glance to my left, where a photo of Young Decay is, along with a framing of their first gold record after signing with Dead Tower. As usual, I give the record two subtle pats before filing in line for the elevator.

The mere thought of going home has my insides twisting. I shouldn't get myself worked up. For all I know, Cynda wants to assign me to photograph more indie bands down at The Hole.

The elevator dings, and I file in along with a slew of others, barely dodging the elbows of a few when they hoist their heavy bags up on their shoulders.

It isn't that I don't want the job. I would love to have an assignment as important as this one.

Even still. Going home…

"Andi!"

A familiar voice calls my name from the other side of the doors, and I see my co-worker, Mya, waving frantically at me. I launch forward through two guys and slam my hand on the inside of the doors to stop it so she can shove inside.

"Thanks for that," she says once she's on. "Tough crowd this morning. Fucking Mondays."

"Fucking Mondays," I say with the same sentiment.

She pulls her earbud out and glances sideways at me. "Wait, I thought you were meeting Cynda at nine," she asks.

I look down at my phone to check the time. "Yeah, so did I," I mutter. "Dropped my coffee cup and had to change clothes," I say. "Maybe she's in a forgiving mood."

Mya laughs, her silky black waves falling over her shoulder. "She'll probably forgive you since you're wearing a tee with her favorite movie on it."

I look down at the distressed t-shirt with the movie poster for The Lost Boys on it—a shirt I wore on purpose in the hopes that Cynda will forget about how late I am.

"Oh—did you hear? Jodi got kicked off the Young Decay job," Mya asks.

Must be the gossip of the morning.

"Ah, I heard the job was vacant," I reply.

"Apparently, she was harassing their bodyguard. To think, four sexy musicians in front of you, and you go after the bodyguard instead."

"Maybe she has a type," I say.

Mya nudges me playfully. "Do you think that's the assignment Cynda wants you to pick up?"

I may as well go home and pack my fucking bags.

I know she's right.

Mya laughs as if the reluctance is written on my face. "What's wrong? Isn't that your brother's band?"

"Half-brother," I correct her.

"Half-brother, whatever." The elevator door opens, and we step out onto our floor.

The name of the public relations brand of Dead Tower that we work for is spread across the back of the wall behind the front desk.

Heartless Muse.

"That would be fun," Mya continues. "I mean, think about it. You get to go home, see family, and hang out with the hottest band on the radio right now. Maybe get us a picture of the elusive Mads Tourning while you're there," she adds with a suggestive brow.

I almost laugh. We're at the end of our hall, and I have to

go left to see our boss.

"I don't think any of us are that lucky," I say. "See you for lunch?"

"Yeah. I'm thinking Thai," she replies.

"See you then."

The hall to my boss's office is lined with signed set lists and candid photos of several bands. Her office is glass, and I can see her on her walking pad as she answers morning emails.

Addie, her assistant, smirks at me when I pause in front of her desk. She taps twice on her phone to find out the time. "Six minutes?" she says, referring to how late I am.

"Considering I only found out that I needed to come in to meet her because of a text from you at four AM, I think six minutes can be excused," I tell her. "I was in the building at nine. You can ask Jessie," I counter, and she laughs.

"Sorry about the short notice," Addie says. "Did you hear what happened?"

"Jodi?"

Addie slides her laptop over and leans forward. "Decay's bodyguard, James, called Cynda around midnight asking for a replacement photographer for the rest of the tour. He said Jodi was sneaking onto the tour bus and trying to catch Mads without his mask."

Mads…

Mads Tourning, Young Decay's bassist, as he's known to the rest of the world. To me, he's just Maddox Keynes. My brother's charming and annoyingly hot best friend.

He's never been photographed without his skeletal neck gaiter mask on.

I scoff. *She's lucky Mads didn't break her camera*, is what I want to say, perfectly picturing him breaking it in half and smiling in her face without his mask while he was doing it just to be a dick.

Even so, I know he likes to portray a certain persona to the rest of the world, so instead, I just say, "Oh," while raising my brows.

Addie smiles crookedly and opens her laptop again. "It was *bad*," she adds. "Jodi says someone higher up asked her to get the photo because a tabloid is offering some ridiculous amount of money for it."

For a photo of Mads?

"That's insane," I reply, disgusted by the idea.

"I've been here since five with Cynda trying to figure this out," Addie goes on. "She's tried calling the band's manager and talking to the guys upstairs. However, they're all telling her she needs to find someone safe. The band is talking about canceling the tour over it."

"Shut up," I exclaim.

Though, it didn't surprise me. I know Mads prefers his privacy, and if there's any sort of threat to him, Reed will lose his mind over it.

"It's *wild*," Addie says as she reaches for the phone. She hits two buttons and presses the receiver to her ear, and I see Cynda answer on the other side of the glass.

"She's here… Yep. Yeah, I'll send her in." Addie hangs up as Cynda pauses her walking pad and steps off, the brunette finally looking in my direction. She gives me a small smile and waves, both of which make me squint at her.

Cynda isn't exactly a smiling-waving kind of person. She's more of a 'stab you in the artery with her heel while stepping on your neck' sort of person, and that's one of the things I love about working for her. She doesn't deal with bullshit.

She must be fucking desperate.

I'm still wearing that wary face when I open the door, and Cynda scoffs.

"I'm assuming you heard," she says as she sorts through a few papers on her standing desk.

"I—"

"You know, you just can't find the right people for this job anymore," Cynda cuts me off, her eyes cast down. "Everyone is looking to make an extra buck. No one has any dignity or pride about the people they're covering." She finally looks up and gives me an annoyed, flat stare, and I smirk at her.

"I was going to ask what happened to your face, but I see you've fixed it," I say.

Her lips curl upward in the slightest manner, and she pushes her dark brown hair back. "Was it that bad?" she asks.

"It was terrifying," I reply.

A snort of amusement leaves her. "Andi, you've worked for me, what? Ten years now?"

"Fresh out of college," I reply.

"You've always had a good eye and even temper for this industry. Tell me why I don't have you on tour with one of our larger clients?"

"I like indie gigs," I reply as I take a seat on her dark green couch.

"Do you know what I think you like?"

"What's that, Cyn?"

"I think that *you* think you're forgettable," Cynda says. "And so, it's easier to remain anonymous. One night with each band. Less complicated when you don't get to know them."

I suck my tongue between my teeth, my mouth twisting as I stare at her. My entire body tenses beneath her assumption, and I resist walking out of the room.

"What, are you my fucking therapist today?" I ask.

"My point is," Cynda goes on. "When I found out what Jodi had done and the reaction Young Decay—*rightfully*—had, I started going through my list of more trustworthy photographers to send back on tour with them. Someone I could trust not to take a fat check in exchange for a photo of their most private band member. And then I realized... who better than the lead singer's sister."

Her head tilts when she looks at me, and I realize what she's asking.

"Wait—" I hop to my feet, hands up defensively. "You want me to take over the whole gig? The entire rest of the tour?"

"Well, yeah," she replies. "What did you think I was asking?"

"I don't... I don't know. *Definitely* not that."

No. *No, no, no* —

"Reed and I would kill each other," I tell her.

"You'll hardly see him," she argues.

"Except every minute of the day," I say, knowing how close and personal the firm liked us to get.

"Then, at least do the homecoming run for me," Cynda practically begs. "Please, Andi. I don't have time to vet someone new when they have press beginning this weekend."

"Press?" I ask.

"Mostly radio interviews. A couple of magazines will also be hanging around the theater next week. Before the show on Thursday, they have a small interview with the radio station sponsoring the weekend event. I need you there by this Saturday. Reed and Mads will be heading over to the station for a small promo on their lunch hour."

Fucking hell.

I huff and press my hands to my hips.

There's absolutely no way I can handle six months on the road—internationally, at that—with my brother. Even the thought of going home for a week has bile rising in my throat.

It's been three years since I was home, and that was only for a day. My palms start to itch, the bottoms of my feet sweating as memories that I've been trying to run from invade my mind.

"Pay is triple your usual," she adds, and my eyes lift to hers.

"Triple?"

I need to hear her repeat it.

"I went upstairs to my boss and reworked the numbers for you after I realized you might only agree to two weeks," she goes on. "Hotel and meals paid for. Rental car. We'll pay for your flight… Overtime, bonus weekends… Plus, triple your usual gig rate."

How the hell was I supposed to turn that down?

Cynda smirks. "Not a bad rate for getting to go home and spend some time with family, is it?"

Family…

I want to tell her to fuck off, but dammit. I could actually put this in savings. Get ahead on a few things.

It's just two weeks.

Two weeks.

I tap my foot on the floor for a moment before replying.

"I will do the homecoming run," I concede. "You can find someone else for the rest of the tour. Close quarters with Reed for six months would never work. I love my brother, but he would be a protective asshole and threaten to throttle anyone who I might flirt with—or even smile at, for that matter."

"As if you would be any different," Cynda mutters.

"I mean, no. You're not wrong," I reply, knowing how many people I'd turned away from him.

Cynda grins. "Spoken like a true sibling," she says. "Very well. I'll find someone to start in November. Two weeks gives me enough time to vet a few candidates. I'll have payroll go ahead and send you an advance for your plane ticket and hotel."

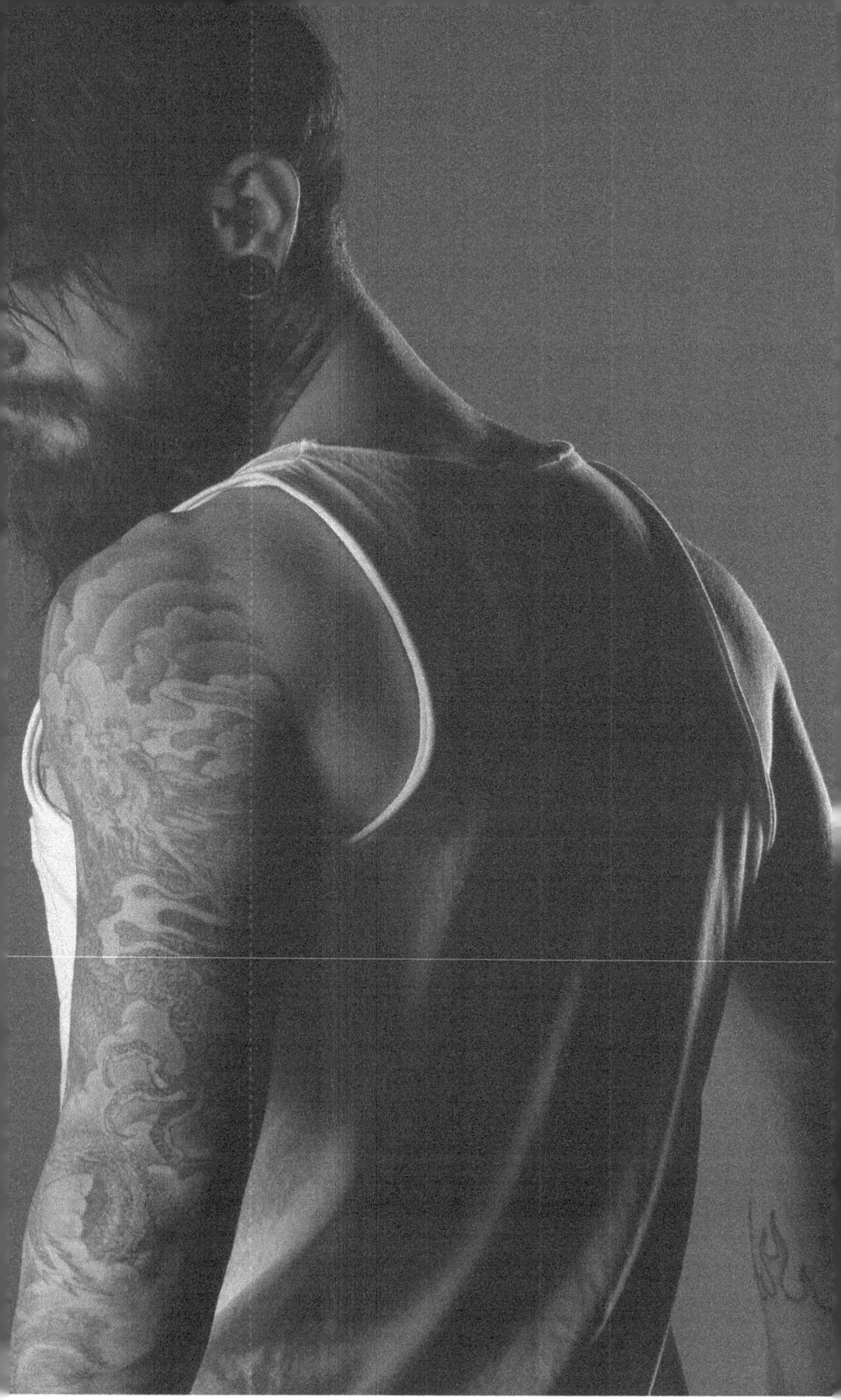

CHAPTER TWO
MADDOX

The screams of adoring fans echo off every wall in the theater.

I strum the last chord and peer at the crowd as Reed jumps onto one of the speakers at the edge of the stage, his long, tattooed arms extended as if he's the only true god in this room.

And as he holds his microphone out to the audience, every single person sings the lyrics to our most popular release back to us.

I'll never get tired of this.

I'll never tire of the euphoria and disbelief that people know our music—*love* our fucking music.

The glee runs through my veins and kicks into every muscle, forcing me to shift on my feet as our drummer, Bonnie, begins counting back the break.

I laugh at the insanity of it all.

It's unreal.

Reed, our lead singer, and my best friend, turns toward me as the crowd continues singing, and he grins my way.

How the hell are we, two poor, sad bastards from the back streets of North Carolina, *here*? How are we standing on the stage at the Tabernacle Theater in Atlanta, Georgia, with a sold-out show—a sold-out *tour*?

Reed can't see me grinning back at him behind my mask. I wave him the horns in front of my bass before strumming a chord.

Bonnie is on her third four-count.

The notes amp up the horde. The strobe lights flicker. Smoke strokes over the stage in billows of anticipatory thrill. Tension rises between us and the crowd as if they know what's coming. Like they know the drop will send the entire theater into a frenzy.

I love this fucking part.

Zeb, our guitarist, plays the leading notes.

And as the fans erupt and we strike into the chorus once more, Reed jumps into the crowd.

He lands on a throng of people ready to surf him through—and he makes it look easy, too. He's never been afraid of the mob, getting brought down, or even breaking a bone. All he gives a damn about is singing that fucking chorus in the middle of the crowd and giving them a show they'll remember.

I have one eye on him at all times.

Always.

The crowd practically screams the chorus back to him as he steps and crawls from person to person. Fans grab onto his hands, his legs, his shirt. It's halfway ripped off him in the five seconds since his landing.

I see venue security in the space between the stage and the barrier trying to get to him, and I laugh. Some hadn't believed us before the show when we told them Reed was chaos onstage and that they'd get their workouts trying to catch him.

The poor bastards.

Our regular security, James, is already in the crowd. He has one hand on Reed's shirt—even if he knows Reed might rip it off and run away.

Reed doesn't give a fuck about security telling him what he can and can't do.

This is his forum. His church.

In this room, for two hours, he's the priest leading you to a salvation that only music can give.

Or at least, that's what music has always been for me.

It's the only thing that fucking saved me.

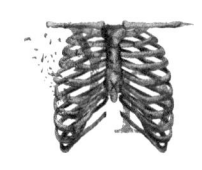

After the show, everything is a blur.

It's *always* a blur.

Coming down from that high is never a steady, gradual slope. It can be a crash, especially on nights like tonight when we don't get to breathe.

We have to be at the airport by two AM, leaving us only enough time to pack up our shit from the dressing room, sign a few autographs out back, and get in the car.

What makes it worse is that tonight, we were rushed out for nothing.

Our first flight was canceled, and now we're waiting on the next.

The voice over the airport intercom is so muffled that Zeb removes his shirt from his face to squint at me.

"Did you get any of that?" he asks.

"Not a fucking word," I reply. "Would have been faster to drive at this point," I add.

"No fucking kidding," Zeb grunts.

He lets his head bang back against the glass and pulls his

black hat down instead, revealing the tattoos on the side of his head and the strip of coarse black curls he had been hiding. He's wearing his glasses for this trip, something he only does when he knows his contacts will get dried out and itchy.

I turn sideways in my seat again and continue scrolling through my phone. The music in my headphones is a playlist of emo and metal bands we grew up listening to—a comfort I've always leaned into and one that influenced Young Decay's sound.

Social media is a bore as I move through the pictures. I wish I had packed my book in my backpack. My eyes might have hated me for squinting at the words. At the same time, learning the ending of the mystery novel I'm halfway through would have been worth it.

It's now six AM. We've sat at this terminal for hours, hiding in plain sight with hats, scarves, and glasses on in the hopes that we'll be left to our privacy. Our manager, Avie, suggested the VIP lounge like usual.

I think our last experience there scarred us forever.

We were videoed and harassed by a creep who thought he could sell the glasses and napkins we'd used, even going as far as going behind the bar and stealing them from the bartender. Security had arrested him quickly. Even still, it had us freaked out.

And honestly, we liked feeling normal once in a while.

Reed managed to be the only one of us spotted by a fan on his way to the restroom tonight, though the guy hadn't followed him back over.

Reed had signed a coaster for him for his discretion.

"Hey—"

My head pops up, Zeb takes down his hat, and we both look over to see our bodyguard, James, standing a few feet away. He jerks his chin toward the gate. "Let's go."

I shove Reed, who's lying across the seats asleep next to me. Reed snorts and flinches, surprisingly catching himself before tumbling onto the ground where Bonnie is lying.

"Hm—what? The fuck, man—"

I nod toward James, who's standing stoic at the end of the aisle, and Reed shakes his shaggy black hair out of his wide blue eyes.

"Time?" Reed asks him.

"Yeah," James replies. "Let's get a move on."

It's a smaller plane, and we're the last ones on. Something about James having to do a secure check of every passenger. I don't know.

I just go where they tell me to.

Reed and I are sitting in the front row. He's so fucking tall that he has to have the leg room, even if First Class in this plane seems to have a decent amount. He lets me have the window seat for this flight, and I shove my backpack under my seat as the attendant comes around.

"Oh shit," Reed grunts, his phone out and staring at a text on the screen.

"What's up?" I ask.

"Just got another text from Andi," he replies. "She said she decided to stay at the house instead of the hotel like she originally planned."

Andi…

Andersyn Matthews, Reed's older sister.

The mere mention of her weaves my stomach into knots. I've had a crush on her for ages, dating back to when Reed and I first met in grade school. She's five years older than us. Though, she's never treated us like kids. Maybe that's why I wrote poem after poem for her in high school and never gave them to her.

I haven't seen her in five years.

Except for her social media photos.

I follow her on my personal account, and each time she comes across the feed, those familiar butterflies swarm my insides.

I'm not sure whether to be excited or not about her staying at the house during this show run. Reed said she's going to be our photographer for the week until PR finds a suitable replacement. I thought I would just see her at practice and maybe flirt a little. Nothing serious because I know better than to fuck with Reed's sister.

Though now…

Mother fucker.

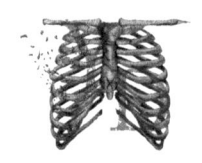

After James drops Zeb and Bonnie off at the hotel, he drives Reed and me into the suburbs where the house we bought his parents is.

"Are you sure it's okay with your mom if I'm there?" I ask, remembering the last time we'd been home.

"She's never turned you away before," Reed replies. "Pretty sure she loves you more than me."

I chuckle under my breath as we turn onto the road.

The neighborhood is a far cry from where we grew up. It was the very first thing Reed and I knew we had to do when we made a little money.

Get his parents out of the house that held too many fucked up memories for all of us.

James pulls into the long, u-shaped drive in front of the two-story farmhouse, and nerves quake through me. Not just because of seeing Reed's mom again after basically telling her to fuck off the last time I'd been there, but because standing on the threshold of the home is the most stunning woman I've ever seen.

Gods.

Fucking.

Damn.

How has she grown even sexier in the last five years?

I can't even open my door for how pointedly I'm staring at her.

Andi is leaning against the doorframe, her dark purple waves over her left shoulder, the right side still undercut with a small braid where her part would have been. She's wearing a slouchy green sweater and black shorts that show off her thick legs.

Reed swings open his door and greets her with a hug that sends her off-kilter. I hear her laugh, see her smile at her half-brother, and then punch his shoulder.

The mere sight of her within reaching distance has my palms itching.

James clears his throat.

"You getting out, or do you want me to take you to the hotel?" James asks as he starts pulling our luggage out of the back.

"I'm going," I reply.

I get out of the car and stretch around to the other side, where Reed and Andi are still chatting, and when her eyes move to me, she seems to falter. I try to keep my cool by stuffing my tatted hands in the pockets of my jean jacket. However, she's already sizing me up, watching me with those doe brown eyes as if she's surprised to see me.

"Maddox," she says, her voice almost breathy, and I know I'm a fucking goner.

I love the way she says my full name. She's always used it. She rarely calls me Mads like everyone else.

"Wow, you…" Her brows raise when she looks me over again. I can't help it when I feel a small smile rise on my lips.

She's looking at me.

For fucking once, *she's* looking at *me*.

She clears her throat quickly, and her gaze darts to Reed. "I thought the rest of the band were staying at the hotel," she asks him.

I chuckle. "Guess that's my cue to leave," I say, only halfway joking.

Because maybe it would be wiser for me not to stay here.

"What—*no*," she says fast, and I arch a brow in response to her practically throwing the word out there.

"Don't worry. He can stay in the pool house," Reed tells her.

"Tina said you were staying in the pool house," she says as Reed pushes past her. "I'm pretty sure she stocked the fridge and bought you new underwear."

He pauses to frown at his half-sister. "Where are you staying?"

"Over the garage," she answers.

"So, what's wrong with my room?" Reed asks.

There's a spot in a tree past Reed's shoulder that Andi's eyes fixate on, and she doesn't respond for a beat.

"Ah, well…"

Determination and confusion swell in Reed's eyes, and he dashes through the door toward the kitchen. "Mom—"

"She isn't here," Andi calls to him.

"What? Where is she?" Reed asks.

"She went to pick up Kamden and Koen from the airport," she answers.

"Ah, fuck. Those little bastards are coming home, too?" Reed asks.

"It's a Matthews family reunion," she says sarcastically. "And Kamden is only four years younger than you. If anyone should be complaining, it's me. Once again, sharing a house with four disgusting teens."

"We're adults," Reed says.

She looks like she might laugh, hands pressed firmly on her hips. "Are you, though?"

Reed gives her a dull look and starts upstairs to the bedroom he'd once claimed.

Andi shakes her head before turning her attention to me again. "God, he hasn't changed any," she says. A glitter of a smile lifts in those pools of brown, and all I can think as she stares at me is how fucking beautiful those eyes would look peering up at me as her lips wrap around my—

"Maddox fucking Keynes," she drawls. "You look…" Her brows raise as her eyes drift over me for the third time, and this time, she swallows before stepping into the doorway. "Are you coming in?" she asks, drawing me away from a perfectly good fantasy.

"Am I invited?" I ask, and a smile flinches on her bow-shaped lips.

She chuckles softly. "You may as well be a Matthews, too," she replies. She jerks her head toward the living room. "I suppose you can crash in the pool house."

I smile broadly and hold out my arms, hoping to god she doesn't realize I want to hug her out of some deep-seated desperation to have her near me.

"Hey, beautiful," I say to her.

She beams, and the way she lights up with that little word makes me restless.

"Maddox," she says before entering my embrace.

I breathe her in and linger in that hug for longer than I should.

If this is the only chance I get to touch her this week, I'm taking it.

And, god, the smell of her hair…

She smells like warm spices, and… is that orange?

I wonder if she tastes this good, too.

A crash sounds upstairs, and we part at the noise of it.

Fucking Reed.

"That'll be him throwing out the exercise equipment," she mutters. Her gaze drifts over me again, those dark eyes seeming to take in the sight of me as if she's trying to find a secret she knows I'm hiding.

"Come on," she says. "I'll help you take your stuff to the pool house."

She grabs my bass before I can tell her I have it, and something about her carrying it away through the kitchen makes my mouth dry.

She isn't yours to take, I remind myself.

I follow her through the back sliding door, finding the cover pulled over the pool for the season. There are a few more fallen leaves on the surrounding deck, and as much as I try to turn my attention away from Andi walking in front of me, it's fucking impossible.

The green oversized sweater she's wearing is falling off her shoulder, revealing a lacy bralette beneath it, and the shorts she's wearing have me needing to adjust my pants. The backs of those thighs may as well have my name tattooed on them with the way I can't stop staring.

She even has little skulls on her tall black socks.

Wait. Not skulls—

"Are those Jack Skellington socks?" I ask.

She smirks at me over my shoulder. "Of course," she says. "Do you want the Sally ones?"

"Abso-fucking-lutely," I reply.

If there was one little thing she and I had bonded on in the past, it was a love for all things Tim Burton and cult classic horror. She never missed a Halloween in the old place, especially when Reed's youngest brothers, Koen and

Kamden, were preteens. It never mattered that she was the oldest. She never treated us like she was too good to hang out with us.

If anything, she protected us.

Looking back, I realize we should have been the ones protecting her.

She opens the door to the pool house and flips on the lights inside, and I almost laugh when I step inside.

Reed's mom, Tina, has a basket of Reed's favorite candies and junk food sitting on the counter, along with a sign stating that she's stocked the fridge for late-night cravings. A balloon is tied to a teddy bear plush with a guitar on the couch. I glance over to Andi, who's biting her lips to keep from laughing.

I can't fucking wait to rag Reed about this.

"I think I'm jealous," I say, and Andi bursts out laughing.

It's still the most adorable and addicting noise I've ever heard. The face she makes when her nose scrunches up, and she throws her head back…

She grabs onto the counter to hold herself together, then wipes a tear from her face as she tries to collect herself. I toss my bag onto the couch and grab the teddy.

"I'll make sure to tell Tina you're upset you didn't get one," she says once she's recovered.

"Damn right," I say. "This is my new good luck bear."

"What, are you going to take it on stage with you?" she asks.

I look at the bear in my hand. "It could use some spike bracelets," I say. "More eyeliner."

"Can't forget the liner," Andi agrees.

Our eyes meet, and Andi clears her throat as she glances at the ground. "This is only my second time here," she says. "To the new house, I mean. It's nice. I love that there's room for everyone."

"Better than sharing the living room with me, right?" I ask, referring to the few occasions when Andi was home from college and slept on the couch when I was also over.

"I don't know. Sometimes I miss our sleepovers," she says, and I can't help wetting my lips at the look on her face.

"What, ah, what about you? When were you last home?" she asks.

"Last Christmas," I reply.

Her phone rings, and Andi frowns as she looks down at it. "Oh. Shit. Work." She holds a finger up. "Sorry, give me a second—Hello?"

As Andi answers her work call, I start rifling through my bag for a set of clothes to change into. The stick of the airport makes me feel as if I'm crawling with germs.

I take my shoes and shirt off without thinking twice, and when I turn back around, I find Andi staring in my direction, her thumbnail in her mouth and the phone halfway against her ear. She appears to be in a daze, and I throw my dirty shirt at her face.

"Hm? Oh, yeah, I heard you, Cyn," she says as she dodges the shirt.

I grin at her and mouth, "My eyes are up here," to her while gesturing two fingers to my face.

She throws the shirt back at me.

"—No, I decided to stay with family. It's easier to catch a ride with the guys from here," she goes on. "Reed and Mads," she says. "No. No, Cyn. No photos of him sans mask. I know."

My gaze lifts to her again, and I find her staring at my shoulders, a strand of hair curling around her finger.

And that little fucking smirk that she gives me makes my dick twitch.

I feel like a teenager again, and I have to remind myself that we're grown-ass adults with a shared bond to this family and equally shitty childhoods that no one can take away from us.

And that we're both doing everything we can to escape the past.

The thought sobers me.

"—Okay, Cyn. Yeah. No, I'll text you tomorrow. Bye."

Andi ends the call and presses it face-down on the counter. "Boss was just making sure what happened to your last photographer doesn't happen to me," she says as she folds her arms across her chest.

I scoff. "Girl snuck up on me in the shower," I say, recalling the incident.

"Maybe she just wanted a taste of you," Andi taunts.

"She's lucky I didn't break her fucking camera," I reply.

Andi snorts, and I lift a brow her way.

"What?"

"Whenever they told me what happened, that was exactly what I wanted to say," she says. "I could see you taking her camera and destroying it with your bare hands, then laughing in her face."

"I still laughed in her face when James found out," I say.

Andi leans against the counter. "I'm surprised you've continued wearing the mask all this time. After your dad died, I thought you might let it slide some."

Fuck, I wish she hadn't brought him up.

I run my hand through my hair and scratch my neck, and she straightens.

"Shit. I'm sorry, Maddox," she says in haste. "Sorry. Being back here has everything stirring up inside me. I have like word vomit, and then seeing you—and Reed—I feel like I suddenly don't know when to shut up. You might have to gag me this week."

My brow lifts, the joke helping to settle me back in this timeframe. Yet, there's something else she said that has my full attention, that ignites a fire in my restless muscles.

"What do you mean 'seeing me'?" I ask.

"I mean…" She fumbles with her fingers, that anxious little smile flickering on her lips. "I mean, you're not… it's been five years," she says with an exhausted breath. "We were at Reed's college graduation the last time I saw you. You both still had your long hair and… and now…" Her voice drifts, and I feel my curiosity getting the better of me.

"Now what?"

"Now you're… god, *look* at you, Maddox."

A nervous laugh leaves her, and I can practically feel my lips curling upward.

"Go on," I urge her, hoping to draw out everything I can get.

She gives me a flat yet mildly amused stare. "You're just not who I expected to see beneath the mask," she says.

I reach into my bag and pull out the mask she's talking about, letting the fabric fall over my arm as I hold it up. "Would you feel more comfortable if I put the mask on?"

"No," she says a little too quickly. "I mean, maybe—no, *no*, Maddox. Don't you dare."

She reaches out to pause me as I start to push it over my head, and a quiet laugh escapes me.

She's never been this flustered in front of me before. Mildly, sure. Never this bad. I can see a few splotches of red creeping up her chest and neck, and it makes me wonder if the rest of her body does this when she's unnerved.

I shouldn't be wondering this.

I shouldn't be thinking of the rest of her body as if I have any chance of ever touching it… tasting it… *claiming* it…

I barely realize I'm staring at her hips when I hear her clear her throat.

This time, it's her who's watching me with a poignant, raised-brow stare, and I snicker when I meet her dark eyes.

"My eyes are up here," she says deliberately, and I want to kiss that fucking smirk off her pouting lips.

"Sorry," I force myself to say. "It's been five years for me, too—though I have seen *you* on social media."

"Oh, yes. I've seen your comments," she says with a tilt of her head.

"What—how?"

Because my personal social media accounts are completely private.

She laughs, and I make it a point to hear that as often as possible this week. "'IHaveTheKeynes.' That's your personal username, isn't it?"

"No…" I lie. "My personal one has always been, 'DudeWheresMyKeynes.'"

Another chuckle sounds from her. "You should have thought of that one first."

I scratch my head and hate myself for not thinking of that fifteen years ago. "That would have been so much funnier."

Her smile softens, and she presses her hand to the door frame like she's about to leave me. "I'm ordering pizza. Anything different or just the usual bacon and onions?"

I don't know why her remembering my pizza order is a big deal, still somehow, it is.

"Sounds great," I tell her.

CHAPTER THREE
ANDI

Holy mother fucking, cheese and crackers and shirt balls.

Maddox. *Fucking*. Keynes.

I walk away from that pool house, fully aware of the way he's watching me, and it makes me wish I wasn't such an awkward walker. I wish I had a confident swagger or knew how to make my hips twist so that he actually had a reason to watch my ass.

I trip over my own feet halfway to the house and nearly tumble into the pool.

Yeah. That's the epitome of my ways of seduction. Falling face-first into a dirty pool because despite how Dad might say he has this cover secure, I know better.

God, that would have been embarrassing.

As I reach the sliding door, I quickly glance over my shoulder, hoping that Maddox is nowhere to be found or that he gave up watching me when he remembered what a klutz I am—

He's leaning against the threshold of the double doors, his arms crossed over his tattooed, firm chest, lips split into a devastatingly smug grin. I let my gaze wander over his torso again, lingering nearly too long on the vee at his hips and the tattoos that seem to melt beneath his belt.

When he sees me looking at him, he pushes off, stuffs his

hands in his pockets, and walks back inside.

When the fuck did he have time to turn into… *this?!*

It wasn't that I was unaware of just how much he'd grown into his previous awkwardness over the last few years—even if the last time I saw him, he only had a bit of stubble on his jaw and still wore that freshly-turned-twenty-one boyish aura.

But now?

Jesus.

His mop of brown waves arches over his forehead to his nose in a natural manner—as if it falls that perfectly when he wakes up every morning.

That part of him, I know. That part of him, *most* people know. Maddox always wears skull neck gaiters over his nose, beard, and neck. He's never seen without one, or at least if he is, no one knows it's him. The only distinguishable characteristics are his eyes, hand, and arm tattoos—which he usually keeps covered at shows.

Seeing him without any of the masks, hats, beanies, or otherwise is like seeing a different person.

I won't lie, though.

I love that skull mask.

Maddox's chestnut beard is somehow perfectly messy, the strands falling over his lips in a manner that makes him press it back when he sips his drink. Tattoos cover nearly every inch of his arms, chest, and neck, most of which he's gotten within the last five years. He has a black septum ring piercing, black nickel-sized gauges in his earlobes, and when he speaks, I swear I see the glimmer of a tongue ring.

Fucking hell.

I lean my elbows over the kitchen island and take out my phone to open the app for the local pizza place, and just as I select Maddox's order, a text comes through.

The boys' planes are delayed, Tina, my step-mother,

says. ***Looks like your father and I will be waiting a few more hours. Don't order dinner for us. We'll just take the boys to the waffle place when we get them.***

I switch over to our text thread and type back. *Okay. Sounds good.*

Did Reed get home? she asks.

He and Maddox got here about a half hour ago, I reply.

Oh, I wasn't sure if Maddox was staying. I made up the office for him in case.

He's staying in the pool house.

Where is Reed sleeping?

I believe he's chucking everything out of the spare room now, I reply, knowing Tina had been using that room for storage.

Of course, he is, Tina says. ***Okay. I'll clean it up for him tomorrow.***

Be safe tonight. We're ordering pizza now.

Okay. I'll let you know when the boys land.

I send her a thumbs-up emoji and click back to the pizza app.

The entire time I'm selecting our dinner, I feel eyes on me.

I refuse to look up.

He is your brother's friend, I remind myself.

Also, a work client as of this moment.

Off-limits.

Shit, why did that make him that much more attractive?

I suddenly wish I had brought more than just one toy to play with.

"Hey—"

I jump at the sound of Reed's voice and whip off the counter to face him as if he's just caught me doing something I shouldn't be. Reed's wide eyes narrow on me, face scrunching up in that comical, confused way that he has.

"The fuck is wrong with you?"

I shove him. "You sneaking up on people is what," I say.

His frown turns into that sideways grin of his that I know he uses to his advantage every chance he gets. "You're still jumpy?"

"Yes," I answer, and he laughs. He doesn't press the topic anymore as he opens up the fridge.

"Tina stocked the pool house fridge for you," I say when he grabs a hard cider. "Why didn't you tell her Maddox was coming?—Oh, grab me one."

After popping the top with his teeth, Reed hands me a drink, then settles on the barstool across from me with a sigh. I pick up the cap, staring at the teeth marks on the aluminum.

"You're going to break your teeth," I say.

A sly smirk rises on his lips. "I've never had complaints before for how I use my teeth."

And I throw the cap at his face. "You're disgusting." I lean over and grab a piece of Halloween candy from Tina's pumpkin bowl on the counter.

"So, why didn't you tell Tina he was coming?" I repeat. "She loves him more than she does the rest of you."

Reed scoffs. "True." He swishes his hair sideways out of his eyes. "Ah. I don't know why I didn't tell her. I guess I wasn't sure how she would feel about him coming this time," he replies. "Last Christmas, they got into it about his dad. She wanted him to go see him in the hospital. Mads basically told her to mind her own business and fuck off."

I would have done the same.

"Why would she think that was a good idea?" I ask.

Reed presses the bottle to his lips and takes a bubbling swig. "You'd think she learned enough from everything with Alice, right?" he says, referring to my mother. "Nah. She kept saying something about facing his demons."

"Some demons are better left under the bed," I mutter.

"In the back of the closet," Reed adds.

"In the cushions of that moth-eaten orange couch in the old garage," I go on.

A soft laugh escapes him. "That couch was disgusting."

"Yeah? It never stopped you. How many virginities did you take on that thing?"

Reed takes another swig of his drink, a thoughtful expression in his eyes. "Four," he answers, though there's questioning in his tone. "No, wait—Five."

"Five?"

"Forgot about Diana Markus," he replies.

"How do you forget about fucking Diana Markus?" I ask, remembering the pretty girl from the high school across town. "More importantly, why was she fucking you?"

Reed holds up two fingers to his mouth, showing off the tattoo on the inside of his forearm of guitar strings under his skin, piano keys tattooed on his fingers, and the chipped nail polish. He sticks his tongue through the two fingers, and I hate myself for laughing.

"You child," I laugh.

Reed grabs a mini Twix and unwraps it. "Mom had this idea in her head that Mads would feel better if he told his dad how he'd made him feel over the years. How his decisions had affected his life with the fights and everything," Reed went on. "Even mentioned forgiving him, but—"

"Why the hell would he ever forgive that bastard?" I ask, feeling my own defensiveness rise. "Why would he give him that peace?"

Reed smirks at me. "I believe that's your own trauma speaking."

I know he's right, and I glare at him for it as I grab another piece of candy. "Suck my dick, Reed," I say with a mouthful of chocolate. "He didn't come back for the funeral, did he?"

"Fuck, no," he replies. "We were onstage in Chicago. I asked him a few times if he wanted to come back, but he didn't want to talk about it. I don't think he spoke for at least a week. Maybe more."

I glance up toward the pool house, glimpsing Maddox as he pulls a shirt over his head, and my heart pains for him.

His father deserved every ounce of agony that cancer had put him through.

The door to the pool house opens as I'm staring, and Maddox stretches across the deck. He's pulled his dark brown hair into a top knot, the sides and back of his hair faded with bold lines shaved at the defining hairline on either side.

I can fully see his eyes now, and I know this look is not going to be good for the newfound, unadulterated lust I'm feeling for him.

Reed glances over his shoulder to see him.

"He still gets kind of weird about it if you bring it up," he says. "Try to avoid if you can."

"Yeah, I already made that mistake once," I mumble against the rim of my drink.

I tap on my phone to check on the location of our pizza as Maddox makes his way through the sliding glass door.

"You can leave it open," I tell him. "Place could use some fresh air."

Maddox leaves it and settles on the barstool by Reed as I open up the fridge and grab a beer for him.

"Orangecraft IPA, right?" I ask, and the corner of his lips quirks beneath the beard.

"How the hell do you know that?" he asks.

"Probably because it's all you post on your Instagram," Reed says.

"Says the guy who's constantly posting videos of his hands stretching or wrapping around something," I taunt my brother.

"People love my hands," he grins.

"I hate that you do that."

"Why?"

"Because I stumbled upon someone trying to market their dark romance book with a recording of one of your videos, and it completely turned me off. I said, 'Oh, that's hot—wait, *gross*.'"

Reed laughs as if he's proud of the blunder.

"I've been trying to get this guy to do them now that he has the new tattoo on his hand," Reed says about Maddox. "Did you see it?"

My eyes narrow. "I mean, I've seen him in pictures while he was playing. You're making it sound like it's more special than that."

Reed jerks his chin at Maddox. "Show her."

"Show me what—*Oh*."

It's all I can manage as Maddox sinks his face into his palm, showing off the skull face and wide smile tattooed on the back of his hand. It aligns with his features perfectly—the hollow nose on his ring finger and bare teeth stretched across his bones. And just like with the skull mask he wears onstage, all I can see is his wicked green eyes when he looks up.

"Remind me to get a picture of that sometime this week," I say, and it's not entirely for the firm's benefit.

I wonder what that hand would look like over my mouth.

Or, more importantly, around my throat.

Maddox smirks at me, and I quickly let my hair fall over my face as I reopen the pizza app.

"Says pizza will be here in ten," I announce.

Reed and Maddox begin chatting about something Maddox saw on his newsfeed, and I turn to grab plates from the cabinet. The breakfast nook table is just big enough for the three of us, what with Reed and Maddox taking up as much space as they do now.

By the time I'm finished setting up and have waters on the

table, the doorbell rings.

Reed pulls cash from his pocket and darts to the door before I can go. When I ask him why he's so eager to get the food, he simply says that the pizza place had a hot girl delivering on this route over Christmas.

I exchange a look with Maddox, who is drawing a container from his pocket with gummies inside, and he just shakes his head as he grabs one out.

"Gummies?" I ask.

He extends the tin to me. "Can't do the smokes anymore. Had to make the switch. It's a whole different high."

I take one and pop it back into my mouth as he chews on a second. "Two?"

"Long fucking day and night," he replies.

Maddox settles at the table, and I sit across from him. "Surprised you two didn't want to nap when you got here," I say.

"You distracted me," he says, and I eye him playfully, causing him to smirk in a manner that makes my thighs tighten.

I expect him to make another clever comment; however, he doesn't say anymore before leaning around the table and cupping his hand to his mouth. "Jesus, fuck, Reed," Maddox shouts. "Are you fucking her against the door or something? I'm starving. Tell her to come back after we've eaten."

I hang my head in my hand and laugh.

Reed slams the door a moment later and comes around the corner with the food in his hands and a grin on his expressive face. He waves the receipt in both our faces, and I see a number written in blue pen on the back.

"You shitbag." Maddox grins at him. "You haven't even been home an hour."

Reed wiggles the receipt tauntingly in front of his nose, then does a dance that is so *very* Reed.

"Thank fuck I'm sleeping over the garage and don't have to hear this girl's fake moans," I say as I take salads and side dishes out of the bag. "Why didn't you originally claim the one over the garage?"

"I'm not taking her upstairs," Reed says, grabbing a slice of pizza. "I'll rail her fucking brains out over the middle console of that pretty Jeep she's driving."

"How romantic," I tease, rolling my eyes at his glee. Even still, I can't get mad at him as he sits beside me and softly nudges my side, the smile I grew up being so fond of radiating on his face.

He's still my little brother, and the sentiment drives deep when I peer across the table at Maddox, whose flirtatious gleam has softened into something resembling sadness.

As if he's thinking the same thing I am.

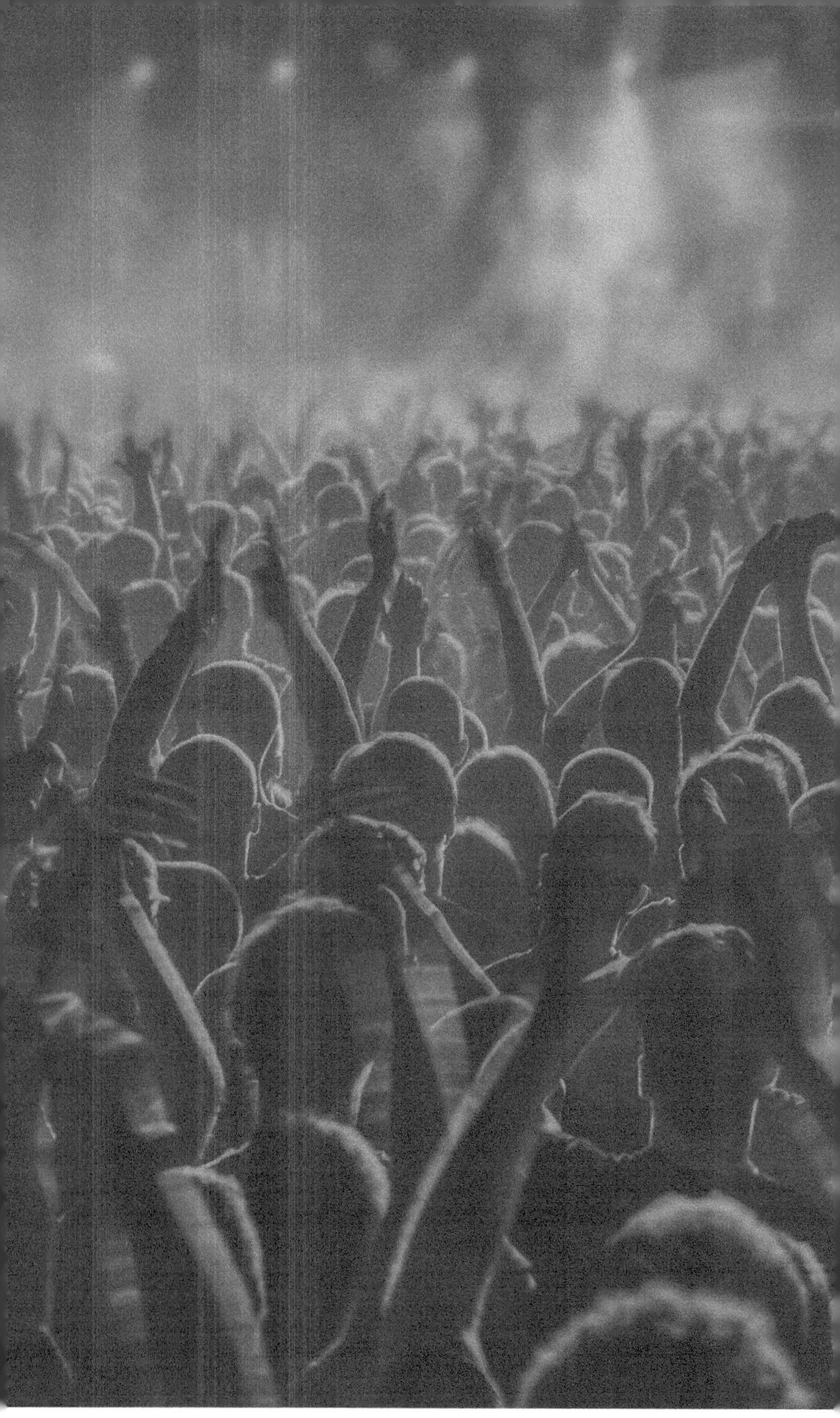

CHAPTER FOUR
MADDOX

"All right, Raleigh, we are back with our special guests today," the radio DJ, Paul, says into the microphone the next day. "Lead singer, Reed Matthews, and bassist, Mads Tourning, of Young Decay are in the house, and we're talking to them about the Halloween homecoming run they have coming up this weekend. If you don't have your tickets, there are a few left for Thursday night's concert. Friday and Saturday are sold out." Paul looks between myself and Reed. "How does it feel being home?" he asks.

I'm still trying to wake up.

Despite the espresso Reed's mother had ready for us once we dragged our asses to breakfast, I'm struggling. It was nice seeing her again. She didn't seem to care about what I'd said all those months ago.

She took me in like no time had passed.

"It's great," Reed says. "We love being home, especially on Halloween."

"Especially on Halloween," I agree.

"What's so special about this holiday?" Paul asks.

"One time a year when the demons get to play, right?" I say.

Reed chuckles. "All the wicked and the witches," he adds. "Honestly, Halloween was always special for us growing up.

I have two younger brothers, an entire family obsessed with horror cult classics—"

"And Tim Burton, as we know about Mads here," Paul says as his eyes move to me. "Don't think we didn't see the Jack and Sally socks when you came in."

"You should see the artwork on his thigh," Reed says.

"You have a Jack tat on your leg?" Paul asks.

I huff in amusement. "Something like that," I reply.

"What's the story on that?" Paul asks. "Why that movie?"

I wring my hands together and stare at the table, thinking of a reply. "Ah… I mean, Reed and I grew up pretty close. It was a movie his sister put on for their younger siblings around this time of year. I guess… I don't know. The music was inspiring."

"It's classic," Reed agrees.

The DJ's grin somehow broadens. "You realize you're going to get a lot of Nightmare memorabilia thrown at the stage this weekend now, right?"

Reed and I laugh. "Bring it on," I say, and I see Andi smirking at us from across the room.

Every time I've looked at her since getting here, I see her smiling at one of us from behind the lens. She's fucking sexy in her faux leather jacket, baggy band tee, leggings, and combat boots.

That goddamn smirk will be the last thing I see before I die, that much I know.

She's finally settled on the bench instead of moving around, and as the DJ pauses to play our latest release, I see him swivel in his chair toward her. I recognize the leer in his eyes when he stares at her. He's been checking her out since she started moving around the room for better angles of us talking.

The predatory gaze makes my jaw tick.

"Did you make sure to get my good side?" he asks her.

Andi gives him a polite smile. "Sure," she replies.

"Will you be stalking them all week?" he asks her.

"All week," she replies.

"You work for Heartless?"

Andi nods, replying, "Yep," and presses her face behind the lens as if she isn't interested in engaging. She takes another photo of Reed and starts scrolling through the images on the back of the camera.

The DJ keeps trying.

"Share the results," he says. "Let's see if you're any good."

Andi lets her wrists cross in her lap and glares at the DJ with a fake smile on her lips that nearly makes me chuckle.

I know that fucking look.

"I work for one of the top PR firms in the nation for the top rock recording company, on assignment with the hottest band on alt radio on one of the biggest weeks of their careers. So, yeah, I'm pretty damn good at my fucking job."

Reed elbows me in the side, and it's obvious he's trying to hold in his laughter, too.

It takes Paul a moment to find amusement in her words and not surprise, and when he does, he beams. "Man, when they say women aren't taking shit anymore, they mean it." He turns back to me and Reed. "Matched with a girl last week who insisted on picking up the tab. It was nice."

"You like assertive women, Paul?" Reed asks.

"Fucking love it," Paul answers. "Nothing wrong with a girl who isn't, but damn. Something about that bratty mouth and I-don't-need-you attitude makes me feel all tingly."

The light flashes in the booth, and Paul signals for us to put our headphones back on.

As Paul reintroduces us and goes through the concert spill again, I open my messages to a number I've never used before.

Having fun yet? I type.

Andi looks down at her phone when it lights up, and her eyes narrow at the screen.

It's Mads, I text her.

Her eyes flicker up to mine. The corner of her lips twitch upward as she sets her camera down at her side before replying.

Time of my life, she says.

Want me to kick his ass?

Andi audibly scoffs, her gaze drifting to me again. *He's harmless. I've met worse.*

Thanks for the socks, by the way. Though, you sneaking into the pool house while I was asleep is pretty stalker-ish.

I took a lock of your hair, too. It's in a special ring box in my pocket. I've been taking it out to sniff your conditioner all morning.

That's hot.

Still can't decide if I want to keep the Polaroids to myself or sell them.

Only sell the ones with my clothes on. Keep the naked ones.

Embarrassed of something, Maddox?

Nah. I want you to have something to look at when you use your toys.

How do you know about my toys?

You're not the only one with stalker tendencies.

That's hot, she says, and our eyes meet across the room.

There's a dark playfulness in her eyes that I want to fuck out of her, and I have to clear my throat and force myself to pay attention to the interview starting back up.

Enjoy the mindless flirting all you want, I tell myself. *That's all you'll ever get.*

The reminder sinks the smile on my lips.

"—back with lead singer, Reed Matthews and bass player, Mads Tourning," Paul says. He swings in his chair to look at us. "All right, guys, let's get personal. How do you relationships on the road? How does that work?"

"It doesn't," Reed says. "We try to keep personal separate from the band life."

"What about inter-band relationships?" Paul asks. "Mixing business with pleasure."

"Nah," Reed answers. "I think all of us are too close for that."

"So, dating apps, they're out of the question?"

"It's tough being on those when so many people know your face." Reed glances at me. "Mads had the right idea from the beginning. But, I mean, yeah, occasionally we have a stop long enough to have more than a backstage fling. It's rare," Reed adds.

"Sex, drugs, and rock and roll," the DJ chimes in. "Mads knows what I'm talking about," he says, grinning my way. "Listeners, this guy even keeps his mask on in a private booth where everyone has signed an NDA, phones taken at the door. Starting to make me think we're hiding a serial killer under there."

Reed laughs.

"I like my privacy," I say with a shrug.

"What about you? You have a partner on the road?"

For some reason, my eyes swivel to Andi across the room, and I look back at the table before anyone can notice. "Ah, no. No, nothing. Like Reed said, getting to know someone is hard when you're only in a city for forty-eight hours. By the time you exchange numbers, you're in a different city with new people and so busy that you barely have time to eat."

"Realities of the road, everyone," Paul says. "I was on the road with a band in the early 2000s and the same thing. New partner every night. The lead singer was married. Back then, the drugs were the only way some of them made it onstage. Do you guys have any before-show rituals?"

"Are you asking if we do drugs before going onstage,

Paul?" I ask.

Paul laughs. "Not entirely," he says.

"No hard drugs," Reed answers, waving him off. "Bonnie's been sober for…" He looks at me as if he can't remember.

"Three years," I say.

"Yeah, three years," Reed says. "Right after the first tour. She's amazing."

"So fucking amazing," I add, genuinely proud of her.

"Really?" Paul asks. "Now, she and your guitarist, Zeb, didn't make it today. They'll be in here on Thursday, right?"

"Yep, we'll be back Thursday," I say.

"You have a lot of press this week?"

"Something like that. We go where we're told," Reed says.

"Usually, we show up not knowing what the hell is going on," I add. "It adds a less rehearsed element to our interviews."

"More chaos," Reed says with a wide smile.

The DJ laughs. "I love chaos with you guys," he says. "That reminds me. I hear you all have nicknames for one another, and one of you is, in fact, Chaos?"

I point to Reed. "This guy," I say.

Reed raises his hand. "Guilty."

"Yeah? So, what does that make the rest of you?" Paul asks.

"Mads was easy… Madness," Reed adds with a sideways grin. "Bonnie is Bedlam. And Zeb is Havoc."

"Havoc? Really?" Paul asks. "Here I thought he was the quiet one of you four."

"That's why his nickname is Havoc," I reply.

"Absolute devastation," Reed says.

"All right, I like it. I like it," Paul decides. "Now, speaking of havoc, I've heard a rumor about this weekend's shows. I hear there's a group trying to get the run canceled."

Reed and I groan. It's only the second time we've heard

about this since our manager said they were handling it.

"I thought people were done protesting music," I say.

"We're not too worried about it. It sounds like they don't appreciate good music," Reed replies.

"That's what we think, too. And if for some reason this guy succeeds, we'll get a permit and let you rock out in the park out back," Paul says.

Reed laughs. "Fuck yeah," he says.

"All right, that's our time with the band for today—"

I tune Paul out as he goes through his sign-off. My phone is vibrating in my pocket. I take it out to see another text from Andi, who vanished from the room in the thirty seconds I looked away from her.

Boss wants a photo from today for socials. I'll see you guys back at the house, she says.

What, no goodbye kiss? I ask.

Play your cards right, maybe you'll get a goodnight kiss.

I smile at the screen. I know she's joking. Even so, it's no match against the restless fluttering in my stomach. A text from James comes through, letting me know he has the car out back and is waiting for us in the next room.

I don't click over to his thread.

Tease, I reply to Andi.

Must be my bratty attitude, she says, and I chuckle out loud.

"Is that Bon?" Reed asks. "Are she and Zeb still at the hotel?"

"Ah... It's James," I answer fast. "He said your sister went back to the house to send in a few things. He has the car waiting on us."

We shake hands and part ways with the DJ, assuring him we'll be back before the concert on Thursday with Bonnie and Zeb. He says something about him booking a private party for the radio and the band tonight at The Red Attic—one of the town's few VIP clubs, and I hear Reed agree for all of us.

Guess I'll be wearing this mask a little longer today.

A photo Andi took of us during the interview shows up on our official social media pages within an hour. It's a great angle, showing off both of us in front of the mics, Reed mid-smile. It's black and white, and I wonder what we're talking about as I take a seat on the couch. We're at a local studio owned by the record company—one of the only places they trust to let us jam out this week and hang with some press without renting out something.

"Damn, I can't believe we didn't get the invite to this," Bonnie says as she holds up her phone. "Pretty fucking rude."

"Didn't you get to hang out with a hot journalist this morning?" Reed asks.

Bonnie twirls her drumstick between her fingers, shakes her blonde shaggy hair out of her eyes, and grins his way. "Yeah, she was," she says.

Zeb shakes his head as he plugs into his amp. "Someone is being modest," he mutters. "Tell them what you did."

I lean over my knees and grin, knowing what she's about to say before she says it.

Bonnie chews her gum with an open mouth in a cocky way. "I don't know what to tell you. She tasted fucking divine."

I laugh as Reed drops his microphone, and as he begins asking for details, I open up my messages to text Andi.

I shouldn't be texting her.
I shouldn't be thinking of her as much as I am, trying to figure out ways to ensure that she's in the same room as me every moment of every day this week.

It doesn't fucking matter.

I'm obsessed.

The photo looks great, I text her, wishing I had something more clever to say.

You sound surprised, she replies almost instantly.

Blame it on my own self-criticism, I say. **What are you doing now?**

She sends me a photo of her sitting on the deck with her laptop, a plate of pumpkin cookies, and a warm mug of orange liquid. I can just see the tops of her bent legs.

My mouth dries. Fantasies of those legs wrapped around my face had kept me up a few hours last night.

Working, she says.

What are you doing later?

Tina mentioned dinner. Why? Is there something on the agenda that I missed?

Work event tonight at The Red Attic. The radio station is sponsoring. You should come.

My boss hasn't mentioned it. I can ask if she wants me there.

No, I mean just as yourself. Not on official duty.

No camera?

No camera.

Does Reed know you're inviting me?

I glance up at Reed, who's doing his mic check, and I know I only have a couple more minutes to waste.

I can make it seem like it's his idea, I reply.

Three dots strum at the bottom of the screen for a moment, then disappear and reappear a couple more times before she finally responds.

Why does this feel secret?

If it was secret, I'd find an excuse to stay behind instead.

I wonder what her face is doing. We've always flirted, yet something about this feels different. She isn't brushing me off like we're just friends as she usually does. She isn't ruffling my hair and nudging my side like I'm just a younger guy her brother is friends with.

The entire notion makes my palms sweat.

I'll be ready when you guys get back.

It's the end of the conversation, and I throw my phone into my bass case.

CHAPTER FIVE
ANDI

Why am I nervous?

I stand in front of the mirror to look at my outfit for the tenth time, ignoring the loud noise of the horror movie I have going on in the background.

Dad brought a television up here while we were out this morning, along with an actual mattress, and while he offered to clean all of his manuscripts out and buy new furniture so that the room could be mine officially, I had to remind him that I was only here for another week.

The same sadness I'd known as a child when my mom would take me away flickered in his eyes, and I felt so horrible about it that we went out for donuts and coffee. I told him everything I could about my new life, job, therapy, and everything I'm doing to try and keep myself level-headed.

It was nice.

Maddox texted just when we got back, and ever since the exchange, I've been so nervous that I took the car to the local shopping center in the hopes of finding an outfit somewhere near suitable for a private party.

"Fuck it," I say out loud.

I use the door that goes directly into the house from this room and wander down the stairs to the kitchen, where I know Tina is busy making more of those delicious pumpkin cookies.

Koen, my youngest brother, whistles when I come around the corner.

"Whoa—where's the party, sis?" he taunts, throwing an apple at me across the room.

"Is Reed not back yet?" I ask as I look past Koen's dark hair toward the pool house.

Koen looks so much like my dad—more so than Reed or Kamden—and the most like me. He and I share Dad's Italian genes and brown eyes, while Kamden and Reed inherited Tina's pale Irish complexion and blue eyes. All of us, however, have dark hair like Dad.

"He's showering," Koen answers.

As if on cue, I spot Maddox exiting the pool house wearing brown pants tucked into his heavy black boots, a black hooded jacket, a white tee, and a denim jacket atop all of it. He's obviously put something in his hair to make it appear fluffier, and I feel myself shift as I watch him head this way.

I know better than to stay in this fucking kitchen where Koen is sure to figure out that I'm suddenly crushing on someone who is essentially our fifth sibling.

I sit my bag on the table and go through the sliding door to meet Maddox instead of waiting in the kitchen.

Maddox is picking a gummy out from his tin when I close the door behind me, and he stops mid-stride. His brows raise as he looks me over—everything from my fishnet tights to my sweater dress with rips that show off the lacy bustier I'm wearing beneath, the thigh-high socks on my legs, and black chunky boots on my feet.

I push the form-fitting forearm sleeves up to try and keep it from falling entirely off my shoulder and pause a few feet away from him.

"Jesus fucking hell, Andi," Maddox says once he stops

gaping. "You should come with a warning label."

I press my lips together in a thin line, and those green eyes gleam at me from where he's still standing.

I really want to know what he's thinking.

His tongue darts over his lips as he finally figures out how to walk again, and he extends the tin to me just as he did the night before.

The high had been just enough to edge me to sleep.

"Not sure that's a good idea to take and go out in public," I say.

He smirks. "Different tin," he replies.

I feel my eyes squinting as I consider it, and as the thought of facing a room full of strangers without a camera to hide behind fills me, I take one from his hand and bite it in half.

"I just need the edge off," I tell him, and his smirk widens.

"Whatever you need, beautiful."

I need him to throw me into the pool house, close the curtains, and fuck me senseless over the back of a chair.

Maybe then I can stop wondering what it would be like.

Maddox reaches for my hand and pulls it up to his mouth. I feel my breath catch when he sticks his tongue out to take the remaining half of the gummy from my palm, his eyes never leaving mine.

Fuck, why was that hot?

"Waste nothing," he says, his voice low, fingers stroking my skin.

I don't know what to do with myself. His gaze is steady upon me, only drifting to my lips when I let my own shift.

"If I was a palm reader, this would look less awkward to your entire family, who is staring at us through the window," he says as his eyes flicker past my shoulder.

Mother fucker.

"Well, you did just lick my hand in broad daylight," I taunt.

"Is there another time I should be licking your hand?" he asks, brow lifted.

I purse my lips, but only to stop from smiling. "No, what I'm saying is, you knew we were in full visibility of... well, everyone," I say.

"I honestly forgot where we were. You're very distracting," he says.

"So this is my fault?" I ask.

"Clearly, this is your fault."

I have to bite my lips to stop from grinning stupidly. "So, why are you the one still holding my hand?"

My head tilts as I smirk at him, and the way he beams back makes my heart ache.

"Did you know that this line signifies how long you'll live?" he says as I hear the sliding door open. "And this one... this is your headline—obviously you're smart, so it's pretty distinct, and then this one is your heart— Ow—"

A piece of hard candy hits him in the cheek.

Maddox looks up and drops my hand, glaring at someone nearby. "What the hell, shithead," Maddox says, rubbing his face where Kamden hit him.

Kamden leans against the doorframe and smiles broadly. "You're lucky it was me and not Reed," he says. His eyes move to me. "Looking cozy, sis."

Maddox runs at Kamden.

Kamden drops his smile and mutters, "Oh shit," before darting to the other side of the pool. I barely register their running figures coming back around this side when Maddox grabs Kamden and wrenches him into a headlock.

"What's.... What's going on?" Reed asks as he emerges from inside.

"Kamden was being a shit," I reply.

"Ah. Guess some things don't change—Hey, let's go! James is out front," Reed shouts.

Kamden is practically squealing and fighting back. Nevertheless, he's no match for Maddox's grip and strength. Maddox wrestles him backward, locking Kamden's arms to the point that Kamden has to yell Maddox's last name as the only way to officially tap out.

I scoff when Maddox stops fighting and holds the younger brother in place. It isn't a look of amusement in his eyes when he takes Kamden's throat in his hand, and whatever he says in his ear, we can't hear.

A knot twists around my abdomen at the display.

Maddox finally shoves Kamden forward, and Kamden glares at him over his shoulder, hand rubbing his neck.

"Jerk off—"

The words barely leave Kamden's lips when Maddox pushes him into the pool.

As I predicted, Dad's tie job was poor, and the cover snaps from the side, sending Kamden into the dirty water below. He's beneath the water for a split second before rising up and yelling something else I don't catch.

"The hell was that about?" Reed asks when Maddox reaches us.

Maddox stretches his hand out and curls it back in as he looks back to find Kamden pushing himself out of the pool.

"Do I need a reason?" Maddox asks Reed.

Reed glances at Kamden. "No, not really. You ready?"

"Yeah."

Reed turns. I follow, catching Maddox's eyes upon passing. A smirk rises on his lips and disappears beneath his mask when he pulls the fabric up to his eyes, and as he winks my way, the swagger in his every muscle causes my muscles to tense.

He pinches my elbow when I pass, and we don't look at each other again the entire ride to the party.

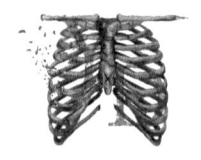

Thank fuck, Maddox gave me that gummy.

If I have to hear DJ Paul tell me one more time about how he loves film cameras more than modern cameras or about the "art of photography" being lost nowadays as if I'm going to debate with him about it, I might lose my goddamn mind.

I sip my Sprite and smile politely for a few more minutes, only because I know I have to be civil with him the rest of the week and because, honestly, I don't feel like having Cynda call me at midnight to tell me to fix my face in front of clients.

The look Maddox is giving me from across the room keeps me distracted enough to hear what the DJ is saying while not fully having to pay attention.

The mask makes him nearly unreadable, even if those eyes are always on me. I can't tell if he's watching because he's suddenly attracted to me or if he's watching out of some protective instinct because of how the DJ tried to chat with me earlier.

Someone bumps into me from behind, and I turn just in time to feel Bonnie slide her arm around my shoulders.

Her blonde hair is braided on the sides so that it falls into a horse's mane mohawk, pink tips gleaming when the different color lights hit them. Her makeup is dark, smokey, and flawless as usual, and the way she wears black lipstick makes me totally jealous. She chews loudly on her gum and gives the DJ a sideways grin.

"Think she's tired of hearing about her job, dude," Bonnie says, her voice hoarse and raspy. She looks my way and proceeds to lick the side of my face. "She's going to come sit on my lap instead," she adds with a wink at Paul. "Maybe my face later. We'll see how this goes."

I fucking love her.

The DJ grins. "See you two on Thursday, then."

And as he turns his back, we both flip him off.

"Thought he'd never leave you alone. Come on," Bonnie says, jerking her head toward the tables overlooking the club below. "Let's go people watch."

A few people pause to speak to her when we move through the crowd to an empty table. She talks to them, insults a few others, and I think I love her more.

Bonnie becoming a member of Young Decay was something that was never entirely discussed. She showed up to a gig that Reed, Maddox, and Zeb were playing a year before they were signed, back when their previous drummer was so high on pills that he could hardly function. The guy passed out halfway through the set. Knowing their music, Bonnie jumped onstage as the ambulance was taking him away, and she finished the rest of the gig without a hitch.

They paid her after and told her when the next practice would be, and she settled into the role as if she'd been playing with them for years.

As we reach the table and she releases me, I have to admire the high-waist trousers and sheer long-sleeve shirt she's wearing, only pasties of skulls on her tits beneath.

"I need you to get me some of these," I say, tapping the bottom of her tit.

"What—the stickers?" She shakes her boobs and grins. "I have a few at the hotel. Text me before practice tomorrow. I'll bring them. Might get these things pierced on Wednesday. Mads mentioned a moth tat."

"Where is he putting that?" I ask as I sit across from her.

"I think he has some blank space on his knee," Bonnie replies, genuine thought crossing her large brown eyes. "Come with us. You could use a new one."

I raise my brow in agreement. The tattoo shop could also be a great place to get a few photos of them. New ink.

I wonder if I can write it off as a work expense.

"Pierce your tits, too," she adds.

I laugh. "When is this?"

"Wednesday," she answers. "Manager said that was the only day press was easy. Our interview is with that one magazine that covers tattoos and musicians."

"Ah." I know the one. "Yeah, I could tag along."

"Hell yes," Bonnie celebrates. "I'll ask Zeb to draw something spicy for you."

"No porn," I tell her.

"Dammit."

I bring my drink to my lips and huff amusedly before sitting up so that I'm looking over the balcony. "I've always wanted to sit up here," I say.

"It's the people watching, right?" Bonnie agrees. "I like to watch and see how many below recognize me."

"Does that happen often?"

"Eh. Depends on the city we're in. We go to at least one of these sponsored parties if we're in town for a few days."

"I don't know how you all do it," I say. "I'm used to being invisible. Being noticed by people would be completely bewildering."

Bonnie laughs. "It was for me, too. Mads told me to wear a mask like him."

"It's the opposite for him, isn't it?" I ask. "He's more recognized with the mask."

"I think that's why he wears his hair back when he's alone," Bonnie replies. "If he's with us, he kind of has to wear the mask in case the rest of us get recognized."

"That has to be annoying," I say.

Bonnie shrugs. "Honestly, we all thought he would stop wearing it after his dad died this past year. You know, less shit looking over his shoulder and whatnot now that he's not here to throw it at his face. At least out in public with us. I know he loves the mask onstage."

"Who doesn't," I mutter without thinking.

"Certainly adds to his aura," Bonnie says. "He's worried about backlash from people finding out who his dad was, I think—"

Whatever Bonnie says next, I don't hear.

A familiar set of blue eyes is staring at me from the bar down below, and I feel my body go into flight mode.

My stomach is on the floor.

My ears are throbbing.

Cold sweat breaks out on my forehead. My palms. I feel the clamminess wash over me, feel myself going pale.

Shit—

"I think I'm going to go home," I say, cutting Bonnie off mid-sentence.

Bonnie says something, her voice concerned as she rises to her feet alongside me.

I can't feel my face, can't tell what my knees are doing, if I'm standing or if I'm falling.

Shit.

Shit. Shit. *Shit*.

Why is he here?

"Andi, whoa, wait—"

I force breath into my lungs as Bonnie reaches for my arm, and I straighten in front of her. "Sorry, just feeling that gummy that Mads gave me earlier," I lie.

"Okay, well, you can at least let us call James—"

I have my phone out. "I already called a car. I'm fine. Really, Bon."

Bonnie's eyes narrow like she knows I'm lying; however, she doesn't press it. "Ah… okay. Okay, I guess… I guess we'll see you tomorrow? Are you sure you don't want me to get Reed?"

"No," I say fast, the mention of my brother sobering me quickly into panic instead of outright fear. "Oh, hell no. *No.*" A nervous laugh leaves me. "God, no."

I manage to get away from her with a kiss on the cheek, and as I make my way to the stairs, I think maybe I've managed to avoid him. Maybe I can get away without a fight. Maybe—

"Andersyn?"

Jesus, mother fucking, goddamn christ.

How is he so fucking fast?

I hesitate for too long. If I'd just pretended not to hear him, I might have made it down the stairs. I might be in the car that's already pulling up. I might be free on my way to the new house that he doesn't know about.

"Andersyn Matthews," he repeats. "That's you, isn't it?"

I slowly turn, plastering a tight-lipped smile on my face. "Adam Vanderhall," I say through my clenched jaw.

Adam Vanderhall, my ex-boyfriend.

He grins his fake, charming smile and opens his arms wide like he expects to hug me.

I step out of his reach with narrowed eyes.

He hasn't changed at all. His blonde hair is still cut tight on the sides, though now he has it swept back like some graduate fresh out of prep school. I still don't understand how I was ever attracted to this prick. Possibly some deep-seated desire to be on the arm of the town's 'good boy' who everyone loves and respects. Who everyone believes to be the epitome of all that is right in this world.

Only to find out that the only thing he's good at is lying.

"How did you get up here?" I ask instead.

He balks. "Don't be hostile, Andi. There are cameras everywhere. Be a good girl and give your old friend a hug," he says through his teeth.

"I'd rather break my neck throwing myself down these stairs," I say, feeling my heels hit the edge.

"You wouldn't be able to do your job anymore if you did that," he says. "How is photography treating you, anyway? Did the classes I paid for help you out? The camera I bought you?"

I cringe.

I sold that camera a long time ago.

"How did you get up here?" I ask instead of giving him the satisfaction of replying. "This is a private party."

"I was invited," he replied. "The radio station thought it might be worth it to have me come and meet Young Decay in the hopes that they might be able to sway me to stop the protests."

Rage replaces the fear, and I feel my nostrils flare. "*You're* the one trying to get them banned?"

"Not banned," he says. "Canceled, yes. Who knows what kind of riots their music might cause during a Halloween run."

"Why?" I ask.

"Violence… drugs… romanticizing suicide and self-harm—"

A laugh escapes me that I know I've been holding in for years. "You're citing them for romanticizing suicide? I don't know, Adam. Someone spends a few days with you, and suicide starts to look pretty fucking tempting."

"What's going on here?"

Reed.

He's at my side in a flash, and I can feel his anger radiating off him.

"Who's—*wait*. I know you."

Of course, Reed recognizes him. I made the mistake of bringing the asshole home for Thanksgiving the year Reed graduated high school.

Reed takes one step in front of me. "See yourself out before one of us does," he warns.

"Reed, I can handle this," I say to him.

Adam grins as if he's already won, and his gaze flickers past Reed to me. "I'd love to discuss you handling me again," he says. "Maybe sometime this week?"

Reed shifts on his feet, fists curling. "Talk to my sister like that again—"

"And you'll what, exactly?" Adam taunts. "Hit me? With all of this press around?"

Reed scoffs, chin dipping narrowly. "Not me."

Maddox steps out of the darkness behind Adam, his stature casting a shadow when he pauses at his back. I have to gulp at the pure anger in his eyes. Adam turns, and despite the fake smile still pressed to his lips, I swear I see a shiver of fear flash in his gaze upon meeting Maddox's stare.

There's a slow, methodical aspect to the way Maddox sizes Adam up, to the quiet way he tilts his head and stares at him like he can break his neck with a snap of his finger.

"What do you think, Reed? Two-twenty-five?" Maddox says.

"Two-thirty at the most," Reed says.

"Might need a few more blocks." Maddox's gaze moves to Reed. "Make sure he stays at the bottom of the river until after the weekend. Don't want to ruin the kid's trick or treating with trash washing ashore."

Something akin to recognition rises in Adam's eyes then. It's enough to make me squirm. Enough to send a nauseating chill down my neck.

Don't remember him. Don't remember him, I chant in my head.

Adam snaps his finger and wags it in Maddox's face, his stare shifting to me. "This is… This is the guy, right?"

Shit.

"It's… Ah, what was your name…" Adam glances at the ground as though he's trying to remember Maddox's name. Fucking asshole. I know he's being a dick. He knows precisely who Maddox is. He knows his name because he searched my phone for it that night. Searched my fucking socials for any trace of a message from him.

Adam takes a singular step forward as he looks up at Maddox. I can see the vein in Maddox's neck straining as he remains rigid.

I swear he isn't breathing.

"It's Maddox, isn't it?" Adam taunts. "Maddox… Ah, what was the last name?"

Maddox's shadow fully engulfs Adam as he rounds over him, daggers in his eyes. "If you know what's good for you, you'll shut your fucking mouth."

Adam grins. "Threatening me isn't exactly the way to continue keeping your identity secret, is it?" he says. "One little call… how do you think your fans will react when they find out the kind of person you really are? Who *Daddy* was?"

Maddox lunges.

A yelp leaves me. Reed grabs my arm as I slap my hand over my mouth, his entire body jerking forward to stop Maddox from doing something rash—

Maddox is utterly still.

He's frozen a whisper from Adam's figure, body stilled mid-swing. His fist is curled, elbow bent.

I've never seen his face as dark and deathly as it is now. I don't know how he's controlling himself, how the very mention of his father and Adam's threat didn't send Maddox hurdling the jerk into the wall and beating him until long after he begged him to stop.

Yet, somehow, Maddox remains steady.

"Mads," Reed manages, and I'm aware that the look in Maddox's eyes has him on edge, too. He doesn't want to see

Maddox fall into Adam's trap.

"Mads," I repeat, though my voice is sticky.

"He isn't worth it," Reed adds. "He's just trying to get a rise out of you."

Adam sneers at Reed's claim, though his stare doesn't move from Maddox. "Go ahead. You'll be proving my point."

I can see Maddox's jaw trembling at the weight of his pressed teeth, see the blackout in his gaze as if Adam had triggered a part of himself that he'd tried to bury.

"Mads," I try again.

Because I know Adam.

I know he's riling inside at this display, probably feeling pure satisfaction at Maddox's reaction and thinking of all the ways he can use this to his advantage.

Maddox finally relaxes his arm.

I don't take a breath. Not yet. Not as Maddox presses his hands to the lapels of Adam's sports coat and straightens them tauntingly, and definitely not as Maddox picks a piece of lint off Adam's shoulder.

"Come anywhere near my family again, and I won't fucking stop," Maddox practically growls in a voice so hoarse and low that aside from Adam, only Reed and I hear it.

Maddox takes one step back and with good timing.

"Hey, there he is!"

The DJ approaches with a broad smile, his words cutting the tense air. He pushes his arm around Adam's shoulders, clearly having no idea what's transpired, and smiles between Maddox and Reed.

"I was wondering where this guy was," he continues. "I wanted you to meet him before you left. This is Adam. We're trying to convince him you guys won't be inciting any riots during your concerts this weekend."

And it visibly dawns on Reed and Maddox as they realize what's happening.

"You've got to be fucking kidding me," Reed says.

Though Reed's words don't draw me out of the daze.

Maddox *laughs*.

The outburst makes my hair stand on end.

"God, you're fucking joking. This is the guy?" He claps his hands and shakes his head, maniacal noises leaving him. "James, can you get someone to start the fucking car?" he asks their bodyguard. "I think we need to leave."

"The fuck do you have against music?" Reed asks Adam.

I cross my arms over my chest. "He's never really liked sex, drugs, or rock and roll," I say, glaring at Adam.

The first bit of anger washes over Adam's face, and he looks at me as if the sentence is a challenge.

"Wait—you two know each other?" Paul asks.

"I think I've heard enough tonight," Adam says, shrugging Paul's hands off his shoulders. He plasters the fake smile back on his lips and shakes Paul's hand, thanking him for the invite before returning his attention to Reed, Maddox, and me.

The way darkness lingers in his gaze makes me uneasy and lets me know I should be more alert the rest of the time I'm here.

"I have a feeling I'll be seeing you boys later this week," he says.

Adam pushes between Reed and me before making his way down the stairs, and once he turns the corner toward the exit, I finally exhale.

Reed is already talking to the clueless DJ, trying to explain what just happened without giving away too many personal details. I don't even look at anyone as I shove past them to the fire exit—where I should have gone in the first place to avoid all of this—and escape the room altogether.

Cold air swarms around me. It's a welcome tickle on my numb skin. I press my hands into the railing and grip it tight, ignoring the ache of its cold metal as I force myself to breathe, to stay steady.

The door opens behind me, and my head droops.

"Reed, don't—"

"It isn't Reed."

Maddox's voice is soft. I inhale deeply, ignoring the overwhelming press of emotion behind my nose, and I face him. His gaze is solemn as he stares, his eyes illuminated beneath the floodlights from the roof.

"Are you okay?" he asks.

I almost scoff. "Are *you*?" I ask, more concerned with how Adam had just spoken to Maddox than how the asshole had stared at me.

Maddox shakes me off. "I'm fine," he says. "It'll take more than him bringing up my shit father to hurt me."

"Maddox, he could tell everyone who you are," I say, almost panicking. "Forget the photographers trying to get a glimpse of you. He—" I sink my head into my hand, the ropes winding around my stomach tightening to the point that I need to throw up. "This is all my fault. I know how much you want that kept private. If he tells the press who you are—"

"Our manager will take care of it," he says, though I can see the fight behind his eyes. It's eating at him, the stress of everyone finding out his past, his father's past.

It's written in every shift of his eyes.

He wipes his face harshly and forces his hands to his hips, gaze lifting to mine.

"Are you okay?" he asks again.

"I'm fine," I answer, though my voice is too soft to be believable. "He's just an ex."

"He's a fucking douchebag," he mutters.

I need to puke.

"It won't be the last time we see him this week," I

regretfully say. "I promise you that."

Maddox huffs in an annoyed manner. He glances back over his shoulder to the door like he's watching for someone before crossing the space between us and pulling down his mask.

I have to swallow as he hovers there.

"I don't know what happened between you two, but the anger and fear in your eyes when I saw you arguing with him made my entire body go cold," he rasps. "Fuck exposing me. He's lucky he isn't splattered on the floor of that club for making you feel that way."

My heart seems to skip, though before I can reply, the door opens to reveal Reed. He looks at Maddox first, then at me.

"Is she okay—are you okay?" Reed asks.

"Yeah," I reply as I start back inside. "I think I'm ready to go home, though."

"James has the car ready," Reed says. "Bonnie and Zeb are going to stay. Avie is already on the phone. I told him we'd call on the way back. You ready to leave?"

"No arguments here," Maddox says.

My lashes lift to Maddox one more time to see him push the mask up over his face again, and he discreetly squeezes the back of my arm when Reed goes back inside.

And for whatever reason, all I can think about is how much I want that squeeze around my entire body, how much I'm craving his embrace and comforting touch.

Fuck, I need to go to bed.

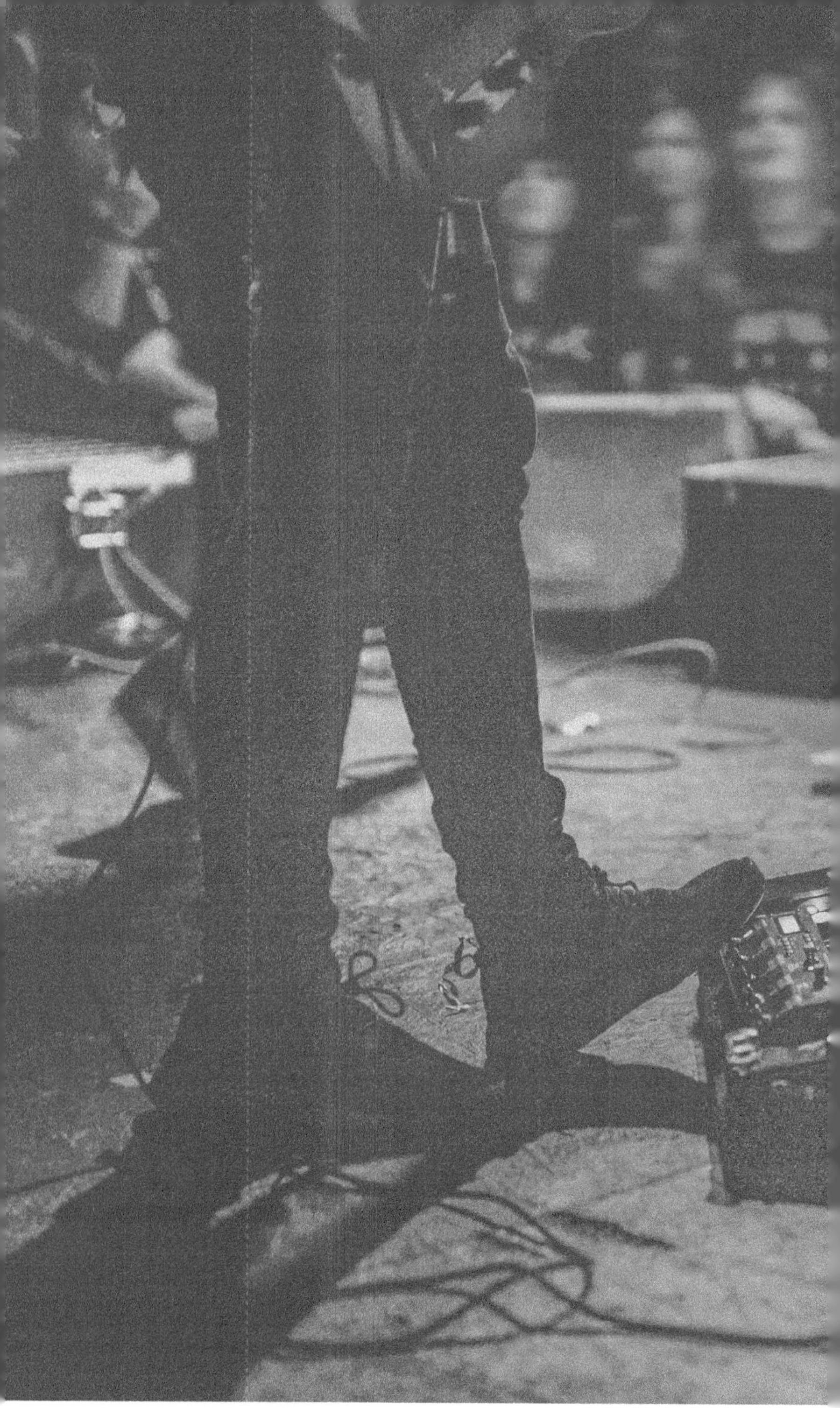

CHAPTER SIX
MADDOX

The Comfort Zone

There's a scary movie playing on the large television. I'm staring at it, yet I have no clue what's happening or even the name of it.

My mind is back at that club, fantasies running through me about what might have happened if I'd gone off on Adam like I should have. I should have thrown him over the side of the balcony or down the stairs.

The entire ride home consisted of phone calls with our manager and the PR firm, along with Reed's outbursts about the ordeal. I barely remember what was said.

The threat of Adam going to the press with my real name lingers. It has my skin crawling with a restless itch that I can't seem to get rid of. Not because of anything I've ever done. Even still, if people knew what my father had done, if they realized the kind of person I'd spawned from…

I pop another gummy into my mouth and sip my beer. It's only my third drink and probably my last. I need the edge off. I need to get rid of this irritation scratching beneath my skin.

As much as I know I shouldn't be stressing over it, it's all I can do to get the look on Andi's face out of my head. She'd been so quiet on the way back, shrank into the darkness with her head lying on the cold glass window, occasionally opening up her phone to text her boss about what happened.

I flop back onto the couch, shove the pillow over my head, and shout into it.

So fucking *fucked*.

When I sit back up, I see a shadow move before the double doors.

I swear if that bastard followed us back here—

It isn't Adam moving around the deck.

Andi is standing on the other side of the glass, her hand pressed against it as if she doesn't know whether to knock.

I launch to my feet without thinking twice and jump over the coffee table to get to the door, terrified that something is wrong, and when I throw the door open, I forget how to speak.

She's wearing an oversized hoodie and those tights, short character socks on her feet. She quickly crosses her arms over her chest and hugs herself like she's suddenly freezing, and the look in her eyes…

"What's wrong?" I ask, fear rushing through me as I look past her into the darkness.

"I can't sleep," she admits. "I saw your light on. I thought… fuck, I don't know what I thought." She threads her fingers into her hair and pulls the roots out of frustration. "I feel fucking stupid. Never mind, Maddox. It's fine. I don't know what I'm looking for—"

"Hey—" I take her wrist when she turns away and draw her back.

An agonizing fright stretches in her eyes when our gazes meet. I feel my jaw twitch when I see it.

I can't let her go back to that empty room alone.

"Hang out with me a little while," I suggest. "Maybe you'll remember what you were looking for."

I see her swallow, and with one more look over her shoulder, she finally nods.

"Okay."

My heart is in my ears.

She's alone with me in the pool house.

She's upset and broken, and I'm not about to take advantage of a shitty situation.

Even still, I can't help the little butterflies inside me at the realization that she came to see *me*.

Her eyes narrow at the counter, and I realize I have a pile of junk food bags and lime water cans sitting on top of it like an outright trash panda. I dart to the mess and try to stuff some of it in the trash. However, Andi sits on the barstool and picks up a Twix wrapper. She doesn't say anything as I gather the mess into the can, and by the time the counter is clean, she's still tearing apart the shiny wrapper.

I don't know what she needs, and that bugs the hell out of me.

"Do you want a drink?" I ask awkwardly.

"Nothing alcoholic," she says with a sigh. "If I start drinking, I'll numb myself into a stupor. And I hate that fucking feeling."

"How about hot cider?" I suggest, and a minute smile lifts in her eyes.

"Cider? Like apple cider?" she asks.

I reach into the fridge and pull out the gallon Tina stocked there, and Andi chuckles softly.

"Cider sounds amazing."

I put it in a pot on the stove because I genuinely don't know how else to heat it, and as I do, Andi shifts toward the television.

"You have music on and a movie? And white noise from the dehumidifier?"

"Ah... helps drown out the voices," I admit, and she nods as if she knows what I mean.

"I do the same thing," she says. "Though, usually, the white noise is the fan in the bathroom."

"It's headphones for me on the bus," I say.

"I use those all day at work, and anytime I'm running errands."

"I did that a couple of times, but I was paranoid that I would miss something," I tell her, and she smirks.

"That's why I keep them around my neck," she explains. "Actual headphones, not earbuds—wow, you went way back on some of these tracks," she adds about my music.

"Comfort playlist," I say.

"I'm totally going to judge you for what's on here. I hope it's the good shit."

"What else would I listen to?"

Her smile sweeps broadly across her lips, and I have to turn back to the stove so I don't pull her across this fucking countertop.

"Are you okay?" she asks. "With everything, I mean. With Adam—"

"It's just a name, Andi."

It's a fucking lie.

An outright fabrication.

Because the thought of Adam going public with my name —my father's name—is eating me from the inside.

"I know, but it's your privacy," she says. "I know how much you value that."

I press my palms into the counter, my back to her.

I hate thinking about this.

What's even more is I hate that *she's* worried about it.

"Avie said they'd take care of it," I tell her, referring to our manager. "He's never let me down. And if he somehow slips through the cracks, I know Heartless will pick it up."

I don't believe myself.

The cider begins to simmer as a tense lull surrounds us, and I'm thankful for the distraction.

"What's the tattoo on your elbow?" she asks as I pour our cider into mugs.

I have to look to remember. "The broken glass or the flower?" I ask.

"Oh, that's broken glass," she realizes.

I set our cups down and bend my elbow to point to the scars buried beneath the ink. "I think you were already at college when this happened," I say.

"Wait—is that when you fell through the window?" she asks.

For some twisted reason, I almost smile at the fact that she remembered, and I pull up my shirt to show her the rest. There's a scar from a three-inch gash down my side from a shard of glass that nearly ended my life.

"Oh my god," she says upon seeing it.

Never mind the way she's staring at the rest of me.

I let my shirt fall before those eyes end all of my willpower. My gaze snags on the tattoo she has on her neck, and I jerk my chin toward it. "What's that one?"

"Oh—Ah… a little hard to show you." She hops off the stool and comes around the counter, pulling the hoodie back so I can see down into her shirt. It's a full rendering of a raven with its wings up, including the iridescent feathers and detail that would have taken hours of work.

"That's fucking gorgeous," I say.

"Ravens have a special place in my heart," she says as she heads toward the couch, drink in hand. "That was my first big one. I think I spent more time in the tattoo chair when I was twenty-three than I have any other year," she says, sitting on the couch and curling her legs beneath her.

"Why's that?" I ask, sitting on the opposite end.

"Had some extra cash with my bartending job on the weekends," she replies. "And the euphoria of that pain was better than the sex I was having—or anything in my life, for that matter."

"I feel that… Was it that asshole from the bar?"

She nods reluctantly.

"He never deserved you," I say. "I remember the time you brought him home for Thanksgiving. I thought your dad would murder him when he tried to downplay your promotion. Reed and I planned out some elaborate scheme to get rid of him that night, but you kicked him out before we could execute."

An expression shifts in her gaze as though the mention of that holiday is too much, like the memory suddenly rushing through her has her on the verge of shutting down.

She takes another sip of her warm cider and looks over the rim at me. "What about you?" she asks. "When did you get most of yours?"

"Ah…" I look down at my arms, my exposed knees. "This last year," I admit.

"Any particular reason? Or just because?" she asks.

I have to run my hand through my hair, eyes moving to the floor. "When I found out my dad had cancer, I pretended it didn't bother me. But the feeling in my gut was like I was the one with cancer, and it was eating me from the inside out. I ended up in the chair every time it crossed my mind to come home and give the asshole even a minute of grief. Somehow… somehow, I was the one who felt guilty. After every fucking thing he put me through, I was the one feeling guilty about not reaching out to him. And then, when he died, it was like now that he wasn't around to put me down and tell me how much of a piece of shit I am, the voices became louder. There was no sense of relief that he was no longer there. If anything, my mind became more of a prison. It's like it felt the need to fill in those gaps. Every time my phone rang and it wasn't his name across the screen, there was this pain in my stomach. I couldn't breathe. Even in fucking death, he made me feel as if I wasn't a good enough son for him to love or stop the madness for."

"And now?" she asks.

I feel my teeth grind slightly. "Being back here isn't as bad as I thought it would be, and maybe that's because we're here and not at the old house, or because—fuck, maybe it's because it's only been a day."

"Do you still hear the voices?" she asks.

My eyes lift to hers. "Every day," I admit. "You?"

A brow flickers up, and she shifts her gaze to her hands. "They never left."

"Sometimes it helps the world not feel so lonely," I say, only halfway joking.

Andi snorts, and it's the most adorable thing I've ever seen or heard. "You talk back to your voices?"

"Don't you?"

"I mean, sometimes," she answers. She stares down at her hands, tension lifting in her eyes. "I think the scariest part about talking back to them is the fear that they'll say what they used to tell my mother."

The thought makes me shift. "Andi, your mother was a psychotic narcissist who self-medicated with the wrong choice of drugs and a string of boyfriends who made it worse. She should have been in an institution where she could get help for the voices in her head. You're nothing like her."

Her brows lift in agreement. "She probably would have conned her way out of the institution," she mutters.

She isn't wrong.

"Even still…" Her voice drifts as she lets out a sigh,

amusement threading in her eyes. "I don't think I've ever told anyone that I hear them," she admits. "For that reason."

"I'm the perfect person to tell," I say. "My voices don't gossip to anyone else's."

A laugh sounds from her. I hadn't even thought it was that funny, and maybe it's the delusion of the late-night, how tired we both are, or how sad the entire notion is.

"How do you do that?" she manages after a minute.

"Do what?"

"Hide it," she replies. "Make people laugh like you do. Laughing through all of your pain. How are you… *you*, when you have so much in your past that could have made you a monster?"

"How do you know I'm not just good at hiding the monster?"

Her head tilts as she smiles at me. "Either way, you're still hiding it."

I fumble with my hands. "Making people laugh helps me feel a little less shitty, maybe less worthless than I was made to believe," I admit. "I never wanted anyone to truly know what was happening behind closed doors. Reed. You. Your family… that was enough people. I think maybe that's why I've continued wearing the mask. If people saw me and figured out my past, what might they think of who I really am?"

"They'd love you just like we do," she says.

Warmth fills my chest at the way she's staring at me, and before I can even think of what to do or say next, the first note of a familiar song plays.

Andi's eyes widen to mine, putting a full stop to our previous conversation.

I almost laugh.

So fucking cute.

"Instant chills," she says as she holds up her arm to show

me. "That one note is like a calling card to an entire generation."

A quiet chuckle leaves me. "We covered it at a show a couple of years back. Fucking hell, you should have heard everyone sing it back."

"I need to hear that at practice tomorrow," she says.

"I'll tell Reed," I say.

Her expression falters, and she begins to fidget with her fingers. "Don't... don't tell him I came here tonight. He gets all weird, and I don't want... I don't want him to think we're anything more than friends," she says.

I want to fall into the deep end of the pool and never come up for air.

I know she's right, and I fucking hate it.

I take a sip of my drink and watch her a second longer. "What else could we be?" I ask.

I know it's a gamble.

I know even mentioning it is stupid.

Being with her could ruin everything. The only family I've ever known. My best friend. The band. My career. It could fuck up everything I've worked for.

Looking at her, I don't know that I care.

Andi sits her cup on the coffee table, and I brace myself for the pain she's about to inflict.

However, the thought of whatever this is goes amiss when the next song comes on.

Andi looks like she can't believe her own ears. Her bright eyes lift to mine, the sorrowful haze that had just been present in them a moment before completely gone.

"Stop it," she says. "This... You have *this* song on here?"

It's an older song, and as the first few beats play, I know why she's in disbelief that I would keep it on my playlist after all these years.

Behind my eyes, all I see is a memory at least thirteen years old of Andi trying her hardest to get Koen and Kamden to dance and rock out with her in the basement of their old home. It's a bittersweet memory, one that makes me fall down the rabbit hole as I look at her and see the same fucked up nostalgia in her eyes.

In a blink, we're back at the old house.

Randall and Tina are shouting upstairs with Andi's mom, Alice, on one of her determined outbursts and episodes as she tries to take Andi away from them.

There's a chair beneath the basement door handle that slides every time someone forcefully rattles the knob.

The boombox is at its very loudest to drown out the noise, to distract the youngest members of the Matthews family, and to protect their innocent ears from the pain happening just above them.

And despite the tears in her bloodshot eyes or the ones silently rolling down her cheeks, Andi is spinning Koen and Kamden and forcing a smile on her face and laughter to sound from her throat. She's moving their arms and playing the air guitar with Reed while I sit on the back of the couch and turn the music up louder and louder.

Anything to drown out the suffocating horrors that eventually cause the neighbors to call the cops.

And Andi... she's trying everything she can to rescue the rest of us from the things she can't save herself from.

I see the same memory swimming behind her now glistening eyes, and I rise to my feet.

"Come here," I say with a gesture of my hands.

She gives me a confused look. "What?"

"It's time someone danced with you."

Something between a laugh and a sob chokes her, and when she doesn't rise immediately, I take her by the wrists and pull her to her feet.

I'm a terrible dancer.

For her...

I'll dance with her all night if she needs me to.

She brushes me off and shakes her head. I reach for my phone and turn the volume so loud that neither of us can hear our thoughts. And finally, after moving her arms back and forth a couple of times, a full smile slips onto her lips, and she gives in.

So fucking worth it.

I'm sure if anyone were to look out the kitchen window and see us, they would think we were drinking. Because for a solid four minutes, we forget who we're supposed to be.

We forget the rest of the world exists.

I spin her. We play air guitar on the coffee table, the two of us back-to-back. There's head banging and laughing and swaying, and the entire time, I can only think that I wish I had done this with her years ago when her heart was breaking. When fresh tears were moving down her cheeks from the arguments and screaming upstairs.

When we jump down from the coffee table, I take her wrists and spin her a few more times until she has to grab my arms to stay balanced. Her laughter rings through the room when I bring her back into me.

She fists my shirt, both of us moving off balance, and I hug her waist so we don't crash into the couch. Her laughter fades through the last bridge of the song, and for the briefest of moments, I feel her clench me tighter.

My heartbeat is in my ears. I widen my hand at the small of her back, and as I hug her close into a sway, I feel her tremble in my arms.

We're clinging to the moments neither of us had control over, the moments that we can't change, the ones that are a part of us now.

It's four minutes of my life that becomes a core memory. I barely realize my forehead is resting against her temple until

I feel her lean into it.

I breathe her in. I feel her pulse in her wrist, and I'm curious what she's thinking. Her eyes are closed when I look down at her. Her jaw is tight, her body tensing against me like she's trying to stop herself from breaking.

I brace my hand against her cheek, causing her eyes to open up at me, and the look within them shatters my heart.

God, I want to kiss her.

I think I might die if I don't.

I want to kiss her and swear she'll never have to feel that pain again. I want to find every scar she's ever concealed so she never feels she has to hide a part of herself.

I thread my fingers in her hair's roots at the nape of her neck and swipe my thumb across her cheekbone, leaning dangerously close to her face. I can feel her staggered breath upon my lips as her gaze darts to my mouth.

"Break, beautiful," I whisper. "Don't be afraid of me. I'll pick up all your pieces."

Her bottom lip quivers. "I've heard too many promises to put me back together again from men who never meant it," she says. "Because they never do."

"I don't mean to put you back together… I mean to hold onto whatever parts of yourself you need me to take, and when they inevitably get mixed up with my own fucked up fragments, we'll make our own masterpiece with all the pieces that don't fit anymore."

There's a pause where she looks up at me, and I feel myself die a little more.

"Maddox…"

Every bit of restraint I have left within me is on its final edge. I need her to walk away from me because if she doesn't move within the next thirty seconds, I'm going to resign into absolute insanity.

The tickle of her fingers in my beard makes my eyes

flutter.

Walk away from her.
Send her to bed.
She can never be yours.

"You should go to bed, Andi," I say, though I can't bring myself to let her go.

I need her to be the one to pull out of my arms.

I need her to be the one to let me go.

She finally nods as if she knows what I'm thinking, as if she can feel the way I'm drowning inside. Before she steps out of our embrace, she leans up, and her lips land on my cheek.

Breath escapes me.

Cold air sweeps between us when she steps back, though she's still hanging onto my fingertips.

"Thank you," she says.

I have to swallow, have to stuff my hands into my pockets because if I leave them out, I'll have her back into my arms again, and there won't be any stopping me from tasting her right here on this couch.

"Wanting to make you smile is purely for my own selfishness," I say, and her lips curl like she knows I'm lying. I run my hand over my beard and huff in amusement. "Seriously, it's never something you ever have to thank me for," I add in a more serious tone.

"Even so." She inhales a deep breath, almost making me think she's been holding it as long as I have. "Goodnight, Maddox."

I watch her grab her drink from the bar, and she exits the room with one more glance over her shoulder.

Oh, mother fucking, god dammit, it all to hell.

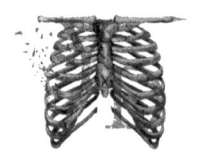

Debate rolls through me as I pace behind the couch, my hands braced behind my neck.

I should have kissed her.

Fuck who we are. Fuck everything that says I shouldn't touch her.

I should have kissed her.

God dammit.

I'm on the verge of pulling my hair out. Every step is in absolute agony. I don't think I've breathed in the thirty minutes since she walked out of that door.

Fuck it.

I pull the hood of my black hoodie up over my head and quietly leave the room toward the big house. I don't even have to go inside to go to the room she's staying in. She claimed the one over the garage because it has a private bathroom, and while Koen tried to argue with her when he and Kamden arrived, Andi insisted she needed the space.

I climb the steps to the room from the outside, and when I reach the stoop, I stare at the door.

What the hell am I doing?

I don't have a plan.

I don't know what I'm supposed to say.

I resist banging my head on the wall for not rehearsing something on my way up here.

However, all that goes awry when I hear a soft noise from the room.

It's brief, almost like a whimper. I step closer and lean my ear against the door, a thread of fear coursing through me. Her room is so easily accessible from the outside it's possible that—

"Right there," I hear her whimper. "Fuck, right there."

My brows narrow. It's only been a half-hour. There's no way she already has someone else inside her room, which means—

She moans again, and I close my eyes to listen more intently, which is when I hear the distinct noise of a vibrator.

Shit...

She whimpers hard and fast, the noise sounding muffled behind a pillow, and I wonder what toy she has getting her off. I rest my forehead against the door, the shadow of the peaked roof swallowing me out of sight from the back lights.

God, this is wrong. I shouldn't be listening to her like this.

I can't stop.

"Just like that," I hear her whisper. "Right there."

I spread my hand across the wood, my dick pressing against the zipper of my jeans as I close my eyes. I want to know who she's imagining between those delectable thighs, who she's quietly commanding to just the right spot.

The image of her lying on that bed, possibly fisting the sheets, fills my mind. It's all I can see in the darkness. She curses again, this time more frantic.

"*Maddox.*"

I shove off the door at the sound of her high-pitched moan. My eyes feel like they're about to bulge out of my head.

My name.

She was moaning...

Son of a bitch.

"Maddox," I hear her continue. "Fuck, right there."

It takes every bit of restraint I have not to open that door and go inside to give her a real reason to whimper...

My name.

My. Fucking. Name.

My forehead meets the door again, my eyes closing as a muffled groan sounds from within me. I wonder how she looks naked on the bed. I wonder if those pouting lips are parted. If her eyes are closed or open as her chin juts toward the ceiling.

She moans out my name again. *Again.*

I ball up a fist and nearly hit the door out of frustration.

I should have fucking kissed her.

Why didn't I kiss her?

Another wonderful little whimper sounds from her. I'm straining against my pants, the ache causing my muscles to tense. The next moan is muffled, the noise of my name once more sounding from her lips is like an echo that I can't tell is real.

Her voice is a broken record in my ears. It's playing over and over. The fantasy of what she would look like beneath me invades my every thought. Her tits bouncing. Her soft thighs squeezing my hips. My hand on her throat. The gasping look of surprise on her face as I plunge inside her tight pussy.

There's another indistinct wail from the other side of the door, and I know she's getting close. I can hear her short breaths—or at least, I can in the fiction running through my head. Her cries sound more frantic. My name escapes her lips again. *Again.*

"Come for me, beautiful," I whisper aloud, wondering if somehow the darkness might carry my plea through this threshold and utter it in her ear as I want to do myself.

I need to know the look on her face as she comes.

I want to memorize it.

"Fucking come for me," I hiss. "Cry out my name."

A plea sounds from inside—a cry that nearly sends me throwing myself into her room to watch that look of satisfaction cross her face. And when she wails out my name…

My fist slams into the door frame.

It rattles and quakes as her orgasm crashes.

Silence swells on the other side.

Shit.

For a single beat, I contemplate staying there and letting her discover me, allowing her to see the state simply listening to her moan has put me in. I consider the consequences of her opening the door and finding me with my rock-hard dick straining to be free of these pants. To be in her hands, her mouth, her pussy. I would kiss her and send her falling back on the bed before taking what I know now is mine.

What's *always* been mine.

Her footsteps reverberate on the floor.

Fuck.

She throws open the door. I'm already jumping over the side of the staircase. Darkness shrouds me as I hang onto the wooden steps a few feet off the ground. I have to get out of here before she or anyone else discovers me.

Her door closes again, and I finally exhale.

My. Fucking. Name.

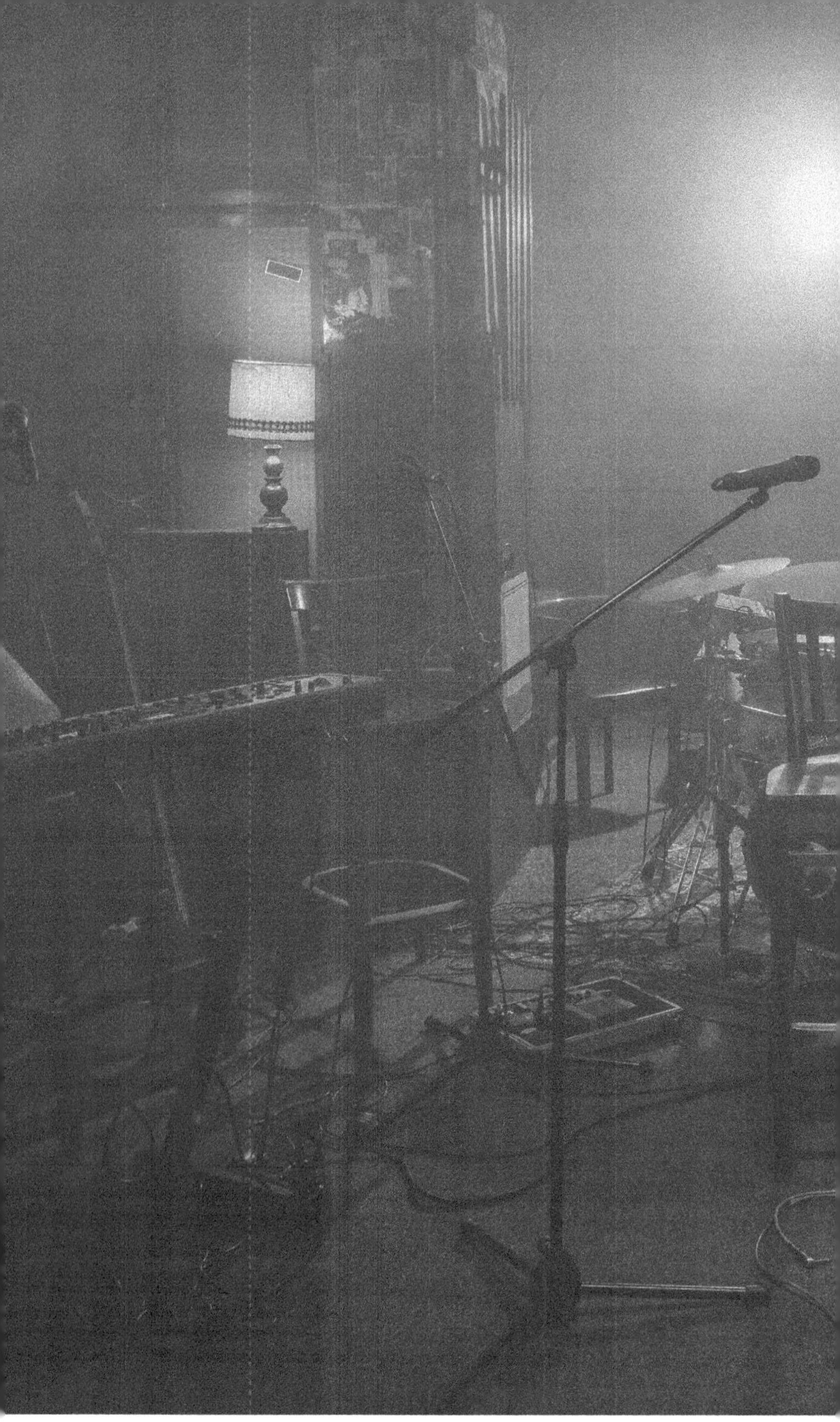

CHAPTER SEVEN
ANDI

There's a lingering tension between Maddox and me that I can't put my finger on. It's almost like a longing for him, to touch him, to smile at him, laugh with him. It isn't in cheesy jokes back and forth or the picking on one another that I'm accustomed to with him.

It's a craving energy.

I felt it in the small smile he gave me this morning over breakfast, in the licentious gleam in his eyes when he stared at me over his coffee cup.

And, most especially, I feel it in the back of the Escalade where we are now. It's so thick that gravity has me edging closer to him each time I shift in my seat.

How are you feeling today? Maddox texts me from the opposite side of the bench.

My gaze drifts his way, and I find him watching me. I wonder if he's as eager to learn if last night affected something deep within my soul as I am to know if it did him.

Because it had.

I'm here, I reply, and it's the best way to describe the numbness I'm trying to ignore. Every instinct within me has told me to shut down and mask, dissociate from the rest of the world, throw myself behind my camera, and ignore everything.

That's the only way I'll survive the anxiety of not only possibly seeing Adam again and being back in this town but also the sudden want to get closer to Maddox.

It's terrifying, and I know I shouldn't want him as badly as I do. I know I shouldn't put him at any risk of his friendship with Reed or the band and the career he's worked so hard for.

I want to be alone with him. I want to know if he's feeling this same thing. However, the very thought of what might transpire is a different sort of scary that I'm not used to. I'm used to the genuinely anxious horror. The monsters under the bed and the creeps at night. I'm used to the scare of physical violence—of a mother screaming and running after me with a knife, of a boyfriend beating me and being so good to everyone else. I'm used to the abuse life has thrown me, and I know how to shout back at it.

However, this couldn't be more different.

Thank you for last night, I text him.

Maddox reads the text, and for a moment, he simply stares at the screen as if he's trying to think of how to reply. A numbness swells inside me. I have to swallow out of nervousness.

Maddox finally moves, and I try not to watch him too closely. He avoids looking at me the entire time he sits up and shifts to the middle of the bench seat, his ass on the edge like he only means to chat with Reed.

"I thought we could have some fun at practice today," Maddox says to Reed as he leans up between the front seats. "Try a few songs we haven't covered in a while to mix things up. Just jam for a bit."

"I could use some range stretches," Reed agrees. "What did you have in mind?"

Maddox is talking to Reed and reaching for me in the back. His fingers graze against mine, and the moment we touch, we flinch as if we've never touched one another before. It's charged and tense. I inhale sharply, yet I can't take my eyes away from the side of his face or draw my hand away from his, and when our palms sink together, my heart leaps into my throat.

Reed mentions an older song, and Maddox takes out his phone as if he's looking it up. He connects his phone to the radio and plays it, and while it plays, I see him pull up his messages again.

I mean it, he says. ***Every piece, beautiful.***

"Is that Bonnie?" Reed asks, turning in his seat and referring to who Maddox is texting.

Maddox drops my hand as if it's on fire and pretends he was just scratching his side. It's so abrupt that the surprise nearly makes me flinch. I quickly pull out my camera and pretend to be going through photos from the day before.

"Yeah," Maddox lies. "She said she and Zeb are at the studio already."

Reed seems satisfied with the answer and swivels back to the front. The pair begin discussing details of the music they hope to play today, and I zone out the rest of the car ride.

Bonnie and Zeb are already at practice when we arrive. Bonnie is warming up with her usual bounces to 'get the blood flowing to her muscles' as she puts it.

I'm busy finding my settings while Maddox and Reed go through what they want to do today, which Zeb and Bonnie are fully on board with. By the time they've all settled into their positions, I realize I've been detached from reality the entire time. Even when I found myself laughing at one of their jokes or speaking with one of them, I can't even remember it.

I hate this.

I hate the moments when I can't connect back with reality. When no matter who or what is standing in front of me, I can't comprehend it. I'm going through the motions, yet in the back of my mind, a stressor anchors me beneath the waves. I can see the sky but can't swim up and out of its depths.

Thankfully, looking through the lens of my camera helps bring me back.

Maddox is watching me as he pulls his mask over his nose and lets his sleeves down to cover his tattoos so they won't be visible in the photos. The mechanical hand rendering covering the back of his left hand is still visible, along with some of the face on the back of his other. His black nail polish is chipped, and I'm pretty sure it's intentional. He settles on the stool, rests his foot on the amp, and then brings his bass onto his lap. Bonnie sets the beat, and as they begin playing a familiar ballad, I feel it move through my bones.

Someone once told me I should ground myself through a higher power. That I shouldn't think I'm the greatest force in the universe or that I'm the only person who can save me.

My initial response was for them to fuck off and mind their own business.

However, something about the sentence stuck with me.

Once I started therapy, and we dove deeper into my past, I started to uncover some childhood memories I had blocked out and buried in the deepest corners of my soul, and I began to realize something.

Music had been my grounding force. It had been my higher power. It carried me through moments I didn't think I'd recover from.

Moments I still haven't recovered from.

Maybe that was why I gripped onto Adam the way I did. Because, at the time, I thought I needed fixing. I thought a knight in shining armor was the only thing that could help me. Cover up the past and forget it ever happened. Run away and ignore all the ways it shaped me.

I'm so tired of running.

The band jams well into the afternoon. They take a few breaks for snacks, try out some new material Maddox has written over the last few weeks, and play a few familiar favorites. It's interesting to watch them work. The concentration and creative juices flow through as they collaborate on the new stuff or plan out new segments for the upcoming concerts—anything to make the nights seem original and not the same as the last few gigs.

"I think we should change up the setlist every night," Zeb says during their last break. "Some people bought tickets to all three shows. We can't do the same thing every night."

"Obviously, do the big three," Bonnie says.

"We can interchange the final song," Reed says, his mouth full of a handful of French fries. "Change up the effects or the breaks. Bring the big piano out on the last night."

"Yeah, you'd like that, wouldn't you?" Bonnie teases him.

Reed grins crookedly in response.

"We're at the venue most of the day tomorrow," Maddox adds. "We can talk to Rock about anything new he can do with lights and special effects. Especially for Saturday."

"Halloween show," Reed says. "Thought about doing the entire show in a Scream mask."

Bonnie arches a pierced brow. "Are you trying to cause a scene?"

"Fuck yeah," Reed says. "Radio is already calling it a Halloween party."

"That's going to be amazing to see from the stage," Maddox says. "Just waves of costumes."

"It makes my spooky heart happy," Bonnie grins.

"I'll be sure to get photos of the best ones," I tell them.

"You guys want to do anything else, or are we done for the day?" Zeb asks. "I need to go to the shops and get a few things."

"Mm… same," Reed says, closing his styrofoam box. He nudges Maddox with his knee. "Want to go with?"

Maddox's eyes flicker to me, but it's so brief that when I blink, he's looking the other way. "Honestly, I need a fucking nap," he says as he rubs his face. "I might have to raincheck you guys."

"Yeah, same," Bonnie says.

"Why? You have a date with that journalist?" Reed asks.

A sly smile slips onto Bonnie's lips. "Maybe."

The rest of the band throws fries at her when she rises, and Bonnie sticks out her tongue. Laughter sounds from each of them, but with the scrape of their chairs against the floor, they all stand to pick up their trash and go their separate ways.

"What about you, Andi?" Reed asks me. "Want to go shopping?"

"I have to get these into the computer," I tell him, holding up my camera. "It would be my luck that something would happen to the card, and I'd be fucked."

"Okay." He takes out his phone and starts texting someone. "Mads, you want James to drop you and Andi off at home before he takes us to the shops? Or call my mom?"

"Ah…" Maddox hesitates slightly. "No. We can get a car," he says as he looks at me.

"Oh. Oh, yeah, I'll get us one," I say as I collect more trash around the room.

The butterflies are flapping so vigorously that I don't know what my body is doing when I look his way.

I can't feel my face as they all chat a few more minutes while waiting on their respective rides, coming up with a plan for the next day and talking about what they should get to wear for the gigs.

And by the time everyone has left the room except for Maddox and me, my entire body is on alert.

"Did you call a car for us?" Maddox asks.

Mother fucker.

"Shit," I say as I pull my phone out. "Sorry. In my head today."

Yet Maddox is smiling at me.

I tap a few times on the screen, fucking thankful that he still has his music playing in the background because if it was silent in here, I might have short-circuited already.

"Three minutes," I announce once it's on its way. "Driver is Corey."

Three minutes is just enough time for me to say something ridiculous and scare him off.

I hurriedly grab the rest of the takeout and shove it in the trash by the wall as Maddox closes his instrument case and grabs his backpack.

Or at least, that's what I thought he was doing.

The trash has barely left my hand when his fingers wrap around my wrist. He pushes me back, my shoulders and ass hit the wall, and it's all I can do to keep my composure as he suspends over me.

He's as close as he was last night. So close that the fantasy I'd filled myself with after I left him flashes behind my eyes. He pins my wrist into the wall, and I have to coerce myself into speaking.

"What… what are you doing?" I ask.

It's a stupid question. Even so, it's all I can think of.

"Every time you watch me like you do, I can't feel my ears," he says.

I blink.

Can't feel his…

"That sounds awful," I say. "Wait—*What?*"

His lips curl upward, tongue swiping between them as the dark pools in his eyes bloom.

"I know that's weird, but… When you look at me, I get

butterflies in my stomach, and there's this itch on the back of my neck like all of my hair is standing on end. I never know what to do with my hands, and I end up shoving them in my pockets to keep from fidgeting."

I stare at him, thinking of how cool and collected he always appears to be.

"I would love to see you fidget," I say. "It might make you seem less perfect."

"I'm not perfect," he says exhaustedly. "If I was perfect, I'd be able to walk away from you. I'd be able to ignore the feeling in my heart and the absolute need to be near you."

My mouth dries.

I don't know what my face is doing as he shifts on his feet and leans closer.

"If I was smart, I'd be able to remember the vow I swore to your brother years ago in your stupid little basement on Halloween when he and I were sixteen and you were home from college. When you pranced around us in that godforsaken referee outfit and the tiny shorts that made me *lose. My. Mind*."

I recall that night. I know exactly which shorts he's thinking about.

And as I remember him and my brother playing video games in the basement while I took my younger brothers around the neighborhood, I also remember his gaze lingering on me from that couch for a few seconds longer than ever before.

"And somehow… ten years later, you're still making me feel as if I can't catch my breath," he admits.

My eyes dart to his lips.

I want to tell him I can't catch my breath when he's around either.

"Is that a bad thing?" I ask.

"Horrible," he says, though his voice sounds like he's

straining to compose himself. His throat bobs beneath those fucking tattoos as he watches me, and I feel his chest rise against mine.

"Put me out of my misery, Andi," he almost begs. "Tell me you're out of my league. Tell me this crush I've had on you for years is all in my head, and what I heard last night was you calling another Maddox's name."

My face is on fire. "You heard that?" I pant.

"Every *fucking* word," he replies.

It explains so much—each look he's given me today, all the teasing… He heard me saying his name. No, *crying* out his name.

Heat consumes me.

"I heard every fucking moan and that… god, that little whimper," he says in an agonizing tone. "Do you know how much restraint it took for me not to go in that room and help you finish?"

"You should have," I breathe.

His face inches closer. I can feel my heartbeat in my ears, his breath on my face. All it would take is one more push, one more shift forward.

"No, what I should do is run from you," he rasps. "I should run far, far away. I should run as if touching you will ruin my entire life."

"Would it?"

His tongue darts over his lips, so close that it nearly touches mine. "It might," he says honestly. "If your brother found out…"

His gaze washes past my shoulder, and I know what he's implying. I know he thinks being with me could break up the band or, at the very least, put him and my brother on bad terms.

"I won't let you ruin your life for me," I say.

"Then tell me to run."

I can't.
I can't.
I'm too weak to push him away.

"Dammit, Andi, tell me," he says as his forehead sinks against mine.

"I can't," I whisper.

His hands are instantly on my neck, his mouth opening—*trembling*—shoulders drawing up like they're the last bit of restraint he carries. I take hold of his wrists, wondering if he can feel the way my heart is pounding beneath his thumb on my throat.

"Why?" he breathes.

"Because—"

My phone goes off with the alert to let us know the car is waiting out front.

CHAPTER EIGHT
MADDOX

I've never had a more significant urge to throttle a phone into oblivion as much as I do right now.

"Goddammit," I snap as I step back and forcefully shove my mask up. I grab my hat and backpack from the table, and when we're both ready to exit, I yank her into me again. She staggers and falls against my chest, eyes blown up at me.

"This isn't fucking over," I tell her.

"Oh, thank fuck," she breathes.

The little catch in the back of her throat almost has me telling her to cancel this car and call another; however, I don't.

Because I know I won't be able to contain myself when I kiss her.

I know I won't be able to keep my composure enough not to wreck this entire room trying to get her out of these clothes and sliding onto my dick.

I'm fucking feral for this woman.

Deep breaths are all that keep me walking down the hall and out into the sunset behind her.

I didn't realize it was so late in the day.

That's perfect.

I have to sit on the opposite side of the car from her just to keep my hands to myself.

When we arrive at the house, Tina is putting out the pumpkins she carved on the front porch.

My restraint is shit at the moment. Nevertheless, I can't *not* speak to her.

"Hi, Mrs. Matthews," I say as the car drives off.

"Oh, hi!" She opens her arms and points to the pumpkins. "What do you think? I believe these are my best yet."

A small smile slides on my lips, though my hands remain in my pockets because I don't know what the hell else to do with them.

"Where is Reed?" Tina asks.

"He and Zeb went shopping," Andi says. "Hey, is my computer still on the counter from this morning? Or did you have to move it?"

"I took it up to your room," Tina replies. "Kamden was helping me with a few things this morning, and he's so clumsy sometimes."

"Ah. Okay." Andi smiles knowingly and glances back at me. "I just need to grab it, and I'll meet you in the pool house."

"Showing him a few images?" Tina asks.

"Have to make sure we have all his parts covered," Andi replies.

Thank fuck, she has a level enough head for this.

I'm dying.

"Will you have dinner with us tonight?" Tina asks as we start to head around to the side fence.

"Maybe," Andi says. "Just text me, and I'll let you know. I have a lot of work."

"What about you, Mads?" Tina asks.

I have enough sense to rub my stomach and grin at her. "Just had something, Mrs. Matthews," I say. "Maybe later. Thanks, though."

I'm on Andi's fucking heels as she leads me around the

corner and through the gate. I take inventory of our surroundings for the younger brothers, who might be lurking somewhere on the deck just to scare us.

She's walking with her head slightly down, her hand opening and closing at her side, gait faster and longer than I'm used to her taking.

"I need to get my computer," she says, glancing at me.

My breaths are too short to stay steady.

"I'll meet you at the pool house," she adds.

Her foot is on the step. However, before she can prance her perfect ass up those stairs, I take her wrist and yank her around. Her back hits the wall. My hand wraps against her neck.

And my lips crash upon hers before I can lose my nerve.

God fucking *dammit*.

I'm dead.

I've died.

I've died, and my ghost is lingering behind just to savor one more second with her.

Because this can't be reality.

She can't be kissing me back with as much greed for me as I have for her.

It's chaotic and licentious and every fucking thing I ever thought it might be. Her hands fist my shirt and somehow pull me closer. I'm gripping her hair, her throat, her waist, her hips. I'm falling deep under her spell and saying 'fuck it' to whatever shit ending this might have for us.

I ignore every alarm going off in my head telling me that I shouldn't be here. That I shouldn't be outside her room. And I sure as fuck shouldn't be kissing her.

Yet, I can't stop.

She groans into my mouth, and I nearly lose it. This need for her is almost uncontrollable. Every cut and burn on my tattered soul seems to mend with the press of her lips against mine. Her kiss makes me feel like I don't have to scrape and itch and pick at the scabs on my heart—to keep bleeding the wounds that have festered over the last two decades.

An ache swells in my chest, and my dick responds to this carnality with the strain I held myself to the night before.

And finally, as her chilled hands move beneath my shirt and hit my stomach, I slow the rapacity between us, deliberately sucking on her tongue as our lips part.

Gasping breaths leave us both, and I rest my forehead against hers for a quiet moment that only lasts long enough for me to find my voice.

"Maddox…"

"Tell me you want me," I say before she can push me away.

She pulls back, her head tilting as my thumb presses beneath her chin. Her lips are swollen from our kiss. Bruised from the passion and brutality warping our senses.

"I want you," she practically begs.

A heavy, almost growling sigh leaves me. The hair on my neck stands.

She wants me…

"I want you, too," I breathe.

Her gaze darts to my lips before meeting my eyes again. "What about your promise to my brother?" she manages. "The band? Thinking it could ruin everything?"

The question barely reaches my ears. It's all I can do to keep my cool as I say, "Fuck your brother," and then kiss her again.

Because right now, with the way she's staring at me—*kissing* me—the damn memory of her whimpering my name… Seriously.

Fuck Reed Matthews.

"Get your fucking laptop," I tell her when I force myself away, knowing if I keep kissing her that I'll take her right here against the wall. "I need to taste you before anyone gets the bright idea to interrupt us."

She swallows and nods, and when I release her, she darts quickly up the steps.

I don't wait for her to come back down. I head toward the pool house and start tidying up, looking for any way to draw the curtains and lock them in place without appearing suspicious.

I turn on the television, my playlist, and the white noise of the dehumidifier in the hopes that it'll drown out any noise or at least make it seem like we're just hanging out if someone came knocking.

I'm covering the windows in the bedroom when I hear the door open and shut. I still haven't caught my breath, and when I see her standing by the counter, turning on her laptop, I stretch across the room.

I can see her fingers trembling as she takes the memory card from her camera and puts it into the slot.

Her eyes drift twice in my direction, and she exhales a short breath, her chest caving.

It's the smile in her dark eyes that nearly does me in.

"Wait—" she says as I start to kiss her. "Give me… give me one second. I actually do need to get these uploaded. It takes a while, and I don't want to forget."

"Take your time," I say as I slide my arms around her waist from behind. She tilts her head when I kiss her jaw and throat, my tongue sliding along her skin before drawing it into my mouth.

The urge to mark her entire neck is nearly strong enough to break my self-control.

I move my hands beneath her shirt and unbutton her jeans, causing her to inhale a sharp breath. I should probably wait, be nice, and let her do what she needs to instead of edging her like this, but I can't bring myself to stop touching her.

Her ass presses into my hips, and this time, it's me who has to groan.

I squeeze her ass in response and slap it harshly enough to draw a whimper from those beautiful lips. And when my fingers dive under the fabric of her jeans to the warm center between her thighs, my head drops onto her shoulder.

She's *drenched* for me.

"Fuck, Andi," I hiss against her throat, my middle finger swirling over her clit.

She grabs the lip of the counter as she starts to limp forward, and I know she's entirely distracted from the task she's supposed to be doing.

I kiss her cheek. "Breathe," I tell her. "Relax for me, beautiful. I have too many things I want to do to you for you to pass out now."

Something like a nervous chuckle sounds from her, and as she brings up some app to upload her photos, I hook my hands into the waistband of her jeans and tug them down.

I have to bend to get them all the way off, though the squat isn't only to get her pants off. I can't resist this sight. Her bare ass is in full view, only scarcely covered by the black lacy boy shorts riding so high up her ass that I can cup her cheeks and not touch the fabric.

With her pants around her ankles, I lean forward, unable to stop myself from biting her ass as she steps out. She flinches at the surprise of my teeth marking her skin, a curse hissing from her lips.

She's too damn delectable to leave like this. I grab her cheeks with both hands and squeeze, parting them just enough that the lace falls between them.

The high-pitched gasp she makes when I lick her goes straight to my hardening dick.

I need to hear that again.

"Maddox…"

I'm back on my feet behind her when she calls my name, and I wrap my hands around her waist as she turns into me. Her gaze moves to my lips, and in a breathless voice, she says, "It's loading."

I stare blankly at her for a beat, causing her to smile.

"That means kiss me, Maddox," she almost laughs.

Hell fucking yes.

She doesn't need to tell me twice.

And when our lips meet, it's as wild as the kiss outside the garage was.

My hands slide over her waist, her hips, her throat. I can't decide where to touch her first. I need to memorize her body's every scar, every little crease and adorable dimple. There's an urgent need to bite and bruise her so she remembers all the ways I had her tomorrow.

So that she never forgets tonight.

I groan into her mouth as my hands meet the band of her panties. They dip perfectly below her soft belly button. I curse and breathlessly capture her lips repeatedly, speaking between every embrace.

"I love these," I tell her as I grab the lace fabric and hike the panties higher on her hips.

I feel her smirk against me each time we kiss. She pauses and leans up on her toes, her tongue licking mine. "I love this," she says, and I know she means my tongue ring.

"You have no idea how much you'll love it," I say.

I bend and pick her up under her ass, then carry her over to the back counter out of view from the door. When her feet hit the ground again, she starts to push at the waistband of my joggers, yet I grab her hands before she can have me undone.

"Not yet," I tell her.

She almost looks hurt when she pulls back. Confused.

I chuckle.

"God, you're fucking cute," I say before kissing her again.

"Wait—You don't want—"

"Oh, I want it," I assure her. "But I've waited years to have you. Years that I've thought of all the ways I want you. So, right now, I'm going to taste you. I'm going to lick and suck and bite every inch of this gorgeous fucking body. And when I'm done doing that, I'm going to fuck you until the only word you can say is my name." My nose grazes against hers, our open mouths just whispers apart.

"How does that sound?"

"Yes," she breathes.

A little huff sounds when my grin brushes her lips. "Get your ass on this counter and spread your fucking legs, then."

I'm too consumed with wanting to lick her pussy that I don't bother taking off her sweater. She hops up, and I square myself between her thighs, kissing her so hard that her head hits the cabinets. It's a short ledge for her to perch on, while it's perfect for me. I grab the band of her underwear and tug.

"Lift your hips for me," I rasp against the corner of her mouth.

Goosebumps rise on her skin. I feel them beneath the hand that I have on her thigh, and it makes my lips curl upward. She presses her hands into the counter, shifting just enough to allow me to strip her of the lace, and I push them into my back pocket before kissing her again.

My hands land on the backs of her knees. I yank her forward, sliding her ass to the very edge, and she tightens her legs around me. I can't help my greed as I brush my thumb against her pussy, only to find her somehow wetter than before.

With a drag of my teeth over her bottom lip, I finally move away from her mouth and sink to my knees. Her intense gaze is on me the entire time, causing my heart to skip as I kneel before her. I swear she isn't breathing.

God, this body.

Her legs are spread wide for me to feast on her glistening pussy, and fuck... *I'm starving.* I pick her thighs up over my shoulders. She sucks in two staccato breaths, biting her lip as she stares down at me.

"Maddox, plea—*oh fuck*—"

My mouth is on her pussy, and Andi slams her head back into the cabinets.

"Oh—*shit*—right there." Her words are barely more than gasps, high-pitched noises sounding between each and every one.

It's music to my fucking ears.

She curls her fingers in my hair as I lick her in deliberate strokes, occasionally sucking her clit into my mouth and nibbling those nerves in a manner that has her squirming against my face. Her voice is breathless, her nails dragging against my scalp.

Pleasuring her is my new religion.

Her legs begin to tremble, her thighs squeezing against my face. I have to snicker against her, and as I do, I blow on her clit.

She jerks, crying out, "*Maddox!*" in an elongated wail that broadens my grin.

I don't stop.

And with each hungry lap of my mouth against her cunt, she limps further. Her incoherent words cry out to the ceiling. I know she's close. So close that I slide two fingers inside her, only to gasp at how her pussy tightens around them. I rise to my feet and kiss her desperately, swallowing her moan into my mouth as I pump my fingers deeper, harder. The noise of my palm slapping harshly against her clit echoes around us.

She braces her hands against my face when we part, and our eyes meet.

"Are you coming for me, beautiful?" I ask.

She nods and bites her lip as if she's holding back. "More," she pitches out.

My brows raise, a smirk toying on my lips. "More?" I taunt her. I know she's on the verge of begging for that release, at the very edge of her willpower.

And yet, she wants fucking more.

I love it.

I slide another finger inside her and press my thumb against her clit. She grips the counter on either side of her hips, her knees bending as high as my ribs, heels hitting the marble, and dammit, the noise her pussy is making in response to me…

Fuck, the *noise*.

Her hips rock. Her chest shudders as if the air filling her lungs isn't enough.

She scrunches her face in the sexiest way, eyes shutting tight. I lean forward and take her chin between my fingers, and when her eyes open to me, I place a fleeting kiss on her lips.

"Watch me, beautiful," I tell her. "Watch the way you're about to come for me."

"Maddox—" A screech leaves her, though she doesn't look away from my eyes. Her jaw drops as my knees hit the ground. I replace my thumb with my mouth, dragging the tongue ring against her clit, and inciting a cry that sends her past her peak.

She comes over my face and soaks me in the most beautiful fucking way. Her body rolls, back arching as she releases in waves, her hand above her head and gripping the cabinet door as the music of my name rolls off her tongue.

"Maddox… *Maddox*…"

Fuck yes.

Her voice is a plea, and I savor all of her. She scratches through the strands of my hair, pushing them back off my forehead and sending tingles down my spine. I bury my tongue inside her to taste and drain every drop of her orgasm, and the way she flinches makes me suck her clit back into my mouth.

Just to test her resolve.

Her entire body springs upward—knees rising, hands gripping achingly tight on my scalp, her back straight—to the point that I ascend to my feet, finding her exhausted, lopsided smile, and I chuckle as she relaxes against the cabinet.

She appears entirely satiated. There's a glisten in her eyes, an exhaustion over her muscles.

And the fact that I gave her that satisfaction has me desperate for more.

Because I wonder what else I can pull from her.

I wrap my arms around her waist and kiss her lips, and she sighs at the taste of herself on my tongue.

"I'm not done with you, beautiful," I say between those long embraces.

A soft huff of amusement leaves her. "I hope not."

Andi sinks from the countertop, and I grab her waist as her knees wobble, catching her from falling to the ground. She peers up at me in a haze and laughs as I take both of her hands in mine to lead her to the bedroom.

"Wait—" She grabs her pants from the floor and hugs them in her arms, only glancing out the door briefly to ensure no one is on the deck.

I leave the bedroom door open.

Just in case.

My dick is fucking straining. I'm so hard that it hurts. And it doesn't help that her hands are on me the second we're in the bedroom together. She tugs at the hem of my shirt and pulls it over my head, barely allowing me to take a breath before her hands are on the waistband of my joggers.

I'm powerless to stop her, yet I try to slow her down as much as I can.

I grab the bottom of her sweater and pull it up, and as her entirely naked body is revealed, a jagged curse leaves me.

God, this is better than I ever dreamed.

A greyscale tattoo wraps from her ribs down her left side, over her hip, and to the top of her thigh. It's a broad depiction of a ram's skull, roses, and three crows. They bend and arch into a bare tree stretching from her foot to her back, where the raven is perched upon her shoulder.

I hadn't realized both of her arms had full sleeves. The art is so intricate that I don't have time to go over each and every detail right now.

The lapse in my concentration allows Andi enough time to finally get her hand beneath my joggers and my boxers. I have to lean my forehead against hers to stay upright. However, as I utter her name desperately, I hear her gasp in surprise.

"Oh my—" Andi pulls back and looks at me with wide eyes, and I feel a smile flinch upon my mouth. I settle my hand on her throat again, thumb pressing gently on the side of her trachea. Our lips graze as she strokes my dick languidly.

"All for you," I say before kissing her again.

She moans into me, her curled fingers deliberately stilling at the tip of my cock.

"Dammit, Andi," is all I can manage. The movement makes me take a sharp breath, and my eyes roll.

I need her on this bed.

I need to sink into her pussy and fuck her until those beautiful tears run down her blushed cheeks, and she swears she can't take anymore.

My hands spread wide on her ass, and I throw her onto the bed. She collects herself and leans onto her elbows, giving me time to slide my snug pants off.

I have to stroke myself a few times as I peer down at her.

Shit, she's *stunning*.

Her bottom lip draws behind her teeth in the most mind-numbing way. It's all I can do to not grab her ankles, throw her onto her stomach, and slam into her from behind so that I can watch her ass bounce against every thrust.

I'll do that later.

I want to see the look on her face when she comes around my dick this first time.

I climb over her, settle my hands on either side of her ribs, and kiss her deeply. In the back of my mind, I know I shouldn't take my time like this. I know I should fuck her quickly instead of drawing out every second that someone could walk in on us.

I don't care.

I want to savor her.

My lips move down her jaw to her throat, leaving marks behind with each pull of her skin between my teeth. I've dreamed of tasting her like this for so fucking long, of seeing her bare in front of me, her nipples perked and brushing against my chest.

Goddammit, her fucking tits.

She arches back as I suck on one of her nipples, a quick gasp leaving her as I bite. Down and down, she hugs my head against her chest as I lick the bottom of her right tit and squeeze the other.

"Maddox," she groans into me.

I continue kissing down her stomach, licking her tattoo, stretch marks, and soft skin. She arches into me, her head throwing back as her knees rise. I slide my hand between her legs again, and as I feel just how soaked and ready she is for me, I bite the underside of her breast.

Amber light cascades over us from the window to my

right. It shines perfectly over her body, highlighting the angles of her as she responds to each lick of my tongue, each suck of her skin into my mouth. I leave a trail of hickeys across her stomach and on the bottom of her breasts, pricking her with indentions of my teeth in every inconspicuous place that I can.

Those fucking little whimpers... The buried parts of her that I intend to uncover... Every inch of her body, her mind, and crease of her soul...

It all belongs to me.

"Maddox."

I start to rise to her face, to kiss her lips, and slide inside her; however, there's a scar on her side that makes me pause.

It looks like the one on the back of my hand. Perfectly circular. The size of a dime—a burn scar.

I rub the pad of my thumb over its raised surface, knowing exactly what that had felt like, knowing it had likely come from her mother on a bender during one of the nights Andi stayed with her when she was younger.

Although, when another scar catches my eye, my entire body stiffens.

It's on the vee of her pelvis. Faint. As if she's been trying to cover it up and heal it for some time. The word is carved crudely into her skin, more than likely with some shitty pocket knife. I brush my finger over it, realizing I'm trembling upon seeing the letters.

Whore.

Whore.

Someone carved...

A rigid feeling swells in my chest and pushes out to my extremities.

It isn't jealousy. It isn't contempt.

It's fucking *rage*.

Rage that some idiot thought he deserved someone as

perfect as her.

Rage that another man tried to ridicule her for…

"Who did this to you?"

The words sound as dangerous as I mean them to be. And even if I already know the answer, I need to hear it from her. I need to hear her say his name so I know exactly who to wipe from existence.

Andi avoids my eyes altogether. She sits up and scoots totally out of my grasp toward the headboard. Her back hits the pillows, her knees bending up to her chest. There's an embarrassment in her eyes that causes my fist to curl.

As if she thinks she actually deserved this.

"Andi…"

I lean over and sweep my hand along her jaw. I need her to know she's safe with me. I need her to realize that I'm not him.

Her eyes lift to mine. Fucking stress hives are swelling all over her chest and rising up her neck. Muscle twitches in my jaw, and even though I want to shout and seethe about the bastard—possibly get in the car and hunt him down—I'm aware that anger isn't what she needs from me right now.

"All the broken pieces?" she asks.

I exhale, grateful it at least takes the edge off my temper enough to appear normal.

"Every single one," I swear. "I'll pick them up with my bare hands."

There's another silent beat between us, and I crawl up the bed to her side. Taking her hand in mine, I kiss her knuckles and squeeze her fingers reassuringly.

I don't want her to feel like she needs to hide or cover it in some way to protect me from the things she's gone through. I want to share this scar with her. I want to share every scar she's tried to ignore and push away.

We'll be broken together.

"It actually happened on that orange couch in the garage at the old place," she finally says. "That Thanksgiving that he came over. He thought I was flirting with you."

My heart jumps into my throat.

He did this because of…

The look in Adam's gaze the night at the club flashes behind my eyes. The recognition. The jealousy. He knew who I was because he thought…

Shit, no wonder the bastard knew every fucking detail about me.

"Is that why you kicked him out?"

"Once I got free, yeah," she answers. "I hit him with Reed's microphone stand."

"He tied you up for this?"

Andi puffs nervously. "I thought he was being playful," she admits. "I thought… I thought he was finally giving in to one of the games I'd asked him to play in the past. Role playing. Chasing. Masks. Bondage… He was always so tame in the bedroom, and I… *god*, I wanted so much more. At first, I was too embarrassed to tell him, but as the relationship went on, I assumed I was safe enough to voice those desires. I remember getting my hopes up when he roped my wrists and gagged me that night… then he started hitting me."

Unwavering fury sweeps through me.

"I should have known that night was different with how he kept watching you during dinner," she says. "It was the same jealous stare he wore when we would go out anywhere. Yet, that night, he pulled his knife on me and went through my phone for any texts between us. And when he didn't find anything, he swore I was hiding it. That was when…" She pauses to toy with her fingers.

"He threw me down onto the couch and… and he cut me. He said no one would want me when they found out I was a lying whore."

I want to get in my car and find the bastard.

I want to fucking wreck him for what he's done to her, for everything he put her through after all the bullshit she dealt with growing up.

"Fucking asshole," I mutter, knowing the words are nowhere near encompassing enough for what he truly is.

"He moved here a few years after we broke up," she goes on. "He said it was because of some council job opening, but I've always felt it was something else. It's like he's been waiting for me to come back. Knowing that he's here is one of the more frightening parts about coming home—along with facing memories of... *everything*," she says. "It's one of the reasons I've avoided coming back for so long. I know I shouldn't let it all get under my skin or control my life, especially when I know I need to come home more, but..."

"Home isn't easy," I say as I look at my own burn scar.

Andi reaches over and slides her other hand into mine. "Erase him from me," she whispers as our eyes meet.

The plea wedges itself between the shards of my broken heart.

I lean forward and brace my free hand around her cheek, my fingertips finding the roots of her hair. Her jaw drops slightly, and I release my own jagged breath.

"Give me time, and I will."

Andi throws her arms around me and climbs onto my lap, her legs straddling my waist as she kisses me. All it takes is a few shifts of her hips, a few strokes of my hands along her body, and my dick is aching to finally sink inside her.

Her back hits the mattress, and she arches her hips to meet me, her wet pussy sliding against my length. The feeling makes me shudder. I barely have the strength to part from her lips, the strength to hold myself back from taking everything she has left—

And as I slam inside her, I'm reminded of something.

She isn't meant for me.

She's meant for someone wholly good and honest. Someone who will bring out the light that's been dimmed in her soul for years. She's meant for someone who will wipe away every scar. Someone who will show her that life can be beautiful if she gives the sun a chance.

She isn't meant for someone scarred beyond repair. For someone who craves to know her every visible wound and discover the ones hiding in crevices that no other being has ever touched. She isn't meant for someone who wants to rip open her scars so that they heal beneath the stitches I thread through them. Someone who will worship those lacerations and show her life is just as beautiful beneath total darkness and the pouring rain as standing in the blinding sun.

She isn't meant for me.

Her soul wasn't made to soothe mine.

Her body was never made for me to claim.

But I've never been a believer in god or fate or even fucking unicorns.

So, fuck all the things that say we aren't meant to be.

I'll make us fit.

Andi throws her head back with a gasp. She's so fucking tight, so fucking tense. I lean my forehead against hers and groan as I hear her whimper, as I feel her angle her hips toward me. My lips land briefly upon hers, and I thrust inside her again, drawing out another gulp of breath.

"Maddox…"

"You can take it, beautiful," I tell her. I grab the back of her thigh and hike it higher, and when I plunge deeper, she presses her hands to my face and kisses me hard. I swallow her words, her moan, her quaff of air. I devour all her fears and anxieties.

With her next whimper, I grab her ass and squeeze. She gasps into me with every deliberate thrust, and I feel her relax a little more every time I penetrate her.

"Right there," she whines. "Maddox, *right there*."

"Right…" I angle myself and push her knee over my arm, keeping her locked in place. Her chest caves with the motion, her nails digging into my side. Her jaw drops, eyes closing shut. Something of a mix between pain and pleasure sounds from her lips, and I let the noise roll over my shoulders.

So fucking addicting.

Every thrust is deeper than the last. She's arching her hips to meet mine, and as my pace quickens, I see a smile flash on her perfect lips.

"What are you smirking at?" I ask.

She throws her hand over her head and braces her palm against the wall. "You feel so fucking amazing," she nearly wails. "Ah—shit. *Maddox*." Goosebumps rise on her arms, and she blows out an audible breath with tears in the corners of her eyes.

"Look at you taking all of me," I say as our foreheads meet. I run my hand up her body, stopping only to squeeze her tit before wrapping that hand around her throat. She opens her mouth to gasp for air, and I lick the tears from the side of her face. The little smile flinching on the corners of her lips does something to me. It ignites the darkest parts of my soul, and I know I have to give her more.

I grab her and roll us so that she's straddling my waist. Her knees pull to either side of my hips, though I don't let her sit back. I hold her at a slight hover, my other hand still encompassing her throat, and I pull her face toward me just enough to flick my tongue against hers.

Her nails dig into my chest so harshly that I'm sure I'll have the most adorable claw marks on my skin when this is over.

I might get them tattooed.

Her pussy tightens around me, and I slam hard enough in

her that she yelps. My fingers fasten on either side of her throat, squeezing just enough that I know the roll of her eyes isn't just from my dick impaling her tight cunt. Her mouth drops open again, moans and cries sounding from her that are stifled and hoarse. She shuts her eyes tight, her face straining. I strike my hand across her ass, and she shudders at the licentious pain.

Shit, seeing her pussy devour my dick sends me teetering on that edge. She frantically slaps my arm, and I know she's on the verge of collapsing. I can feel her release right there—

"Come for me, beautiful," I tell her.

My grip around her throat relaxes, and her whole body paralyzes when it does. Her pussy pulses around me, the waves causing my body to erupt with hunger for more. And when she collapses into my arms, I catch her.

I brace my hand against her face, my motions slackening to a deliberate stroke. Tears slide down her cheeks, prompting me to kiss them away.

"Hold onto me," I say before kissing her nose.

My arms wrap around her back, and I hold her firm against my chest as I drive hard and fast into her. She whimpers in my ear, still riding her own orgasm, and with just a few more strokes, I come deep inside her.

I think my soul has left my body.

I think it escaped and sank itself into her somehow.

Because that moment is confirmation enough that I'm all hers—that I've always been hers. She's always held my heart in her hand. And now, she's manually pumping blood to the rest of me.

She picks her head up once we've both nearly caught our breath, and her tired, satiated smile meets me.

"Did you lock the door?" she asks.

I almost laugh. "That's what you're thinking about?"

"I'm asking because I don't want to move," she says, her

nose brushing mine. "And I wonder how long we have before one of my brothers burst through the door."

Even with the mention of our predicament, there's nothing anyone can do to bring me down from this high. I cup my hand around her cheek and kiss her unhurriedly.

"Probably about five minutes," I say, and she chuckles.

She lays her cheek against my chest and closes her eyes. "Two-minute cuddle, then."

The butterflies still haven't stopped fluttering. "I'll set a timer."

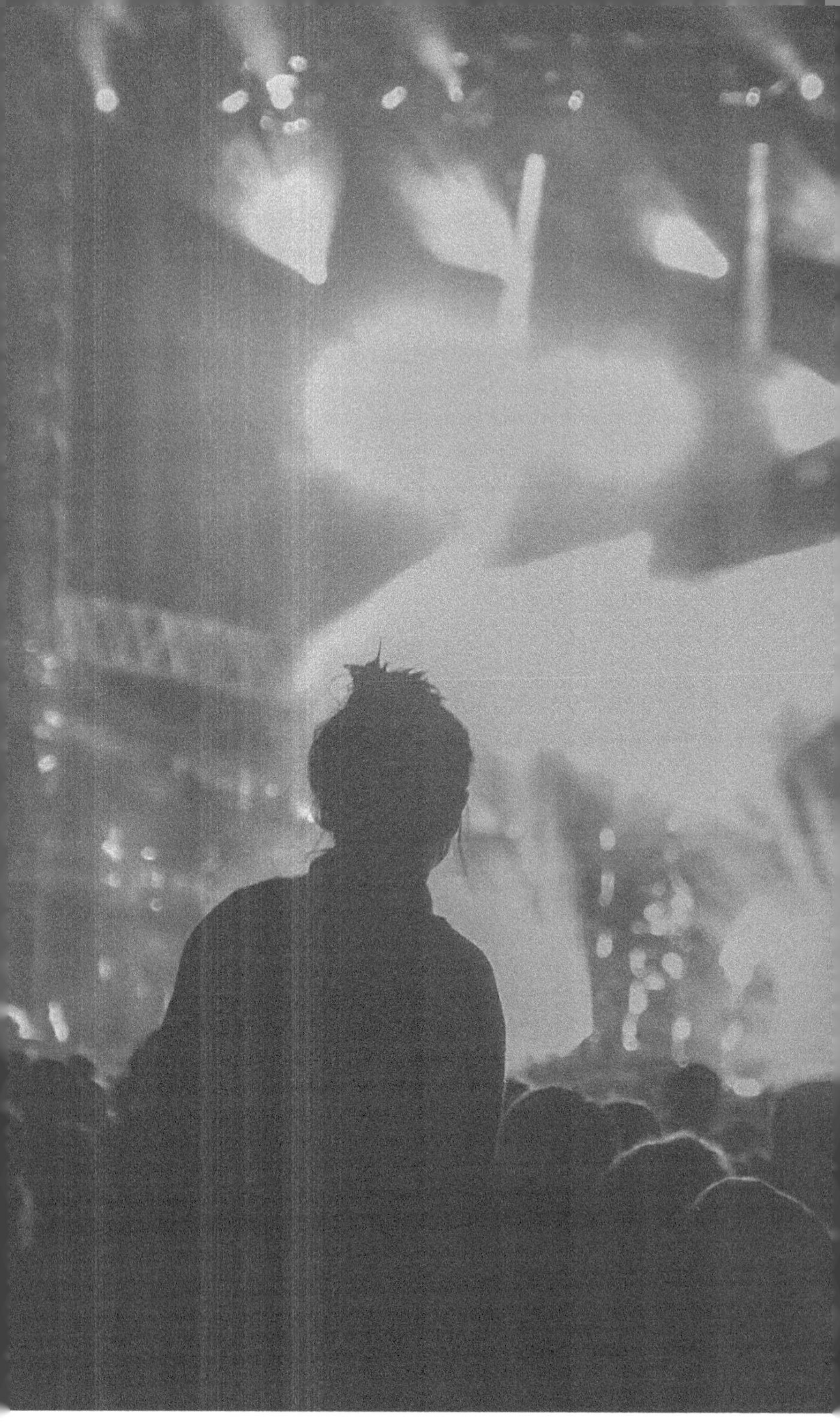

CHAPTER NINE
ANDI

I can't stop staring in the mirror at my naked body.

Last night... *fuck*, last night...

Somehow, Maddox and I had ourselves cleaned up only a few minutes before Reed knocked on the pool house door. I was back in my sweater and a pair of leggings I found in the closet and sitting at the bar with a half-empty beer and bowl of popcorn like I'd been working the entire time. We'd removed all the sheets on the windows, and despite the fact that I could still feel Maddox's cum leaking out of me when my brother sat on the stool at my side to look through photos, there was no other evidence that anything had happened.

Of course, had my brother seen Maddox's display of absolute assertion upon my body like I was looking at it now, he would have thought differently.

The warm water feels like a massage over my sore muscles, my swollen and bruised skin. I stay in the shower longer than usual, replaying every kiss and touch.

No one has ever looked at my body or seemingly worshipped it as he did. Even the stretch marks on my soft belly and the dimples on my thighs... he looked at them like they were just as sexy as someone with none of those blemishes.

Last night, Reed mentioned the band having breakfast with

the journalist Bonnie's been fucking all week. It's a meeting that the manager insisted they all be on just in case Adam had gotten to the press without them knowing.

The last thing they want is an ambush, and the possibility of Maddox losing his privacy has them all on higher alert. They're even combing through social media sites for any mentions of him.

I hear the car in the drive when I get out of the shower. Reed is yelling something, and as Maddox shouts back, I look out the window to see the Escalade. Bonnie and Reed are hanging out of the windows while Maddox grabs his pants as if he forgot something.

"Come on," Reed says. "Just forget about it. We can come back after breakfast."

Maddox presses his hands to his jacket and his back pants pockets again. "I forgot my—fuck—"

"What, did you forget your wallet?" Bonnie asks.

"Mask, dude," Maddox says. "Go ahead. I'll grab a car and meet you there."

"You sure?" Reed asks.

"Yeah. I think it's all the way in the laundry in the back. Go ahead. I'll catch up," Maddox says as he turns on his heel.

Reed considers him one more time before slapping the side of the vehicle twice. "Okay. You can wake my sister up for a ride if you don't want to call a car. Or Mom—"

"I'll text you when I'm on the way there," Maddox says.

Reed rolls up the window, and Maddox disappears through the side fence as the Escalade pulls out of the drive.

Weird.

I throw my towel on the ground and grab a flimsy, long-sleeved tee from my suitcase, along with a pair of underwear just to sit around in. I wish I had coffee up here. I could use a cup to read emails and get some work done.

The thought of going downstairs right now makes me

pout. Tina is so chipper in the morning, and I'm not ready for her yet.

I love mornings, but I also like my mornings to myself to listen to music, drink coffee, and work in peace.

A knock sounds on my door.

My heart feels like it drops to my feet. The knock is from the outside door, meaning it's not my dad or Tina checking on me from the other side.

It's…

Hurriedly, I try to do something with my hair so it doesn't look like a flat mop on my head.

"Andi?"

The sound of Maddox's voice awakens every inch of my still-tingling skin. I open the door slightly, finding him standing with his hands in the pockets of his slim black joggers, those piercing green eyes staring at me.

Yet all I can think about is how satisfying his beard tickled my inner thighs and how that tongue ring sent pulses through me that I didn't know were possible.

"Maddox." I swallow. I can't discern the look in his eyes, and it nearly sends me into a panic. I open the door wider and step back to let him in.

"I needed to talk to you," he says as he quietly shuts the door.

"Oh… Okay."

I'm not sure I like where this is going.

He runs his hand anxiously behind his neck, and I have to shift on my feet. It's a far cry from the Maddox that railed me sideways the afternoon before.

"Mads?"

"Last night was a mistake," he says, and my heart flips.

He held back from going to breakfast with his friends to tell me…

"Or that's what I should tell you," he continues.

Fucking hell.

He's trying to kill me.

I don't know whether to breathe yet or not.

"That's what the dick move would be, wouldn't it? To tell you that last night was nothing, and we shouldn't see each other again. That your brother means more to me than you ever could."

"It would," I manage.

His jaw tightens, and he advances a single step. "I love your brother, Andi. But dammit, I've wanted you for as long as I can remember, and last night… last night, it felt like all the gaping spaces in my heart were healing. Like your touch was mending the broken pieces of my shattered soul."

Goddamn songwriter.

He takes his hands from his pockets as he reaches me. His palm braces against my neck, thumb pressing beneath my chin to tilt my head back. I'm met with hunger in his pale sage eyes, and as much as I want to agree with him, I know I can't. He was right the first time. This can never be. We should never have let last night happen.

"You're best friends with him. Brothers, even. Closer than family. I don't want to be the reason—"

"Do you want to be with me?" he asks.

I do.

None of this felt like one night.

None of this felt like a quick fling of lust.

This felt…

"Yes," I manage.

His tongue darts over his lips, and he shifts the weight on his feet. "Then you'll have to rip my heart from my chest and stomp on it before I let you go. Run it through the shredder until it can't be put back together, Andi. That's the only way I'll walk away from you."

"What about Reed?" I ask.

"I'll tell him when we're ready," he answers.

"And until then?"

The right corner of his lips quirks upward. "Until then…"

He leans down, his open mouth pressing to mine, his tongue sweeping across my own in a teasing, claiming manner. I groan into his possessive kiss, my knees weakening beneath it. His hand moves to the back of my neck, fingers tightening in my hair and causing me to suck in a sharp breath. He parts from me, his nose brushing against my cheek until he reaches my ear.

"Until then, I'll enjoy every illicit second with you," he says against the shell. "Every second that I know you're thinking of me when you shouldn't… Imagining my tongue sliding along your center… my dick buried inside that tight pussy of yours…" He moans as if the very thought has him in agony and nibbles my earlobe.

"Can you keep us a secret, beautiful?"

My eyes close, neck craning as I lean into him.

Fuck my brother.

"Yes."

His other hand squeezes my waist, and just as I think he'll kiss me, he steps back. The vacancy splashes over me like ice water.

He's grinning when I open my eyes.

"Wait—where are you going?" I ask in a more desperate tone than I mean to.

"God, that's cute," he mutters. "I'm actually late," he adds as he starts cracking his knuckles, eyes running over me in a manner that makes me want to drop to my knees right there so I can taste the dick that had me crying from pleasure last night.

"I just needed to straighten all of this out before having to pretend like I'm not dying inside the rest of the day," he explains.

I try not to smile. "I think I like you in agony."

His smirk lifts into his gleaming eyes. "Fuck, I do, too," he says.

"I could drive us if you want," I say as he takes his phone out to call a car.

He chuckles. "It's adorable that you think I'd behave alone with you in a car."

"I didn't say that," I reply.

He stares at me for a long enough beat that I know he's debating it. "What kind of car did they give you?"

I laugh. "It's Death Tower Records, and I'm working with a popular rock band who could very well get in trouble or need a lift out of a sticky situation. What do you think they gave me?"

"Something large and blacked out?" he asks.

"Something like that."

Upon arriving, I had parked the brand new, customized, blacked-out Jeep Cherokee in the garage, as I hadn't wanted to mess anything up on it. It belonged to the venue, though Heartless had told them I would need it to chauffeur the band back and forth.

Cynda had sent a wink-face emoji when she had the car waiting at the airport for me.

Maddox whistles upon seeing it. He jerks his chin my way and holds up his hands. "Keys."

"You do have your mask, don't you?" I ask, remembering the excuse he'd given Reed.

Maddox grins sideways and picks it out of his pocket. "Would you like me to put it on?"

I drag my lip behind my teeth. "Maybe."

He snickers and shoves it back into his pocket.

"Tease," I say.

"Maybe later," he tells me with a wink.

I toss the keys over the hood and climb into the passenger

seat while he does the same on the driver's side. As he cranks up the car and music blares over the speakers, I grab him by his shirt, and my lips land on his.

Maddox pulls on me, and I climb over the console to straddle his lap. It's tight and a struggle. My knees hit the seatbelt clip and the door panel, my foot brushing over the steering wheel. He laughs at my clumsiness, his shirt stretching slightly as I accidentally pull on it to straighten myself out. And this time, when he kisses me, it's carnal.

I feel like I'm trapped in a box with only his lips as my escape. His hands are everywhere, running up my sides, my spine, grasping at my throat and my ass. I can't keep up with him. He's everywhere all at once, desperate passion exuding between us like we know these few minutes are all we'll have the rest of the day.

I'll take every second I can get.

Between my thighs, I feel him growing. The thought of his large dick makes me whimper. Fuck, the pressure it had put on me... I had felt it everywhere.

I needed it again.

He pushes me so my back is against the steering wheel, and his mouth moves from mine down my throat, between my breasts.

His tongue ring has me whimpering at the memory of it dragging up and down my pussy, and my hands tighten in his hair.

A ding sounds from his phone.

He grunts about it like he wants to ignore the noise and continues nipping at my skin.

It dings again, and the way Maddox snaps and practically snatches the phone out of the cupholder makes me snort. I lean into him and kiss his jaw, his long beard tickling my face as he reads the messages.

"Mother fuck," he says. "Reed."

"Asking if you got lost?" I ask.

"Yeah." He taps a few buttons to message Reed back before moving his eyes to me. "Fun's over."

I eye him, and he raises a brow as if he can tell what I'm thinking. I capture his mouth again and reach between us to slide my hand beneath the waistband of his pants, and his groan is glorious in response.

I need him in my mouth.

"Drive," I tell him.

Maddox bites my lip before releasing my waist so that I can swing my legs back over into the passenger seat.

He squints in wicked delight upon watching me sit up on my knees. He hits the garage opener, and as the door rises, he reaches beneath my chin and tugs it upward.

"The restaurant is just five minutes away, beautiful," he says. "You going to make me come in that time?"

I nod desperately. "Yes," I plea.

He threads his hand into my hair at the back of my head, and I can see the licentious gleam practically pouring into those blown pupils. For a beat, I think he's going to say something. Yet, his dark gaze is enough to have me crawling across the floor to him if he tells me to.

And before I can steady myself, he accelerates out of the driveway, brings my face to his for a quick kiss, and then pushes my head into his lap.

I reach for the volume wheel and turn the playlist up, blaring metal through the speakers.

Despite the sunlight flaring over the tinted windows, I know we're concealed. I know no one can see me bent over his lap and taking his attentive length into my mouth.

"Fuck, Andi," he mutters, his fingers massaging my scalp.

His dick hits the back of my throat as I bob my head and swirl my tongue around his tip. A quiet moan escapes me when I feel him shift his hips up, hear the engine roar as he speeds through traffic. He's sucking air through his teeth and cursing, and I know he's trying to hold out.

Though, when his fingers take ahold of my head so tight that I can't move, I finally have to squirm.

I *love* it.

He pushes me, his dick moving past my gag reflex, and I force myself to relax my throat, drop my jaw, and allow him in. A scratchy noise sounds from me that I try to stifle.

It sends him cursing.

"Swallow," he says in an aching voice. "Swallow all of me, beautiful. I want the back of your mouth bruised, your jaw aching, and my cum still dribbling down your throat when we join the others."

I hum a plea around him, saliva dribbling from the corners of my lips as he loosens his grip and lets me suck him to the tip.

A tear streaks down my face as I gasp for air.

Determination moves through me when I take him into my mouth again.

I wrap my hand around his base and envelope the rest of him with my mouth, working him in more urgent motions, more urgent swallows.

"Shit." He grabs the waistband of my leggings and pulls, the seam wedging in my ass as if he's using it as a handle. "Mm… fucking hell, Andi. Just like that—"

We pause at a red light, and he slams his head back against the headrest, hand coming off the steering wheel so that, for a beat, he can use both of his hands to push his dick all the way down my throat.

I gag, choke, and squirm against the pressure, and yet...

I want fucking more.

The light changes, and as he accelerates, I feel him shudder.

"Are you ready for me?"

I'm frantically sucking him up and down, taking as much of him as I can without the press of his hands, my own fingers pinching his balls enough to make him groan louder than he did last night.

I hum my response around him. He's jerking; his muscles seem to flinch as he finds that end, and he shoves my head down once more.

I choke and sputter at the surprise when he comes down my throat. His grip slackens, allowing me to draw up enough to swallow and suck his release until he whips into a parking place and slams on the brakes.

He yanks me up by my hair, revealing my smile, and glances over my face as though he's seeing it for the very first time.

"Fucking *vixen*."

His cum drips from the corners of my lips, still soaking my tongue when he pulls me into a deep kiss. He wraps his arm around my waist and back, nearly pulling me into the seat with him to share one more embrace before we pretend that this never happened.

"How are we going to go all day without this?" I ask once we part.

He brushes his nose against mine and then kisses the tip. "I don't know that I can."

CHAPTER TEN
ANDI

Throughout the day at the venue, I have to keep checking myself.

I'm here to do my job, not make out with Young Decay's elusive masked bassist behind every corner and in the shadows of places that have us both checking for onlookers over our shoulders. Every close call makes us jump, has us parting ways with awkward excuses to anyone coming around the corner.

The chase is exhilarating, and every time he looks at me, adrenaline winds through every ounce of my blood.

By the time we make it back home, I'm so pent up with tension that I can hardly eat anything.

It's three AM when he sneaks into my bedroom to fuck me from behind and stuff my face into the pillows to the point that my only choices are to tap out or suffocate. Relief sweeps over me when he drags me out of the pillows by my neck. I'm coming, and yet, he doesn't stop. He lays down and pulls me backward onto his lap, my ass slapping against his abs as he maneuvers my rocking hips up and down his length, his cock brushing the sensitive spot inside me with each impale.

I grip his thighs, and I nearly collapse when his release finally spills inside me.

Maddox sits up to wrap his arms around me, catching me

from my slump. He kisses my shoulder, my neck, my jaw, and I drop back against him. His fingers find my clit again as he holds me, and I whimper from the delicate touch.

I swear, he's going to make me come again.

"You're doing so well taking me, beautiful," he whispers, the words skimming chills along my skin. "So fucking well."

I think I'm addicted to him.

He makes me feel alive. He makes me feel as if the scars on my body aren't something I have to hide or run away from. It's in the little smile on his lips beneath his long beard that causes my knees to weaken, the smirk in his gaze across the room, and the way he strokes that fucking tongue all over me.

I'm present and living and *fuck*… I can't get enough of it.

I crash around him again with the toy of his fingers, and he cuddles my exhausted body after, refusing to leave me until the sun finally threatens to expose us.

Reed is lying on the breakfast nook bench when I throw on a sweatshirt and shorts to go downstairs the following morning. I smile as my eyes drift to Koen, who is flipping pancakes on the stove. He returns my smile and reaches beneath the cabinet for two pans. My grin widens when I take them from him.

There's nothing like a bit of morning revenge for every time he used to wake me like this when we were younger.

As quietly as I can, I stalk around the counter, and when I'm standing over Reed's body, I clash the frying pans together as hard as I possibly can.

Multiple times.

Reed jerks up and hits his head on the table lip. A slew of curses sounds from him. They're muffled behind mine and Koen's laughter. However, when Reed sits up to find me responsible, he launches out of the booth.

I scream and run outside—

He's too fast.

He grabs me just as my feet hit the deck, and I'm whipped into the air by my waist.

I don't remember Reed being this strong.

He throws me upside down over his shoulder, making it like he's going to throw me into the pool, and I scream again for him to let me down, kicking my legs in an attempt to squirm out of his grasp.

Maddox emerges from the pool house and catches my eye as I shout his name.

He appears entirely happy to see me in such a predicament.

"What did you do?" Maddox asks, smiling broadly.

"She—" Reed tickles my stomach, and I jerk in his grasp, trying desperately to get away from him.

"Mads, help—Help! Reed, *no!*"

I can't stop laughing.

"She woke me up with the pans," Reed says. "What do you think? You think the pool destroying her hair is good enough punishment?"

"I don't know, man. You might have to jump her off the diving board," Maddox replies.

"Wait—no!"

Reed grins. "Get the tarp off."

"Reed, put me down! No—*I'm sorry!*"

Because I really don't want to get wet in this dirty water.

"*Maddox!*"

However, Maddox is grinning as widely as Reed, and he's pulling the tarp back just enough that I don't get caught in it from the board.

"Reed—don't you dare." I smack his shoulders and kick the air but to no avail. Reed is already carrying me around the edge of the pool. Kamden and Koen come out of the house to see what's happening, and now, the four boys are chanting, "Throw her in!"

And when Reed pauses at the end of the board, I glare sideways at him.

"You're such an asshole," I say, though I can't help laughing.

"Don't worry, sis."

It's the last three words he says before he jumps off the board with me in his arms, and together, we go plunging beneath the water.

It's dark and full of leaves and slimy, and when I rise above the surface, I want to puke. I slosh water at Reed's grinning face, mouth open to insult him when two more figures run in our direction.

Reed grabs and shields me as Koen and Kamden jump into the pool after us.

As much as I hate Reed for throwing me in, it's a moment that I know I'll hold onto. It's so rare that all of us are home. I'm surprised Tina or Dad aren't outside to see what the commotion is all about.

Looking up, I find Maddox laughing with his hands stuffed into his pockets.

"Come on, Mads," I call out to him. "You're a part of this craziness, too."

"Yeah, come on!" Reed splashes water Maddox's way and whips his own shaggy hair out of his eyes.

"No fucking way," Maddox says, smoothing his beard. "I just oiled the beard."

"Come on," Kamden and Koen yell.

Something is burning.

I sniff the air, and the culprit dawns on me.

"Shit. Koen, did you leave the stove on?" I ask.

His expression falters in an instant. "Fuck—"

"I got it." Maddox darts inside, and I push myself out of the pool to run to the sliding door.

I pause at the threshold as I don't want to get the floor sopping wet. Maddox has the smoking pan off the glass stovetop and shakes his head when he looks my way.

"Good catch," he says. "Another minute, and the thing would be on fire."

"Fucking Koen," I mutter.

Maddox smiles slyly my way before his eyes rake over my soaking body. "Want to use my shower?" he asks, and I can't tell whether it's because he wants me there or because he knows there's no way I can take this hoodie off in front of my brothers to walk upstairs—bra or no bra.

Because my entire body is covered with his claim.

"Ah… don't really have much of a choice there," I say nervously.

"That's right, beautiful," he says in a low voice, his lip smugly drawing behind his teeth as he tosses the pan in the sink.

My heart flutters at the memory of last night, and I know he's thinking the same thing when our eyes meet.

Reed, Kamden, and Koen already have their shirts and shorts off, leaving themselves in only their boxers as they hose down beneath the outdoor shower.

"Feels like we never grew up," Maddox says, peering outside to the three brothers.

I smile over my shoulder at them, recalling how much I had wanted to protect them when we were younger. I remember the loud music in the basement and trying to do anything to distract them from what was happening upstairs with my mother.

Maddox's hand lays over mine when he steps to the other side of the glass, and I clench my teeth.

"You did everything you could, Andi," he says softly.

Emotion swells behind my eyes. My mother's face comes into focus, and with it, a pain rises in my chest from all the times I thought she would get better.

"Reed was two years old the first time he asked me who the crazy lady was who came to steal me away on the weekends, and he wanted to know why he couldn't go," I say as I watch my younger brother towel himself off and joke around. "He was so fucking innocent about it. He just wanted to be where I was."

I shift on my feet as Maddox continues to watch me. As if he remembers the first time he met my mother, Alice, as well.

"I don't want to go," I say to my mother, standing in the foyer. "Dad… He said he'll be back soon. He just went to the store."

I don't want to go.

Your boyfriend is a creep.

You'll ignore me all weekend and get high in the next bedroom.

You'll forget I'm there.

You never have any food in the house.

The couch smells like piss from the dog you don't take care of—

Is what I should have said.

Alice shakes her head and pulls my arm. "I don't have time for this, Andersyn."

The blaring car horn is an echo against the rain.

I tug out of her grasp.

"Reed is upstairs," I argue, on the verge of tears. "Kamden, too. I can't leave them. They're too young. We have to wait—"

"Oh, please, what is the boy now? Seven? Eight? He's fine on his own." She grabs me again as her boyfriend shouts from the car. "We're coming!" she shouts back. "Let's go, Andersyn," she tells me, her voice rising. "I don't have all day."

"She said she doesn't want to go," comes a young voice from the dining room.

Alice's eyes narrow on Maddox—the bright red lip, the scrape on his face, his hair matted to his head from the rain. Recognition rises in her gaze, and her lips split into a taunting grin.

"You're Darren Keynes's boy, aren't you?" she asks. "I see he

finally made it home from Harry's," she says, referring to the local bar. *"Bastard's been drunk there most of the day. Still had enough sense to punish you for running off yesterday, though, didn't he? You scared him."*

"He passed out on a park bench," Maddox snaps. *"I hoped he was dead."*

Alice balks. "I'm going to have to talk to Darren," she mutters. *"Tell him he should have taught you better manners. Don't you know better than to speak about your elders like that?"*

"Leave Andi alone," Maddox says. *"She said she doesn't want to go with you."*

"Let's go!" the boyfriend yells from the car.

Alice scoffs when she looks at Maddox again, then grabs my arm. "Come on, Andi."

"No," I argue. "I don't want to go. I can't leave — Stop—"

Alice's hand strikes across my face. "You get in that fucking car, young lady," she snaps as I hold my stinging cheek. *"Let's go."* She grabs me again, with both hands this time, and in my shocked stupor, my feet slip.

"No—" Maddox runs forward and shoves my mother back. "She said she doesn't want to go!"

Alice stumbles. Her eyes grow wild upon Maddox, and she launches at him. I'm back on my feet in a rush to come between them, but I'm not fast enough. Alice pushes Maddox with all of her strength, and despite his fight, he goes flying into the staircase.

"Maddox!"

"What the fuck is going on here—" Alice's boyfriend says as he reaches the door. *"What's taking so long? Let's fucking go, woman. What's the hold up?"*

I can't take my eyes from Maddox. He's groaning on the steps and holding his head. Forget the boyfriend now trying to grab me. I swing his arms off, my heart jumping into my throat.

"Maddox? Maddox, are you — No! Wait! I don't want to go—"

My pleas fall on deaf ears. I'm thrown over the boyfriend's shoulder. I barely hear whatever my mother is saying. I'm kicking. Shouting. Screaming louder than I ever have before. As if seeing Maddox try to save me ignited a fire within that I had long forgotten about.

The door is getting smaller and smaller. Maddox finally gets to his feet. The back door of my mother's car opens. I'm thrown into the back seat as Maddox comes rushing out into the rain.

I can't open the door no matter how much I kick the window and jerk on the handle. I'm trapped.

I don't want to go.

I don't want to go.

I don't—

I force out an audible breath and blink away my tears.

"I never thanked you for that night," I say softly to him.

Our eyes meet, the same sorrowful glisten reflecting back to me, and he leans against the door. "Which night?" he asks.

"The night you tried to stop her," I manage.

He swallows as the memory visibly runs through him, then squeezes my fingers behind the curtain. "It wasn't enough."

"It was," I tell him. "It was enough to remind me that I could fight back, too."

Maddox appears as if he's about to say to hell with all three of my brothers standing a few feet away.

I push off the door and release his hand before we do anything rash.

"I'm going to go shower," I say.

"You can grab one of my hoodies if you want," he says when I take a few steps.

"She'll steal your boxers, too," Reed says as he sees me heading to the pool house.

"That was one time," I argue.

Even so, his smile is enough to lift some of the heaviness from my heart.

There's so much slime and dead foliage on my clothes that I feel horrible about the trail I'm about to leave in the pool house, though the floor is easy to clean for a reason, and luckily, the bathroom is only a few steps from the door.

As I turn on the shower, I get a text on my phone.

Let's jump on a Zoom today, Cynda says. **Do you have a minute?**

I groan inwardly. I hate work video calls.

Yeah. Give me a half hour.

Call me when you're ready.

I drag my wet clothes off and pile them in a heap atop one of the oversized towels so all I have to do is gather the edges once I'm clean.

I try not to allow the thoughts of Alice back into my mind and instead push more recent, positive reflections through me to try and put a band-aid over those open scars.

I get another glimpse of a hickey on my boob as I wrap the towel around me and quickly exit to go to Maddox's room.

I don't even notice that he's rummaging through one of his bags until I turn to close the door.

I jump and clench my chest, the towel falling halfway off. "Fucking hell, Maddox," I manage breathlessly.

A quirk of that lopsided smile shows itself as he pulls a sweatshirt from his bag, his gaze wandering over me in a manner that makes me think he's seriously considering taking my towel off and clothing me himself.

"I told them I was coming to make sure you didn't take my concert underwear," he says. "Of course, then Tina gave me these."

He extends his arm, holding a pair of warm leggings from the dryer, and I smile.

"Why doesn't it surprise me that she's been up there looking for dirty laundry," I say as I move behind the door and drop the towel to put the clothes on.

"Mom of four boys," he replies. "She's used to cleaning up our messes."

Because he's as much a part of this family as I am.

I turn my back as the towel falls to the ground, only because I know if I can see him staring at me the way that he does, there's no way either of us are walking out of this room without a quick fuck against the wall. I tug my damp hair out of the sweatshirt and adjust the oversized sleeves as I face him again.

His gaze is dilated. The sage appears crystallized in the morning sun coming through the front windows. He strides toward me, then pauses to look over his shoulder as if he knows we're being watched.

"We're heading out to meet Bonnie and Zeb for tattoos in a few. Reed booked them the entire day and gave them tickets to the show on Saturday. Do you want to ride with?"

"Ah, I think I'll just catch up," I reply. "My boss texted me. I need to hop on a face call with her."

"There's the most terrifying sentence in existence," he says, and I huff amusedly.

"Seriously. Like, couldn't this have been an email?"

Maddox chuckles at the joke, and I can tell by the stretch of his fingers that it's taking everything in him not to touch me in some way.

"Are you okay?" he asks.

I glance toward the ground and coerce a full breath into my lungs. "Yeah," I tell him. "Yeah. Nothing a little tattoo therapy can't fix."

The smile he meets me with sinks its way into my knotted stomach. "I need you to do something for me," he says, and my eyes narrow when he reaches into his pocket and pulls lipstick from it, along with a piece of paper. "Kiss this."

I'm so confused. "What?"

He chuckles at me. "Put the lipstick on and kiss the paper."

"Why..."

"Amuse me," he says.

I oblige with narrowed eyes, using the mirror on the back of the door. "Where did you get this lipstick?"

"Part of Reed's Halloween costume," he says with a wink.

"Who's he going to be?"

"Joker," he replies, and my eyes widen.

"Holy shit. He's going to make the best Joker. Do we get to dye his hair on Saturday?"

Maddox grins. "There's a Halloween shop by the tattoo place. Our manager called to see if they had wigs and makeup and shit, so we're grabbing everything we need today."

"Who are you going to be?"

There's a sinful glare in his eyes. "Bane," he replies. "As long as I can find that vest and the long coat."

"What about Bonnie and Zeb? Who are they going to be?"

"Poison Ivy and Scarecrow."

"Bonnie is going to be Poison Ivy?" I ask.

"She's going to break a few hearts in that one," Reed says as he sticks his head through the door. He gives Maddox an upward nod. "You ready?"

"Yeah." Maddox gently folds up the piece of paper and slides it into his wallet. "Andi is meeting us later."

"No tat today, sis?" Reed asks.

"There will be a tattoo," I correct him. "But I have a call this morning, so I'll drive out later. I hear I get to torture you with hair dye on Saturday."

Reed grins in the most characteristically Joker-ish smile I've ever seen on anyone. It creases his dimples and bares all his teeth, and I chuckle.

"There will be fainting," I say.

"One can hope." Reed taps the door frame twice and pushes off, his head nearly raking the top of the door. "Let's go, Mads. Bonnie is already texting."

Maddox gives me one more look, and I don't know what to do with myself other than stare as he leaves the room and follows Reed to the front, where I know James is waiting for them.

My phone dings with a text from Cynda, and I groan.
Can we chat now?

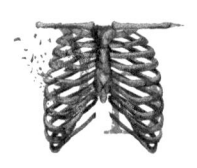

The sting of the tattoo needle on my back is exultant bliss.

It's just me and Bonnie in the studio right now. Maddox, Reed and Zeb are over at the Halloween shop.

"Did you find a wig for Ivy, or are we dying your hair also?" I ask Bonnie from the backward chair I'm sitting on. She's lying on her stomach for her tattoo a few feet away from me.

None of us are very particular regarding our bodies, and we were happy to choose from the badass, intricate sketches the artists put together specifically for us.

"I thought it would be just as fun to dye it," she says. "I've never been a redhead before."

I smile. "It's going to be so hot."

"I can't wait." Bonnie closes her eyes and takes a deep breath. "If I fall asleep, don't wake me up."

The tattoo artist grins. "You're almost done."

"Freehand a little more, if you want," Bonnie says. "I mean, if your hand isn't tired. I know you had Reed earlier."

"Might take a break and come back to you," the artist replies. "We have you until five."

"Same with me," I mutter, my cheek smushed against the round face pillow.

"Yeah, girl," Bonnie says.

"There's something to be said that both of us are like, 'keep drawing on us with a needle,'" I say, halfway joking. "Or that we're both on the verge of a nap."

"I blame the music," Bonnie says about the metal music playing. "They put on the relaxing shit."

The door opens then, revealing Reed and Zeb grinning ear-to-ear at us when they stride through the door with large bags in both hands.

"That looks dangerous," I say.

Bonnie rests her chin on her hands. "Damn. Did you buy out the store?"

Reed looks as though he's just gone shopping for his own birthday. "Got some things to make Saturday's show epic."

"The rest of the bags are in the Escalade," Zeb says.

"Shit. What did you buy?" I ask.

"Oh, you'll see," Reed grins. He steps around and pulls up a chair beside me. "Bonnie's journalist wants us to head over to The Red Attic after we stop by the venue to drop things off. You in for another party?"

"As long as there are no surprises at this one," I reply.

Reed's eyes shift to the door, his teeth set. "If he fucking shows up, I'll kill him."

"Whoa," Bonnie mutters.

"Mads is on the phone with our manager right now," Reed goes on. "There's extra security inside tonight. They just want to make sure he's okay with going out. And to remember to keep a level head."

"Last time wasn't his fault," I argue.

"Yeah, they know," Reed says.

"It's only a reminder," Zeb says. "Rumor about some protesters trying to crash the party is circulating on a few boards."

"Are you sure he should be going at all?" I ask.

"That dick isn't keeping him from having a good time," Reed says. "We'll be fine."

I'm still uneasy about the entire thing.

"Maybe I shouldn't go," I say. "If I'm not there, maybe Adam will leave you alone."

"I think he'll be just as much of a problem whether you're there or not," Reed says. "They swear they're taking care of it."

I chew on the inside of my mouth for a beat.

If I know Heartless and Death Tower, I know that Young Decay means enough to them that they'll do whatever they need to ensure they're protected.

"Okay," I finally agree. "What's the plan?"

"I'm going to go put this stuff in the car," Zeb says with a jerk of his chin to the door. "I'll make sure he's still cool."

"Yeah, do that," Reed says as Zeb leaves. "So, we'll go to the venue and drop this stuff off while you two are finishing up," Reed says. "Then we'll get ready and head to the party around… 9? Sound good?"

I know I'm getting old when the thought of attending a party that starts at nine p.m. literally makes me groan.

"That's past my bedtime, Reed," I say.

Reed looks at me flatly. "Come have a drink, and then you can leave," he says. "We'll have you in bed by eleven."

I sigh. "Fine."

CHAPTER ELEVEN
ANDI

Are you okay with tonight? I text Maddox from my room once we're all back at the house and getting ready.

Yeah, he replies. **I need five minutes alone with you before we leave, though.**

Why? I ask.

Because I might lose my fucking mind and expose us if I don't see you before we have to go another few hours pretending like we're nothing.

My core flutters at his impatience. *Sounds like you're in agony.*

I'm at the edge of my restraint.

I hear Reed shouting up the stairs for me, and I know that Maddox will have to wait.

Reed is yelling that we're leaving.

Fingers strum softly against my door.

I almost giggle as I shout to Reed that I need another minute, and then I open the outside door.

Maddox throws himself into the room and slams the door behind him as his lips land on mine. The ferocity of his kiss catches me off-guard. Even still, he's so consuming that I give in as if he's the very air I need in my lungs.

Because *fuck*. Maybe he is.

His hands brace around my neck and hold me steady, the

touch breaking my entire body out in goosebumps that make me grasp his waist to stay upright.

"This is all I've thought about today," he says between kisses. "Just… Only you."

I give his hair a gentle tug as a groan escapes me. "Everyone is waiting," I manage.

"Let them fucking wait," he hisses.

He grabs me by the hips and throws my back against the outside door, his chilled hands already reaching for the button on my jeans. I flinch at the cold, prompting him to smile against my lips.

"You're going to love how they feel on your warm pussy, beautiful," he says as he slides his hand beneath my underwear and between my thighs.

Shit, he couldn't have been more right.

The cool nip of his touch causes me to weaken in his grasp. I weave my fingers into his hair and hold his head against my neck as he pumps his finger into me and drags my heated wetness over my clit. A whimper leaves me from the sensation, and I desperately rock my hips against his motions.

Three knocks boom on the other door.

My heart skips, and Maddox throws his hand over my mouth.

"Let's go!" Reed says on the other side.

Maddox's eyes meet mine. "Say you need five," he mouths, slowly beginning to slide his calloused finger in and out of me in the most tantalizing way.

I can hardly keep my eyes from rolling back, let alone muster up the voice to say anything.

"Andi? Come on, let's go," Reed says.

"I'm changing pants," I have enough sense to say.

Maddox smirks against me, his lips landing on my cheek almost praisingly. There's a delight in his green gaze that has me nearly forgetting that Reed is on the opposite wall's other side.

"So bad," I mouth to him.

He grins. "You love it," he claims with a fleeting kiss. He curls his fingers and plunges aggressively inside me, making my mouth drop and my chest cave. His nose brushes on mine like he knows exactly how fragile he's making me. Over and over and over, picking up speed to the point that I have to clamp my fists around his shirt. I want to let go of the noises threatening in the back of my throat. The strain of denying that whine and plea has me shaking in his arms.

Reed pounds on the door again.

"Give me five minutes!" I cry out. "I can't decide what I want to wear."

"Open the door," Reed argues. "I can help."

"I'll be out in a minute—"

"I'm coming in."

"Shit," I hear Maddox hiss.

I shove him back, my heart pounding as I search for any place for him to hide.

Maddox throws himself into the bed and under the covers. He motions to the pile of dirty laundry and my suitcase, and I quickly throw all of it on top of him as he pulls the bedspread over his curled-up figure.

It's a chaotic mess; however, it'll have to do.

Because the door is opening.

Reed sticks his head in as I shove my shirt down over my open jeans. "Jesus fuck, Reed—"

"What's wrong with what you have on?" he asks as he peers over me.

I gawk at him. "It isn't what I was wearing thirty seconds ago," I say as I button my jeans. "You didn't have one more minute of patience?"

"When have I ever had patience?" Reed asks, and his

genuine look of innocence makes me shake my head.

"Give me another minute to make sure I have my bag together," I nearly plead with him.

Reed nods and takes out his phone. He taps the screen a couple of times as I grab my purse from the floor, and when he presses the phone to his ear, I frown.

"Who the hell are you calling?" I nearly balk.

"Mads," he answers.

Oh fuck, I hope he doesn't have that ringer on.

"Why are you calling him?" I ask as my heart skips a few times.

"Because he isn't answering my texts," Reed says.

"Okay, so can you do that in the hallway?"

Please go in the hallway.

Please just go.

The distinct noise of a vibrating phone sounds from the bed.

I need to vomit.

Shit.

Shit. Shit. Shit.

It stops the second Reed frowns toward my pile of clothes, and I pull my own phone out as though it was mine buzzing.

"Cynda," I claim, waving my phone. "Maybe Maddox is out front," I suggest.

"Yeah, maybe," Reed says, his brows furrowed. "Probably forgot his phone in the pool house."

"Great. By the time you find him, I'll be downstairs," I say in an attempt to rush Reed out of the room.

"Yeah." Reed is still frowning at the phone, yet he turns on his heel to leave anyway.

I don't take another breath until my brother is finally down the hall and taking the stairs at the end. The instant he disappears, I quietly click the door shut and lock it.

Maddox throws the bedspread off at the sound of the latch.

"Son of a bitch," he mutters.

"That was entirely too close," I manage, my heart still pounding in my ears. "You have to go before he sees you coming down the outside stairs."

Maddox meets me at the end of the bed. He slips his hands around my waist and neck, his lips landing upon mine for a kiss that almost has us falling onto the bed.

"I'll finish this tonight," he says as he releases me.

"I can hardly wait."

He pauses at the door and glances back at me, and my resolve debilitates at the gleam in his eyes.

"Get out of here," I tell him.

He twists the nob and starts out, though not before crossing the room once again to kiss me. I laugh into his mouth and grab his arms as he swings us off balance, my heart somersaulting at the eager embrace.

"Fuck, the next few hours are going to be painful," he says.

"I think you can manage," I reply.

"I don't know. I might die from not touching you," he argues.

I shove him slightly, almost rolling my eyes, though it doesn't damper his grin. He kisses me again and then disappears out of the door before either of us can say to hell with this party.

I know he's right.

This *is* going to be painful.

Out front, James is waiting for us. Bonnie and Zeb are already in the car, so I climb into the third row, feeling like a child as I do. Maddox starts to clamber in after, yet, Bonnie gets out of her seat to climb over the second row bench seat and sit beside me, teasing Maddox about his long legs when she does.

Maddox cracks his knuckles and thanks her, even if there

is a strain in his voice.

I almost laugh at his disappointment.

The press party on the second floor of The Red Attic is already in full swing—to the point that it appears the band is late. I hang back with James as cameras flash in their faces, hoping to stay out of sight from any photos.

James smiles at me when I hide behind him. "Not used to being in front of the camera?" he asks.

"Hell no," I say. "You?"

"Hate it," he replies. He reaches into his pocket and hands me a card, seriousness in his eyes. "If you find yourself in the situation that happened here the other night, text 'SOS.' I'll be in and out tonight. I have a few more guys stationed inside just in case."

I take the card. The notion of Adam being there makes me nauseous. "Hopefully, he's not idiot enough to try it again. I was surprised they weren't at the venue protesting yesterday."

James gives me a look that lets me know he's the one who took care of it.

"Oh… that bad?" I ask.

"I didn't want the band worrying. But yeah, he was there," James tells me. "Along with about twenty-five others."

"That's very protective of you," I say.

"I don't do it just because they pay me," James says. "They're good kids. A lot easier to work with than some of the pricks I've worked for in the past. Someone hurting them is personal."

I glance over and notice the band is heading up the stairs, surrounded by a gaggle of press trying to chat. James cusses under his breath.

"Here we go," he mutters. "Text me, Andi. I mean it."

I nod at him one more time before he sets off to thin the crowd of people encircling the band. I tap the card against my palm and glance around the room to all those with their phones out taking photos or already posting on social media, and then I make my way up the stairs.

There's no way to get a word in with the band for over an hour. I chat with a few people I recognize, but eventually, I make my way to a booth by the far corner that overlooks the club below. I'm nursing my second whiskey-ginger ale, scoping out the people in the crowd who have chosen to wear Halloween masks tonight, and tapping my foot to the music playing when I feel someone sit beside me.

I don't even have to turn around. I can smell Maddox's woodsy scent.

"Bored already?" I ask, chin moving toward my shoulder.

"Thirsty," he says, and I chuckle at his honesty.

I slide my drink to him. "You can hide in my shirt long enough to take a sip."

Only his eyes move to me, a smirk visible within them. He shrugs his coat off and hands it over. "Hold this for me."

I scoff and hold it up over his head—just long enough for him to pull the mask down, slurp my entire drink, and then push it back up.

"The tedious things you do to maintain this image," I taunt him.

"Exhausting," he says.

I start to hand him the coat, and he gives it back. "Hang onto it for me?"

I'm not about to refuse.

It's warm and smells too much like him.

I fold it up and lay it on the table between us, letting it hang off the side. Even just sitting beside Maddox has my body on alert, my neck heating. I take out my phone and pretend to scroll through social media so I don't appear too fidgety. I'm itching to touch him, for him to touch me—

His hand moves to my thigh.

The unexpected, yet so-fucking-welcome, touch shortens my next breath.

Maddox's fingers catch in the rip of my jeans and slip beneath the fabric toward the inside of my leg as if he can't stand another moment. It's soft and promising, not entirely lustful. He squeezes my thickness. I don't dare look his way. Even though everyone else is too busy and deep in their own conversations to notice us.

I'm running out of things to pretend to do on my phone when a text comes through.

Push me away, Maddox texts.

Squeeze me harder, I reply.

He does, and I try to disguise my jagged breath.

It's taking everything in me not to drag you into a bathroom stall and hold my hand over your mouth while I fuck you.

Romantic, I tease.

You bring it out of me.

Whenever I look at you, I have to think of disgusting things just to keep my mind from wandering to the noises you make for me. And that little face scrunch when you're coming on my tongue.

I gulp, the fluttering nerves moving out to my extremities.

Sounds terrible, I force myself to text.

Excruciating, he says. **I feel the urge to punish you for it.**

Touching me like this is definitely a start, I say as a sharp ache moves from my fluttering abdomen to between my legs.

I can't stop thinking about your taste, he replies, and I wonder if he can feel the goosebumps rise on my skin beneath his fingers.

I should have found the time to fuck you over the edge of that bed before we came out, he continues. **Maybe then, I wouldn't be in such agony over not being able to kiss you right now.**

"You liar," comes Bonnie's voice.

I flinch at the sound of her, turning my phone face-down on the table faster than I should have, judging by the coy look on her face. Her eyes practically dance with delight as she grins and sits across from me.

"What?" I ask, trying to keep my composure when Maddox pinches my thigh. His hand drifts over my knee, and he pretends to bend over to tie his shoe under the table.

"You said you were single," Bonnie says, referring to our conversation at the tattoo studio.

"I am," I reply.

"Really?" She scoffs. "So, what's this little smile on your face about?"

"What—I'm not smiling," I say as I cover my mouth.

"I saw it, too," Maddox says, straightening up. He leans his elbows over the lip of the table and eyes me sideways. "I wonder if your brother knows."

Asshole.

"There's no one," I argue, and I want to smack his stupidly grinning face.

"So, who were you talking to, then?" Bonnie asks.

"My cat-sitter," I answer. "She sent me an adorable picture of Patches."

Bonnie's chin lifts smugly, and she settles back into her seat. "Sure," she taunts.

"She did," I argue before opening up my phone and showing Bonnie the photo my sitter had sent me just an hour earlier.

Bonnie raises a poignant brow in response and sips her drink.

"Let me see that," Maddox says as he takes my phone.

I don't know what my face is doing when I glance at him.

He's playing this much cooler than me.

Of course, he's also much more skilled at hiding things

from other people.

"I remember this cat," he says. "Damn. He's old by now, isn't he? He's the stray that came that one Christmas."

It's times like this that I'm reminded just how long I've known him.

"Ah, yeah," I say.

Someone comes over then, and Bonnie rises to her feet with her arms wide, bringing the person into a hug. I'm back to pretending I'm not dying to get home already—with or without Maddox.

Do you want to get out of here? Maddox texts me.

Thank fuck.

You read my mind.

I'd like to read other things on you, he says.

I smile at the screen, noting that he peeks at me when I do. *I'll call a car and meet you at home.*

Not a chance, he counters. ***I'll text James. He can take us.***

I'm fine by myself. I have my pepper spray.

Please, Andi.

Something in me wants to argue. To tell him that I'm perfectly capable of catching a car on my own.

You don't always have to face the big, scary world on your own, Maddox texts.

Maybe I think my demons will protect me.

I'm your demon, and I will.

I almost smile. I nudge him slightly with my elbow so he knows I hear him. *Out front in five, then*, I text back.

Put your spray in my jacket pocket, just in case.

I don't bother telling anyone else that I'm leaving. I know Maddox has to make his rounds, and maybe he'll tell Reed that I'm going with him because I'm tired. At least I had already put the bug in his ear that I wouldn't stay more than a few hours.

James isn't on the staircase when I make my way down. I

spot a couple of the other guards on the bottom floor. Nevertheless, none notice me when I slip out the front door.

I slip on Maddox's jacket when the chill hits my skin, hoping he doesn't need it. His smell wafts over me, and I bring the long sleeves to my face, my eyes closing as I imagine all the things he might do to me later.

A body presses up behind me and wraps their arms around my waist. I smile and lean back, thinking it's Maddox. "You're trying to get us caught," I say as I pull slightly away from him. "You know you can't—"

My insides drop as I turn, and I realize it isn't Maddox behind me.

Shit.

"Ah… Adam." I can barely get his name out, let alone catch my breath. I back away and glance around us. "I thought you were told not to come here."

Adam has a Michael Myers mask in his hand, a knife in the other.

"I just want to talk," Adam says.

"I don't," I reply. "I don't care what you have to say to me. I don't want to hear it."

There's still a scar on his eyebrow where I whacked him with the microphone stand.

Good.

"Andi, please," he says. "I've been doing a lot of thinking. I want to apologize. I want you back. I think… I think I've figured out what you were looking for all those years ago."

I blink. "Excuse me?"

He takes a step in my direction. "I wasn't the person you needed me to be back then," he says. "I wasn't willing to explore the things you wanted. But I think I know how to be that person now."

"You have no idea what you're talking about," I counter.

My phone is in my hand. I need to text James, but I'm too

terrified to look away from Adam, even if we are on a street with people around us.

I don't trust him.

"I'm going to turn around," I say slowly. "And if you follow me, I will scream."

A glimmer rises in his eyes that I don't like. "Seeing you with that scum the other night brought back a lot of memories," he says, referring to Maddox. "It reminded me of everything you'd ever asked me to do with you. The games. Your little craving for bondage and role-playing. It got me thinking—realizing, really—that maybe... maybe *he* was the kind of man you'd wanted me to be."

"Maddox is ten times the man you are," I manage.

Adam chuckles. "We'll see if the rest of the world agrees once I tell everyone who he is."

"Don't take your anger out on him," I argue. "Leave him out of this. This is between us. Maddox has nothing to do with it. He's never hurt you—"

"He took something from me. Something that he doesn't deserve," Adam interjects. "I plan to get it back."

"God, you're such an idiot," I snarl. "I'm not a toy you get to pick up and put on a shelf as if you've somehow rescued me."

"Aren't you? Little Andersyn Matthews. Mommy's broken girl, only looking for someone to shield her from her past, and yet still craving the monsters in the shadows." He slides the mask over his face, and bile rises in my throat. "How's this for your craving?" he asks with a tilt of his head.

"Adam, this isn't fucking funny," I counter, my voice rising.

Mother fucker. Everyone's going to think this is a bit. A scary fucking bit.

I back away a few more paces, but he advances. A few people snicker at the exchange outside the building, egging

Adam on.

My chest is tight. I don't know when I last took a breath.

"Go ahead," he says. "Run."

Fuck.

I do.

I. Fucking. Run.

I bolt through the throng of people standing outside and head down the street. I can hear Adam's boots hitting the sidewalk at my back, hear the voices of people thinking this is a joke, laughing as I pass them by.

I don't know where to turn, where to flee.

In my panic, I run out into the street. Horns blow. One car slams on its brakes a second too late. Its nose barely nudges my legs—

I don't stop.

I *can't* stop.

My phone hits the ground.

I start to run back for it and realize Adam is too close. I have to leave it.

The lapse in my attention is just enough time for him to catch up with me. I run down a dark alley, hoping I can lose him in the shadows—

He grabs my arm and flings me into the wall. My head slams into the brick. It knocks my brain, my vision. Lights glimmer behind my eyes. I have to blink over and over just to grasp reality again.

A hand crushes over my mouth.

The force shoves my cheek into the jagged wall. I squirm and kick. He's ripping at the tears in my jeans. I thrust my hand to his face and push him back, making him yell as I wriggle and fight and cry out.

The cold of an actual knife hits my stomach, and I freeze.

Adam yanks the mask off and hovers in front of me, his free hand over my mouth, the other now using his knife to tear through the fabric from the top of my thigh, across my stomach, to my waist.

It pierces my skin, and I yelp behind his hand.

"This is what you wanted, isn't it?" he hisses at me. "What you always *begged* me for?"

I want to speak.

I want to scream.

A tear stretches down my numb face. I'm trembling, trying to figure out any way to get out of his grasp without the knife cutting clear into my hip. Thread by thread, the jeans rip.

I lose a little more of myself with every fiber that comes undone.

And then I remember…

Carefully, I reach into Maddox's pocket. My jeans fall open. Adam grins and holds up the knife to my face. The silver glimmers in the light at the end of the street, yards away from where we are—

I can just make out my blood on the tip.

"What else should I carve on you when I'm done?" he asks.

I unclip the safety on the pepper spray and pull it out fast. He sees my movement and starts to swat my hand down. His hand grabs my wrist. The knife flails in the air. I hit the button on the spray, not caring that it isn't in front of his face.

Some still hits his eyes.

He yells and staggers back. The knife clatters to the ground.

"You fucking *whore!*"

"*Andi!*"

Maddox is a whirl in my vision as he tackles down the alley. I stumble off the wall and throw myself into his arms. He's calling my name and touching my face.

Yet in a blink, Maddox launches himself at Adam.

I sway and catch on my knees. My palms and knees land in

a wet puddle of asphalt and grime. I hear the pair topple onto the ground behind me, hear a punch strike one of their faces.

"Maddox, he has a knife!" I yell.

It's all I can get out. I'm faltering, blood trickling down my face and hip.

Maddox looks twice at me over his shoulder, and upon seeing me, he slams Adam into the ground once more, then bolts to his feet.

"Andi—*Andi*, look at me—"

He grabs my face and pulls me to look at him, and when our eyes meet, a fury beyond anything I've ever seen swells within his black pupils.

"Mother fucker." Maddox looks back at Adam, yet before he can launch again and throttle Adam into the next existence, Adam is on his feet. The bastard scrambles into a run, footsteps pounding on the damp alley street.

Maddox rises like he's about to sprint after him.

"Maddox…"

My ass hits the ground. I don't know what he's saying. All I know is that his hand is on my face, and I'm on the verge of puking. I blink repeatedly. I don't know whether it's from the hit on my head or simply a hazy reaction to the brawl.

I can't catch my breath.

"—you stand?" I hear Maddox ask. "Andi, can you move?—"

Can I stand…

Can I stand?

Wait…

We're in an abandoned alley in the middle of town, merely a block away from where the press is swarming, looking for glimpses of the band. I don't even know how Maddox managed to leave the club without being seen, without there being a gaggle of photographers on his ass right now.

I *have* to stand.

He can't be seen like this.

"Yeah," I finally say.

Maddox takes my hands and hauls me to my feet. I see him watching around us for any onlookers. He pushes his hoodie over his head and turns his mask inside out as we approach the street. I don't know where he's taking me, and I don't care. I force my legs to move one after the other down the street until we can no longer hear the club or people.

It's a few minutes before either of us says a word.

This new street is dark and quiet. Maddox pulls his phone from his pocket and dials a number, pausing us on the sidewalk.

His fingers are *shaking*.

The sight causes tears to line my eyes. I reach out in some desperate attempt to help him settle, to assure him we're okay, even if it's futile.

Maddox's gaze lifts. Our eyes meet, and he laces his fingers into mine, then draws me into his arms. And as he waits for the person on the other end to answer, he kisses my forehead and each of my knuckles.

Blood is running down my cheek, my stomach. Somehow, my pants are still on my hips. I'm trembling, though I don't know if it's from the chill in the air or the ordeal.

I only know I'm crying because I feel the tears dripping onto my chest.

"Hey—" Maddox says as someone answers. "Hey, yeah, it's me. I need you. I sent you my location."

I hear James on the other end, concern lining his tone.

"No, the others are still at the bar," Maddox goes on. "No —no, *fuck* no. Don't get them. Something's happened. Yeah. Thanks, James."

As Maddox ends the call, he presses his hand against my cheek. I hear him curse, see the glisten in his gaze.

It's all I can do to stay steady in his arms.

The black Escalade pulls up beside us a moment later. Maddox quickly reaches for the back door handle as James gets out. His eyes widen upon seeing me. He looks down at his phone, and I know he's searching for missed calls or texts from me.

Maddox doesn't speak.

I climb inside, Maddox after me.

James doesn't drive away the instant we're all in. He turns in his seat as Maddox pushes the hood of his jacket off my hair, and rage pools in his eyes when he sees me.

"I'll fucking kill him," he seethes.

"Maddox—leave it," I almost beg. "He's not worth you losing everything over."

"No, but you are." He swipes his hand desperately over his face like it's the only thing calming him. "God fucking dammit, Andi, *you are*," he repeats in an anguished tone. "If I'd just walked out of the fucking bar with you, you wouldn't be hurt."

"I'm okay," I assure him.

The veins in his neck are straining. He bears his fingers down on his eyes and inhales a deep breath, and I hesitantly brace my hand against his cheek.

Frustration slides from his gaze as our eyes meet. Jaw clenching, he kisses the inside of my palm and closes his eyes as his forehead leans against mine.

"He'll never touch you again," he says. "That much, I promise you."

"You can't know that," I whisper.

"I do," he replies, and his voice seems to shake. "Goddammit, Andi, I do. I swear."

His lips press to my forehead once again, and he tugs me into his chest.

"Do you need the hospital, Andi?" James asks, and his eyes appear as sorrowful as Maddox's.

"Yes," Maddox says.

"No," I argue. "No. I think I just need a shower. I don't want to make a fuss out of it. It's just scratches. I'm more traumatized than anything."

James meets Maddox's eyes, and reluctantly, he nods. The bodyguard puts the car in drive and pulls out onto the street toward home.

As we're moving away, Maddox reaches for my chin and tilts my head back so that I'm looking up at him again.

"I'm so sorry I wasn't there."

"Actually, the pepper spray in your pocket saved me," I tell him in an attempt to lighten his mood.

"Poor shot at humor," he says, and it's me that almost smiles.

There's a bandage on his neck that I squint at, and I realize I haven't seen him without the mask since the tattoo studio. "What's this?" I ask.

"Take it off," he tells me. "I need to put that ointment on it at home anyway."

I reach for the edge of the bandage and tug it back, and when I see the tattoo beneath it, my eyes widen.

"You had my kiss tattooed on your neck?" I ask.

His thumb swipes across my cheek, the smallest of smiles in his dark eyes. "I did."

My stomach unknots, body warming.

My kiss.

He has my kiss—my lips—on his neck for everyone to see.

I lean closer, but before I kiss him, my eyes drift to James, knowing we shouldn't be like this in his presence either.

Maddox gets my drift.

"Hey, James?"

"Yeah?"

"You never saw what's about to happen," Maddox replies. James looks at him through the rear-view mirror, and without a word, he simply nods.

The kiss Maddox plants on me is more than the lust-fueled frenzy we've met each other with the last couple of days. It's deep and passionate and threaded with promises of safety within his arms.

And that is nearly enough to make me forget about the pain of my new wounds.

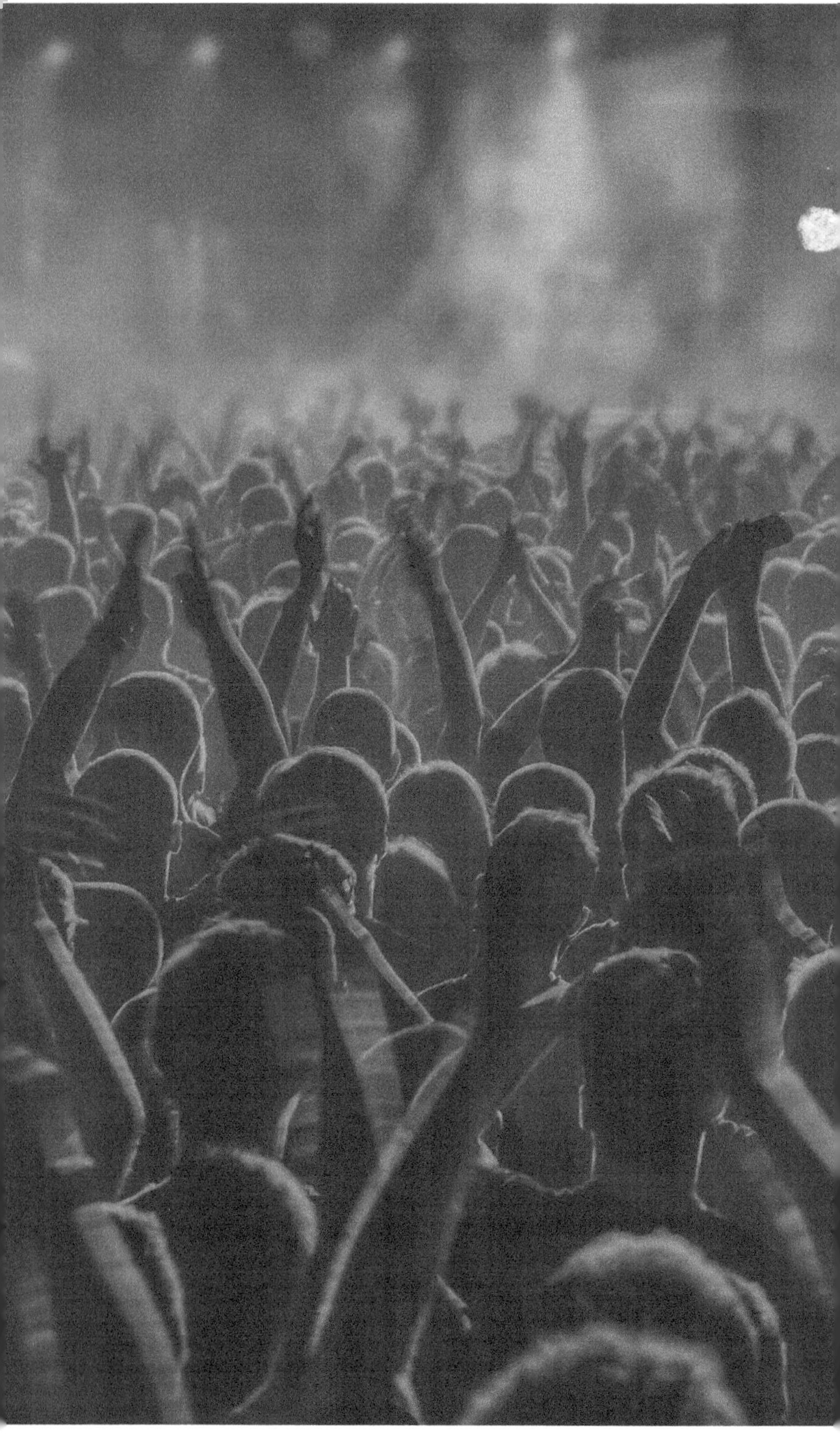

CHAPTER TWELVE
MADDOX

I've never been more livid in my entire life.

I think the stars behind my eyes are from my fury, though I can't be sure. They could be left behind from nearly blacking out at the sight of Andi against that fucking wall.

I should have hunted the bastard down right then and there and left his body in the trash.

But seeing her curling on the ground blinded me.

"I can manage upstairs," she argues as we leave the car. "I don't want anyone to find us. I can't let you—"

"Hey—" I tug her chin so that she's looking up at me, and my fist tightens at the sight of tears in her eyes. "I'm not leaving you tonight," I tell her. "Garage or pool house."

She swallows as if she finally realizes I'm not giving up this argument. "Pool house," she decides.

James pauses at the door. "Do you need me?" he asks.

"I think we're okay," I reply. "Thank you," and I hope to hell he knows I mean it.

As James quietly turns out of the drive, Andi and I head through the side gate to the back deck and pool house. Once there, I draw every curtain and drape across the windows, lock the doors, and press a chair beneath the front handle.

No interruptions.

She shouldn't have to answer questions she doesn't want

to.

Not until she's ready.

As soon as everything is secured, I sprint to the bathroom for towels, the fridge for an ice pack, and alcohol in the cabinet. I'm frantic. My mind races with everything I need to help clean her wounds.

The one I'm most scared of is the one on her hip.

Fuck, I hope she doesn't need stitches.

When I return to the sitting room, I notice that she's pulling her shirt over her head, and her jeans have fallen open at her waist.

Everything appears so much worse in this lighting.

"Don't—Wait—" I halt her before she sits on the couch. "Lay down so I can look at that one," I say, nodding to her stomach.

She doesn't argue or speak, and I clench my jaw at the fright wavering in her eyes.

I'll fucking kill him.

I dart to her with my supplies as she lays down on the couch and swear under my breath when I glimpse the gash.

"What is it?" she asks.

"You need fucking stitches," I tell her.

My head sinks into my hand. I should have taken her to the hospital, to the police, damn what anyone might have said upon seeing me with her. I can handle one overnight in jail—it wouldn't be the first time—so long as she gets the help she needs.

"We're not going to the hospital," she says as if she can read my mind.

"You need the hospital," I tell her.

"No," she says.

"Why?"

"Because you *know* why," she nearly snaps. "What—am I going to tell them someone on their fucking city council chased me into an alley, gashed me, and then tried to rape me? No. They'll turn it around somehow. And if you're with me, they'll look at you. They'll think I'm defending you. If one of them realizes who you are, if one of them knows your fath—"

She shuts her mouth tight and stares at me as if she's regretting ever saying it out loud.

I sit back on my knees, my insides twisting. "Go ahead. Say it."

Her throat bobs, and I can feel the shame rising in my body.

I scoff. "Dammit, Andi, don't protect me from you, too," I say, my tone soft. "Believe me, there's nothing you can say that I haven't heard."

The beat of silence between us feels like an eternity, and I stretch my fingers to stay calm.

"People around here don't know where you've been," she says carefully. "They all think you've been in jail for fuck knows what, not touring the world as part of a highly successful rock band. They're all too stupid to realize that not everyone turns out like their parents."

I want to shove off the ground and pace, to wring my hands behind my neck and let my frustrations out behind the guise of a knife to my thigh.

Yet, looking at her, I feel that frustration wilt and turn into something ten times worse than rage. A burning sensation presses against my sinuses, and I avoid her eyes when I speak.

I thought I could handle the rejection.

I thought I was tough enough that if she realized what might happen if we went together, I could brush it off and not think anything of it.

God, this fucking hurts.

"James can take you, then," I concede. I shift off of my

knees and grab my phone, ready to dial and somehow keep myself from doing something incredibly stupid after she's left.

"Maddox, that's not what I meant—"

"It's fine, Andi," I say.

Why are my hands shaking?

"I only meant that I can't see you taken away for something you didn't do—something you would *never* do," she says. "Maddox, please, hear me out. That's not what I meant."

But I'm too fucking stubborn to hear her.

"Maddox, hang up the phone," she begs. "*Maddox*—"

"Yeah?" James answers.

She grabs the phone out of my hand and puts it up to her ear, and I don't bother fighting her. I hear James speak again, though Andi doesn't move her eyes from mine as she replies.

"Hey, James. Yeah—no, no, we're fine. Just… we're fine. We'll see you tomorrow," she says before hanging up.

Another moment passes, and I feel the tension between us coming to a head.

"If you're ashamed of who I am, just say it," I say, my heart breaking. "If this is nothing more than a week of wild sex for you, just fucking say it. If you think you can never be seen in public with me—"

"Maddox, you barely allow yourself to be seen in public," she snaps. "What—are you thinking of letting go of your mask? Of letting the world see you for once? How can you accuse me of not wanting to be seen with the real you when you don't even want to be seen with yourself?"

I fucking hate this.

"Maybe I am thinking of shedding the mask," I say. "Maybe I had considered that if I had someone by my side who could look past how fucked up I am, I could free myself of that weight. Maybe…" I pause and twist in a circle, my hands running over my face.

I have to get this out.

Even if it kills everything good in my life.

"Goddammit, Andi," I hiss. "I know I'm not your knight in shining fucking armor. I'm the twisted monster holding you hostage. I'm the shadow curling itself into your bones and snatching you into the darkness I've lived in for two decades. I'm the asshole that never means to save you from your past. I'm the one that craves your tears, your blood, and your scars. I'm the person who needs to know the bits of yourself that everyone else thought were too difficult or immoral to handle. I want the corners you've hidden and the desires no one else understands. And that's... *fuck*, that's something no one on the outside will ever understand," I say desperately.

Her nostrils flare with emotion as she shifts on her feet, our tear-lined eyes unable to move from one another.

I'm splintering inside with the unknown, bearing everything I am to her.

Because fuck it.

"I know I'm not good enough for you," I go on. "I know I'll never be the savior you deserve. No matter how willing you are, I shouldn't be dragging you into the hollows behind me. You're meant to be guided into the sunlight—"

"And what if I'm tired of being blinded by the sun?" she asks, her jaw tight. "What if I'm tired of being burned by its promises? What if flying too close to it has hurt me more than the darkness ever did?" She pauses to wipe the tear off her scraped cheek, and it pains me that I wasn't the one to catch it.

"Dammit, Maddox… what if the hollows are my home, too, and I've been too terrified of my own shadow to see it?"

I'm fucking numb.

She wants…

"Of course, I want to be seen with you," she goes on, her

voice trembling. "I want every person who ever doubted you to know you're not him. I want you to feel free enough that your mask becomes a choice, not a death sentence."

She finishes crossing the space between us. Our fingertips meet in a way that makes us both flinch before we sink into that touch.

"I want *you*, Maddox," she says in a broken tone. "But I can't watch you get taken away from me and everything you love because someone else can't see the same parts of you that I do."

My chest caves, eyes closing as I tug her into me.

"If we're going to share the same darkness, you have to know that you can't protect me from the assholes outside with pitchforks who swear you'll be safer without me," I tell her. "We're not kids anymore, Andi," I say softly. "You don't have to protect me. Let me be there for you. Let me protect *you*—to hell with everyone who thinks I'm dragging you down."

Her body sinks slightly as if she's suddenly weak, and I press my lips to hers for a gentle, promising kiss that has me hugging her for long after our lips part.

"I'm still not going to the hospital," she says into my chest after a few beats.

God fucking dammit.

"Fine," I concede. I release her only to get my phone from the counter, and she frowns when she sees me bring up James's number to text him.

"What are you—"

"I don't have what I need for this cut," I tell her. "Just sending him a list of things to pick up from the store."

Stress hives rise on her neck in splotches of red. She looks down at the ground and tucks her hair back, shame written in her eyes.

I don't want her to be embarrassed by this.

This wasn't her fault.

None of it was *ever* her fault.

I send the list to James, and after he replies with a thumbs-up emoji, I peer at her again.

"I need to clean this," I say. "And... and your head."

She nods without speaking.

Every time the water hits one of her wounds in the shower, she flinches, and as I clean the knife wound, she grips my other arm so tight that my hand goes numb.

James leaves the bag I requested by the door. I have Andi lying on the bedroom floor, a towel pressed to the now open cut to stop the fresh bleeding.

"I didn't realize you were so well-versed at this," she says as she stares at the ceiling, and we hold the towel tight to her side. "I think... I honestly thought Tina cleaned you up most of the time."

"Not every time," I reply, unable to look away from our scarred hands lying atop one another. "There were days when I couldn't move. Days when he was home too long for me to sneak out."

"Never the hospital?" she asks.

"Going to the hospital meant CPS," I say in a low voice. "CPS meant possibly getting taken away from your family. Fuck my dad. I couldn't lose the only people who didn't believe I would turn out just like him."

She sucks air through her teeth when I peel back the cloth from her thigh. "Keep putting pressure up top," I tell her as I open a butterfly closure.

Familiar rage pulses through me again as I see the cut. Even so, I have to stifle it.

"Reed used to tell me if music didn't work out, I should become a nurse," I say after a few minutes, and the smile that raises her lips causes my heart to flee.

"He isn't wrong," she replies.

My hands move as if I've done this a thousand times. I'm reminded in glimpses of memories I've long tried to forget. And not solely memories of my father but of the taunts surrounding me. From early fights in my childhood to the ones in college.

I see myself staring in the mirror and placing these same closures on my eyebrows, pressing ice packs to my eyes, my nose…

Staring back at the kid still running from something that was never his burden to carry.

"You know you're not him," she says as if she can sense my thoughts. "You would never do the things he did."

"Which part?" I ask, my voice sounding nearly comical. "The abusing his kid and telling him he's worthless and will never amount to anything, or the drunken benders and rapes?"

Andi's eyes meet mine for a second too long, and I huff as I shake my head, almost unwilling to answer.

"Did you ever know?" she asks. "About the girls, I mean."

I pause. "No," I admit. "He never brought them home—at least not while I was there. By the time one went to the police about it, I was eighteen and living with your family."

"Hence the college across the country," she says.

"Even running states away didn't stop people from putting together who I was. Every time they did, I ended up in jail overnight for knocking some asshole on their back. The fucking way people looked at me… It's like they thought I would come after them, their girlfriends. Like his fucking ghost was sitting over my shoulder and telling me what to do."

"Is that why you never graduated?" she asks.

"I threw myself into our music instead," I reply. "It was a better home than the classrooms of people who only thought of me as yesterday's trash. Once Reed graduated, I decided

I'd had enough. I cut my hair and started wearing the mask all the time. People were so… god, they were so different. Like night and fucking day. It nearly gave me whiplash."

Andi beams. "Humorous," she teases me.

"You're laughing," I say.

Her stare makes me want to rush the last few closures so that I can get back to healing her in a different way. Instead, I give her a smile that feels almost foreign, the feeling weaving through my abdomen an unfamiliar ache.

Somehow, as my eyes flicker to hers again and again, I feel the anvil on my chest lift the smallest amount. It's minuscule and faint, yet enough of a shift that a lump builds in my throat.

I finish the last few and bandage the wound so that it doesn't dry out or get infected, and once I'm satisfied, I lay down on my side by her.

"I know I'm not him," I say, fingers tracing up and down her arm. "Doesn't mean the rest of the world will believe it if they find out. They never have in the past."

Andi takes my hand into hers and kisses my fingertips. "That was the past," she says softly. "If people knew you— the person you've become… they'd know you're nothing like him."

A heavy sigh leaves me as I stare at our entwined hands atop her stomach. "My terms," I finally say. "If I'm going to take the mask off and tell the world who I am, I want it to be on my terms. Not fucking… not by some asshole with a hero complex—a fucking backward hero complex, at that," I say, referring to Adam.

Her lips flinch in the briefest of motions. "He thought the mask would turn me on tonight," she says. "Because he realized who you were. He thought it would just flip me or something, and I'd fall right into his arms."

"He's a fucking idiot," I say. I lean forward and take her

chin between my fingers. "I'm the only creep in a mask you're allowed to fall for."

It comes out before I realize what I'm saying. Yet before I can take it back or correct myself, I feel her smile against my lips.

"Is that what's happening?" she asks softly.

I release a jagged breath in a shit attempt to keep my cool. "I fucking hope so," I breathe.

Our lips meet with a kiss that warms my chest and aches my decrepit heart.

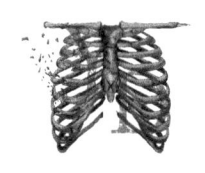

I'm still getting used to the harsh sunlight from the eastern window on the other side of the pool house in the mornings. It cuts over the world's edge and stretches across the ground until it reaches this room, where the amber light seems to melt over every surface. I've cursed it this week. Put a pillow over my head. Tried throwing a sheet over the window to try and stifle it.

But if that light wants to cascade over her beautiful body as it's doing right now, who am I to argue?

Andi fell asleep in my arms, and I hadn't bothered waking her up to go back to her room.

To hell with anyone that might have said something against us last night.

There was no way I was leaving her.

However, with a new day rising, I know we have to leave what we are in the dark. I can't tell Reed before this show run and chance him freaking out.

Maybe after…

I shake my head at the possibilities. It's too early to make life decisions.

With a kiss on her cheek, I rise from the bed, trying not to wake her, and she only stirs enough to squeeze the pillow in her arms tighter.

I need to check out the house and see who's home so I can get her out of my bed without looking suspicious.

My shirt is hanging over the back of the barstool. I grab it and shove it over my head, and just when I start out the door, I see Reed's mom coming out of the house through the sliding doors.

Looks like I woke up just in time.

She meets me halfway across the pool deck with two cups of coffee.

I hope to hell I don't look like I just spent the night fucking her stepdaughter into the next decade.

"Morning, Maddox," Tina says, smiling broadly. She's wearing an oversized sweater and linen shorts, her blonde hair pulled up in a clip at the back. "I was just bringing this out to you. I know that the sun is blaring in the mornings through those windows. It can be hard to get your bearings sometimes. Reed only got home a couple hours ago."

Thank fuck I got my ass moving this morning.

"Morning, Mrs. Matthews," I say, my voice still raspy as I haven't quite woken up. She extends the cup of coffee to me and peers me over the rim as she sips her own. She and Reed have the same stark blue eyes, and it's those eyes that are humorously scrutinizing me right now.

I take a sip of the hot liquid. "Your eldest son is an animal."

"He certainly can be." Her gaze washes over me, lingering slightly on my neck. "Did *you* have a nice night?"

"I did," I answer. "Tried to get back early. I can't party like

I used to."

"No. Though, you can still swoon girls into your bed, can't you?" She tilts her head amusedly, and my brows narrow at the accusation.

"You have lipstick on your collar, son," she says. A soft snicker sounds from her, and she turns on her heel. "It's a plum shade, too. Our Andi likes that shade of lipstick. Perhaps she and your overnight friend can exchange which brand has the best."

Fucking hell.

"Your sweatshirt is dry if you want it," she calls back.

I definitely want it.

I scramble to follow her into the big house. She has one of my band sweatshirts mixed in with Reed's laundry lying on the bench of the breakfast nook.

"I can do my laundry today, Mrs. Matthews," I say as I pull the hoodie over my head.

"Give it to me," she argues. "I'll take care of it."

"I can do it," I tell her.

It's an argument we've been having for over ten years now.

"Maddox, you have a lot to do today. Let me take care of it," she insists. "I miss having the laundry of all four of my boys in the house. Especially when you've all finally grown out of the gross years."

I laugh. The things we did with our clothes as teenage boys makes me question how I don't have a permanent rash—and how she didn't kick us all out.

"At least let me feel somewhat helpful and put it in the washer," I concede.

She smiles fondly at me from the other side of the bar. "Well, now that that's settled, what would your overnight friend like for breakfast?"

I nearly snort into my cup. "Ah... I'm not sure," I reply.

"Groupies don't usually spend the night."

"I hope you're using protection, Maddox," she sighs. "And having them sign an NDA. Especially if you're not wearing your mask around them. I know how much you value your privacy."

Shit.

I should have thought to grab that.

"Always," I tell her.

I hear Randall, Andi's father, coming down the hall. I know his barreling footsteps because I'd had them memorized as a teen when Reed and I used to stay up late or sneak out of the house for a party. And when he comes around the corner, his smile meets me.

It's a broad smile, even if behind his gleaming eyes, he appears wholly haunted. It rests in the creases by his eyes and how he holds his shoulders—as if they once carried the world upon them. Andi shares his complexion, dark hair, and nose, though the rest of her…

Her mother's face flashes behind my eyes, and I blink to shut it out.

Tina sweeps in and presses her lips to Randall's cheek as he grabs a piece of bacon from the tray.

"Looking well-rested this morning, Mads," he says with a coy look over me.

"Oh, mother fuck," I mutter, pressing my hands to my eyes. "I'm going back to bed," I add, only half-joking.

Tina snickers and Randall's grin widens.

"It's your hair," Randall says. He comes around the table and sits in front of me. "Who is she?"

"Just a groupie," I lie, and it feels like an insult.

Randall raises his brow. "You know the road rule, Mads," he says. "No over—"

"—night guests," I finish for him. "This one slipped up."

"Seems like she saw a little more of you than usual,"

Randall says. "No mask?"

Fucking fuck, fuck.

"Again. Slip up," I mutter.

God, between Andi's lipstick and my forgetting the mask, they'll have it figured out by the end of the day.

Randall's smile is considerate, and I stand before he can begin drilling me with any more questions.

"I should... I'm going to check on her while you're cooking," I say.

"Bring her to breakfast," Tina says as I start through the door.

"Oh, god, no," I say with a laugh, though I feel myself panicking as I say it.

I have no fucking clue how to get Andi out of this room.

The entire walk back to the pool house, I can feel the Matthews watching me as if they think the girl I brought back will just walk out and greet me. I notice that the white curtains are drawn across the double doors, and I'm curious if Andi got out of bed to do that in the last fifteen minutes.

She's hiding behind the door when I close it, her eyes wide.

"Are they both up?" she asks.

"Ah... unfortunately," I answer. My gaze wanders over her, noticing she's wearing one of my t-shirts and nothing else. My brows raise. "Good morning to me," I mumble before grabbing her by the hem of her shirt and hauling her into me.

My heart flees when I feel her smile against my lips. I wrap my arms around her waist, holding her tight as I bend her backward, and her arms slink around my neck to secure herself.

Kissing her makes me weaker than anything else.

"I have no idea how to sneak you out of here," I tell her once we part, my hands wandering to her bare ass. "I let us sleep too late."

"Can you distract Tina?" she asks.

"They know I have a girl in here," I say. I point to my collar where her lipstick lingers, and her eyes widen.

"Also forgot to wear my mask out of here," I add. "So, they know whoever I have here has seen my face."

"Well. Fuck. Um…" She takes a step back and pushes her hair off her face. "James?"

"What about him?"

"I can pull my hair back and into one of your hoodies, get in the car with him like he's taking me home, and he can drop me off down the street?" she suggests.

It's not a half-bad plan.

"What will they say when they see you walking down the road back?" I ask.

"I'll… I'll tell them I wanted a walk," she says, though her voice doesn't sound very confident.

I elevate my brow in a questioning matter, and she lifts her shoulders and hands.

"I don't know what else… I mean, I don't normally go on a random walk in the mornings of October, but I can tell them I was doing witchy shit," she says.

I snap and point my finger her way. "Now, that might actually work."

She chuckles in the cutest way, the light in her eyes so different from the night before.

I'm still not over it.

"Are you okay?" I ask.

She crosses the space between us again and entwines her fingers with mine, our palms meeting. "No," she admits. "No, I think… Maybe I should have taken a walk this morning to get out of my head."

I push her hair back, my jaw tightening upon seeing the scrape on her cheek. "Maybe we should muff this up a little bit and tell them you fell on the sidewalk this morning?"

"Oh, god," she groans. She tips her head in her hand. "I have no idea. I can't tell them what happened."

"I know," I agree, though I wish she would.

She picks up her phone from the counter and switches on the front-screen camera to look at herself, even though the screen is cracked now. I had picked it up on my way out of the club, knowing it was hers by the photo of the cat on her Lock Screen, and that alone had told me she was in trouble somewhere nearby.

"Shit," she grunts. "Think James will throw me on the sidewalk, too?"

I give her a poignant stare, and she sighs.

"I'll tell them I tripped last night and fell into the wall," she finally concludes. "Honestly, it wouldn't be the first time."

Our eyes meet for a beat, and she gives me a small smile. "Busy day today," she says. "Major concert later."

"Fuck. It's already Thursday," I realize. "No wonder Tina is making a big breakfast. Shit—I need to get you out of here." I pull my phone from my pocket, bring up James's number, and then lift it to my ear.

"Are you actually calling him?" Andi asks.

"Easier to explain—Hey, James. Where are you?" I ask him.

"Ah... getting some coffee. What do you need?" James asks.

"We need a favor."

CHAPTER THIRTEEN
MADDOX

Maddox's Hype Playlist

Every concert sends my nerves into shambles.

But the first concert of an extended run with the added pressure of it being in our hometown? The weekend of Halloween?

I'm on the edge of a high-rise. Gravity's weight is daring to drag me over the edge. Fear and adrenaline thrive through my tense muscles. I need to jump. To dive head first over this ledge and get it over with. Let this exhilaration pull me through the weightless pressure and onto the other side of life.

A deep breath fills my lungs, and I blow it out through my mouth.

Young Decay.
Young Decay.

The noise of the crowd chanting for us is loud enough for me to hear over the music blaring from the headphones around my neck.

Andi's headphones.

She'd gotten them to James to give to me before the show. I haven't seen her since breakfast. She decided to hang back out of sight before the show tonight, insisting that she didn't want to be a distraction.

I could really use her as a distraction right now.

The last moment we were alone together, I had her bent face-down over the kitchen island with her pussy in my mouth and her hands gripping the other side of the counter.

That sweet cunt of hers is my goddess.

It was a nice way to spend the five minutes we had waiting for James to arrive to pick her up and drop her off down the street.

My hood is up, mask on, as I walk back from the stage to the dressing room to check on the others.

Bonnie is beating her drumsticks on the dressing room table when I arrive. Zeb is bouncing up and down, boxing at the wall, more than likely listening to a cold case files podcast in his headphones.

And Reed…

Reed is sitting in the middle of the floor with his legs crossed beneath him. His eyes are closed, palms up. I know there's a guided meditation playing through his earbuds. He likes to completely zone out before taking the stage so he feels like he's been absent from the world for a while.

Bonnie winks at me through the mirror.

I drink an entire bottle of water before heading back out for another walk.

Moving around backstage with my hype playlist blaring through my headphones is the only thing that helps me clear my head.

I like getting a look at the crowd and watching some of the opening act. A few times, I've strapped on my bass and jammed with them if I know their music.

Maybe I'll do that Saturday.

Tonight is too fucking nerve-wracking.

The opening band is taking down their set now. I pause in the wings, shadows falling over me, and turn the volume down in my headphones to get a better sense of the audience.

The house lights are on.

Fans are beating on the stage barrier.

My heartbeat begins to thud in my ears.

Young Decay.

Young Decay.

Standing here, I feel the tension from the crowd, and the familiar rope wraps achingly tight around my anxious muscles.

A group of people on the other side spot me. A woman in the front points and looks at her friends, prompting them to throw their hands in the air, screaming and shouting at me.

I take my hands from my pockets and flash the horns, and the group roars back.

Something about the exchange amps me up.

Let's fucking *go*.

Young Decay.

Young Decay.

Reed is stretching on the ground when I reach the dressing room again. Bonnie is painting her lips black and checking her makeup one last time. Zeb is taking a single shot of vodka. He slaps the empty glass on the table twice and jumps a couple of times to shake out his nerves.

I grab my acid-wash grey jacket and put it on over my sweatshirt.

"How's the crowd?" Reed asks from the floor.

I pull down my mask and grin at him. "Fucking magical," I reply.

Reed hops to his feet as I take my tin from my bag and grab a single gummy out. Reed holds his hand out for one, and we cheer's them together before popping them into our mouths.

Another deep inhale fills me. I shake out the audible breath and crack my neck as the four of us circle in.

Young Decay.

Young Decay.

Three knocks sound on the door.

The stage manager sticks his head inside. "On in seven," he says.

The crowd is so loud that we can hear them when the stage manager leaves the door open.

Reed and I exchange grins.

"Fuck, that's beautiful," Bonnie says.

Young Decay.

Young Decay.

For a few seconds, I fumble with my phone and connect it to the speaker in the room, eventually tuning into the same before concert hype list I'd been listening to as I walked around backstage. As the first song begins, Reed claps his hands so hard that it sounds like gunfire. He jumps up and down, shakes his hair out of his face, and Bonnie joins him. Together, the pair belt out the lyrics, and Zeb and I take one more shot.

"Let's go! Let's go!" Reed says midway through the song, unable to keep his cool.

"All right, focus in," Zeb calls our attention. He pulls a bean ball bag from his pocket, holds it up in the middle of us, and then drops it.

Reed is the first to kick it up.

And for the next four minutes, we battle to keep it off the ground.

We've played this game every single show for the last four years.

It's four minutes when we can forget about the crowd waiting for us and the nerves that just won't go away. Four minutes when we get to be carefree, as if no one knows our names.

Four minutes where we get to just… *be.*

By the time the stage manager comes back to walk us out, Reed and I are celebrating our team victory with high-fives.

Young Decay.

Young Decay.

We file out of the dressing room, and I hear the stage manager say, "We're walking," over his headset.

I can't stretch my fingers far enough to ease the restlessness.

In. Out.

In. Out.

Every time they shout our names, goosebumps rise on my arms.

Reed shakes my shoulders and proceeds to jump on my back for a stretch, so damn excited that he can't contain himself. The energy coming off him is contagious, and I run us up and down the hall once, letting him high-five and yell at everyone we pass.

He's fucking heavy, yet I barely notice it.

An invigorating humidity surrounds the four of us when we pause together for a final time at the back of the curtains.

The lights turn completely off.

The crowd erupts.

Stage lights cascade from the sides out over the audience. Our emblem is illuminated behind Bonnie's drums.

And with the strobe lights, our intro music begins.

Young Decay.

Young Decay.

"You know I love you guys," Reed says as we huddle. "Tonight is going to be absolute insanity. Everyone will go home after, and they won't be able to shut up about us for the next few decades. We'll have fucking grannies in their rocking chairs fifty years from now talking about how the best concert they ever went to was for four dumb fucks who never should have had a goddamn chance on a stage like this."

"There's a name we missed," Bonnie grins. "Four Dumb Fucks."

Reed shakes Bonnie and me while Zeb laughs.

"You guys ready?" Zeb asks.

"Let's fucking go, man," Bonnie says.

"Fifteen seconds, Bon," Avie says as he passes us.

We look at each other once more, and then, as loud as we can, we scream.

The audience's noise drowns it out. We hug each other again, and finally, we separate to our respective spaces.

I glance back at Reed one last time. "One eye, brother," I tell him. "I got you."

Reed points his long arm at me. "Better keep two tonight," he says.

"Ah, *fuck*," I laugh. "What are you going to do?"

Reed grins. "You'll see."

"Fucking hell. Fine. Two," I reply, walking backward away from him.

"I trust you," Reed calls back.

I trust you.

The sentence drives deep into my soul. I point at him again before turning on my heel to make for my place in the wings on the opposite side.

Bonnie dramatically climbs onto her platform at the back of the stage as I reach the curtains. The audience roars with her silhouette against the strobe lights. She picks up her sticks from the seat and drums a few beats, sending the crowd into a frenzy.

A flash brighter than the phone cameras lights up the stage between the strobes. Even if I know she's there, it's hard to see Andi in the walkway.

The strobes flash faster, and I finally find her.

She's staring at me from the other side, and just before my signal to head onstage sounds, I sign a single word to her.

It might be the lights, but I swear she signs it back, and it causes my heart to skip.

I step onto the stage opposite Zeb to deafening cheers and shouts. It knocks me all the way to my gut.

I can hardly feel my face and hands as I push the strap over my head and strike a note.

And when Reed hits the stage, the energy rises to a new high.

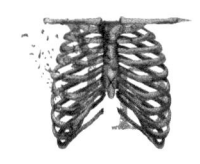

The waterfall of adrenaline racing through me after the show has my vision in a blur, my ears shot to hell. I still can't feel my hands. My face hurts from grinning.

Reed hit a new level tonight that I know will only grow over the coming days.

He's the epitome of chaos.

And with all the excitement radiating through me, it's a wonder I don't throw Andi into the nearest wall and fuck her senseless when I spot her gorgeous self standing backstage and waiting on us when we step offstage.

I'm sweating.

I can't hear a damn thing.

I still have lights flashing in my eyes.

Yet staring at her numbs all of it.

Not kissing her is one of the hardest things I've ever done.

I don't know what to do with myself.

Reed hugs her so hard that he picks her up off the ground and spins her. Bonnie brings her in to lick her face after. Zeb fist bumps her, and when she turns to me, I can see the same turmoil in her eyes as is swimming in mine.

Thank fuck she has enough sense to hug me before I hesitate for too long. The smell of smoke and fire from the pyrotechnics lingers in her hair. Even still, I smell the orange scent of her soap in the crook of her neck.

"The next time you avoid me all day like this before a show, I'm bending you over my knee and turning your ass as pink as your cunt," I say into her hair.

She laughs softly. "There's a threat I wouldn't mind entertaining," she replies.

"I mean it, Andi," I tell her.

"I didn't want to interfere with the band or distract you," she says.

"The only thing distracting me today was the thought of what I'm going to do to you later as punishment."

She pulls slightly out of my arms and squeezes my biceps, the grin on her face nearly causing me to bend her over right here.

"Mads! Party!" Reed shouts down the hall. He thrusts his arms in the air and lets out a loud yell, and I curse aloud.

Andi laughs as if she can tell what I'm thinking.

"Andi! Party!" Reed also shouts.

My brows raise at the face she makes, and she shoves my stomach when I laugh at her.

"Where exactly are we partying?" Andi asks.

"Probably the fucking Attic," I say.

She huffs, both of us staring at Reed as he slaps the hands of every person he walks by, his excitement like an epidemic.

My manager, Avie, clears his throat nearby, and I frown.

"Something wrong, Av?" I ask.

Avie is on his phone already, and I realize he's calling The

Red Attic to let them know we're coming.

And possibly clear the club of any protestors.

"No fights," Avie says, pointing his finger at me. "Something happens—if you even fucking see that shithead—you call me. You call James. You give that asshat no attention. He's a bullet waiting in the chamber. Heartless has a team on his fucking ass, but until he's signed the NDA and paid off, you give him nothing."

Andi balks. "Wait—paying him off? You're giving him money?"

"If we need to—" Avie holds up one finger to us as someone answers the phone, then looks at me "—Hey. I mean it. No fuck ups," he tells me.

Avie walks away, and Andi sinks her face into her hand. "I'm getting too old for this shit," she mutters. "Fuck it. Let's go." She glances back over her shoulder in my direction. "You can ride with me. I'll protect you," she adds with a smirk.

Hell yes.

"Sold."

By the time we pack up and head back to sign a few autographs, my adrenaline is starting to wear. Zeb hands me an energy drink, which I kick back to wake myself up.

Fans have lined up across the back fence, and when we leave through the back door, their cheers echo off the building.

James is waiting with the Escalade at the end of the line. I look around for Andi and her car, though the moment I open the back door, I realize why I don't see her car.

James has her already sitting in the third-row seat.

She looks at me with pursed lips and then at James, who's now standing outside the car. He clears his throat, and I climb into the third-row seat with her.

Because even if I can't kiss her, I need to be near her.

Even if my knees are in my fucking chest.

"No dice on the ride?" I ask low enough that the others can't hear, sitting sideways.

"I was caught," she mutters, glancing at our bodyguard.

I should have known better. "Guess that's what we pay him for."

The rest of the band files in, and as the inside lights turn off and Reed and Bonnie begin recapping the entire show, I reach for Andi.

I need to feel her.

I only mean to touch her, to squeeze her slightly, or massage her knee. But dammit… it's so dark here that I'm curious as to what I can get away with. The second row bench seat is high enough that nothing can be seen if one of the others were to turn around.

I wonder if her heart is racing as fast as mine.

The music is deafening—or maybe that's because I still hear echoes. Reed and Bonnie's laughter is hysterical. I shift in my seat, moving closer to her.

Andi seems to have a better idea.

She turns her back to me, sits between my thighs, bends her left knee in the seat, and pulls out her camera to show me the photos she took at the concert. The back screen glares when she turns it on, and we both wince.

"Oh, shit, that's bright," she mutters as I wrap my arms around her waist. I feel her tense. Nevertheless, in the next second, she's opening her legs wider.

I think I'm fucking in love with her.

I slide my hand beneath the waistband of her leggings. Her breath catches when I maneuver my fingers over her stomach to her pussy, and as if she knows she's staggered too long, she flips through a couple of photos.

"Holy shit," I mutter, and it isn't just because the photo she's showing me is impressive.

She's *soaked*.

I want to groan. Want to lay my head against hers and tell her to lie on her back so I can taste this.

"This is amazing," I continue, trying to keep my voice from hitching. "Fucking amazing."

I stroke up and down her center with two fingers on either side of her clit, pinching when I pull up.

"You like it?" she asks, and I know she doesn't mean the fucking photo.

"Love it," I tell her.

She keeps flipping through the images as I continue touching her clit, continue teasing her in full view of everyone around us.

I reach for her camera with my free hand and wrap my fingers around the outside of hers as I feel her begin to tremble. Her thighs tighten around my hand as I alternate motions, pressuring her pussy harder. *Faster*—without making too much distracting motion.

"Hey—why does he get to see pictures?" comes Reed's voice.

My head shoots forward to find Reed turned in the front seat as if he'd shifted to look back at Bonnie and happened to see the camera screen illuminating in the darkness.

I don't stop touching her.

Andi glances up. "He's beside me," she says. "Do you want to see them?"

"Yes," Reed says.

Andi passes the camera up as if it's on fire.

I almost smile at how quickly she gets rid of it.

Perfect.

I want her coming on my hand before we leave this vehicle.

Her breathing is short. She grabs her knee and stiffens, pretending to pay attention to Reed as he thumbs through the card.

"That one right there," she says, causing me to bite my lips together. "That one. I like that one."

The way she's forcing herself to keep a normal voice makes this so much sweeter.

Because she definitely isn't talking about the photo.

"This one?" Reed asks.

"Yeah, right there—that one," she quickly corrects herself.

Her hand tights on my knee as she trembles against me. She starts to squirm like she's holding back her release.

We turn into a tunnel, and I take a chance to bite the left side of her neck.

"Give me what's mine, beautiful," I breathe in her ear.

We're just minutes from The Red Attic. My pace picks up, the increasing force causing her to dig her nails into my thigh. I can't help my smirk, the absolute triumph of her on the verge of an orgasm in this back seat.

Shit, I'm going to have to think of something to get rid of my own fucking erection.

I wish I could see the expression on her face as her pussy grips my fingers. She rolls her hips toward my hand as if the memory of where we are has slipped her mind. Even so, she's quiet.

She's fucking *silent*.

All except for the sharp breath she sucks in before she comes hard around my digits.

Goddammit, I want to kiss her.

A long exhale leaves her. I swirl that release over her clit, making her flinch before removing my hand from between her thighs and simply leaving them on her stomach.

"So perfect," I breathe in her ear.

The lights of the club come into view. It's packed, and James circles the block once to ensure things are clear before riding around to the back entrance.

I don't want to pull my hands away.

Reed passes back the camera, and as the rest of them open the doors, eager to get inside, Andi fumbles with putting away her things. I pretend to be helping her, though when I look up, I realize no one is paying us any attention. Reed and Bonnie's doors close, and Zeb leaves his open for us to exit.

James gets out of the car and stands by the open door. I hear him lock the others, and the moment I know that door is the only one anyone can get through, I grab Andi's face and haul her lips to mine.

The kiss is insane and desperate and filled with all the yearning I'd felt having to see but not touch her today. I don't even know where my hands are—her face, her neck, her waist, pulling her into my lap. She groans into my mouth as she straddles me, her hands raking through my hair.

"No one's ever made me come that fast in a room full of people," she says between our kisses.

I take her chin between my fingers and hold her face steadily in front of mine. "No one's *ever* made you come like I do," I claim. "I can feel it in the way your entire body quakes with your orgasm, in the way you respond utterly to me. Like you've never known what it means to die of pleasure."

She inhales a jagged breath. "Does this mean you *do* know?"

And there's a twinge of jealousy in her tone.

A smile lifts my lips, and I nudge her nose with mine. "Not like I do with you," I tell her, squeezing her ass. "No one compares to you, Andi."

Andi swipes her thumb over the new tattoo on my neck, and her eyes meet mine. "No one compares to you, either."

Our lips meet again, this time slower, more deliberate.

As if both of us have forgotten where we are.

James clears his throat.

I reluctantly part from her, and she swallows as her fingers

graze my beard.
"An hour?" she asks.
"I think an hour is all I have in me."

CHAPTER FOURTEEN
MADDOX

We're lying naked on my bed just ninety minutes later. I think I counted every minute in that club, almost setting a timer because of my anxiety.

There was no sign of Adam or any of the protestors, which I was grateful that we didn't have to flee because of.

James said little when I texted him about driving us back, though the comment he made when we climbed into the back seat was a simple, "No fucking in my car."

We didn't argue. James was good enough to us that I didn't plan on pissing him off.

It's past midnight, and while the adrenaline is slowly beginning to wane, I'm not sleepy. Maybe that's why I'm holding Andi tightly on my chest, taking my time raking my chipped nails down her side, and staring into her dark honey pools gleaming up at me right now.

This is what I've wanted with her the entire week—to fuck her soul out of her body and hold her while it finds her again.

Andi shifts onto her elbow over me, her thigh swung over my hip, and she brushes her finger over the lip tattoo again before kissing the space beside it.

"Maybe I should get your teeth print on my ass since you like to bite it so much," she jokes.

"It's a nice ass, Andi. I can't help it," I tell her.

"Jiggly and full of dimples," she says with a scoff, mild embarrassment in her tone.

I squint at her, my grip tightening. "You're proving my point. It's a great ass."

This time she laughs, and I swear that little smile is magic.

"Do you not like going out with them anymore?" she asks. "Partying after the show, I mean."

I start moving my hand up and down her back as I speak. "I'm pretty sure I ran out of party energy after our first tour," I say. "We were a fucking mess. We never slept; if we did, it was because we'd passed out on the hotel floor. We still do crazy shit or prank each other when we're bored, but… After Bonnie went to rehab, reality hit home for all of us. We'd barely gotten that fucking record deal, and we were already throwing it away. Reed and Bonnie still love going out, though. Zeb is usually the first to start pranking us out of boredom. Bon has a way of conning Reed into staying out longer than usual. I think he likes the attention."

"You sound jealous," she teases.

"I miss my best friend," I admit. "I go out to appease them. After a few beers, I end up back on the bus playing video games or planning another song."

"That's lonely," she says.

"Nah," I tell her. "It isn't bad. It's nice to have a little quiet to myself occasionally."

"Where is your apartment relative to Reed's? I know he mentioned a few years ago that you two were living in a high-rise," she says.

"Ah. He's on 58, and I'm on 59," I answer, and she smiles at me.

"You two bought identical apartments a floor apart from one another?" she asks.

"We bought the top three floors," I answer.

She leans up, her brows raised, and I wave her off.

"The top floor is open concept and soundproof, so we have somewhere for the band," I explain. "Spent more on setting it up as a prime location for playing than we did on our own decor."

"Do you rent out the space?"

"We haven't. Invited a few other bands to come jam with us, though." I lean back on the pillow and press my hand behind my head. "I can't wait for the break between this tour and the international one. It'll be nice to sit still for a few weeks. Work on new material. I miss the days we used to practice in your garage. Acoustics were fucking terrible, but I wrote some of the best shit sitting on that ugly orange couch."

Darkness flashes in her eyes, and even though it's gone in the next second, I know her memory of that couch isn't what the rest of us remember.

"God, that thing was horrendous," she says. "I don't know who it pained more to get rid of it, though: Dad or Tina. Both of them stood there with tears when the movers removed it. It took everything in me not to burn it."

"Have you been back?" I ask her. "To the old house?"

A solemn look passes over her face when she looks down, her fingers raking down the tattoo on my sternum. "I haven't. You?"

It's a gamble what I'm about to say.

No one else knows, not even Reed.

"Not since I bought it," I reply.

Andi pushes up to her hands over me, eyes narrowing like I've just told her I'm dying. "What? You bought it?" she asks.

"Yeah," I reply.

"Does Dad know?"

"Nah," I reply.

"Does *anyone* know?"

I shake my head.

"Why... Why would you buy it?"

I shrug, a heavy sigh leaving me that raises my chest. "Couldn't let it go."

She's staring at me in a haze like she can't understand why I would want to keep the place where…

I reach for her hand, prompting her eyes to move to mine, and I bring her palm to my lips.

"Do you want to see it?" I ask.

She chews on her bottom lip for a moment. I can see the debate in her eyes, the unrest winding through her.

"Yeah," she finally decides.

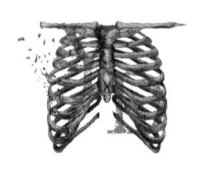

The drive over is quiet.

I'm glad Andi suggested taking the old Bronco instead of the studio's car. The area we all grew up in isn't the worst neighborhood in this town, but it certainly isn't the best.

As we near, I reach over and take Andi's hand. I know what this house is to her. I know the memories and pain gushing through her as it becomes visible beneath the amber street lamps.

It's the house where she once played princess.

The house where she climbed all the trees and got stuck more than once. The house where she watched her father fall in love again. The house where she got her first camera and hid behind doorways to snap photos of her family, feeling more secure behind the lens rather than in front of it.

It's the house where she would take Reed and hide them away in the closet or the basement when her mother would barge in unannounced in a drunken state to say she was taking Andi away—whether for the weekend or permanently.

It's where she tried to protect Reed and their younger brothers from her mother's fever.

Where she once crawled under the baseboards when she was home alone, and her mother chased her while calling her a whore.

Where her father found her crying in the dirt, a knife in her own hand to defend herself, and where she'd shouted to him that she didn't want to live if it meant having to stay in that house alone again.

It's the house where she watched her mother break down the door, then shout and scream and blame Randall for everything wrong with her before taking her own life before them in the dining room.

Andi swallows as she turns into the driveway and shines the headlights on the old garage.

I squeeze her hand. "Are you sure?"

"Yeah," is all she says before she turns the ignition back.

An eerie silence consumes us when we step out of the truck. A low fog hangs over the streets and the dewy grass. Halloween decorations linger on porches and across fences. There's a house two doors down where it looks like some kids had fun streaming rolls of toilet paper in the giant oak tree out front.

"We did that a few times," I say, smiling over my shoulder at Andi.

Her lips twitch when she looks down the street. "To that tree, too," she says.

"It's a hard tree to cover," I say as I come around the car. "It was a nice challenge. These kids, though… they couldn't even wait for Halloween?"

The expression on her face is one I recognize. As if she wants to smile but has forgotten how.

I take her hand as we approach the front door.

The smell of old wood and mothballs hits us when the red door creaks open. It's completely dark, and I take out my phone to shine the flashlight around.

Andi hits the foyer light switch out of habit. The yellow uncovered lightbulb flickers beneath a cobweb above us. And as the room is illuminated, Andi releases my hand.

It's all I can do to watch her reach out for the staircase banister, her fingers running over the dust as if she can feel the past within those particles.

The Matthews only left a few pieces of furniture behind, including the enormous, ornate mirror I remember Tina being obsessed with when we were younger. The rule of 'no running in the house' was solely because she was terrified one of us would fall into it.

Her boundary couldn't protect it from something worse, and they'd left it behind along with the grief accompanying this place.

The glass is still shattered at the bottom corner, with dried blood in the cracks that were ignored for the years after it was broken.

Andi presses her fingertips to her forehead.

"I never apologized to Tina for that," she says softly. "I never apologized to her for *any* of it."

Her voice is breathy, almost short.

She ambles ahead and looks at the door beneath the stairs leading down to the basement and the chair beside it. I can see her fingers trembling when she pushes it slightly, and on the wood floor are two scratches from that chair digging into it.

My heart pounds, each beat feeling like a drum in my chest. It's all I can do to manage her name through my sticky voice.

"Andi?"

She doesn't say anything as she moves into the kitchen through the entryway at the back of the hall. The same cream-colored wallpaper with miniature blue houses and pink flowers is peeling back from the drywall. The cabinets' blue paint is faded and chipped. The linoleum remains cracked and rusted beneath appliances that have long expired.

Andi runs her hand over the counter, almost appearing lost in memory. Her fingernail snags on an indention in the top, and she picks at it like a scabbed wound.

"We never replaced this," she breathes. "We never…" Her chin lifts, eyes darting around the room again. She moves to the wall by the broken-down fridge and spreads her palm over a hole in the partition, though she doesn't speak.

I feel the energy change. I see it swell in her glistening eyes. Her jaw is trembling, invisible strings tugging downward at the corners of her lips as she tries to hold it all in.

She proceeds to the dining room faster than I can catch her.

There's a rectangular spot on the floor where the rug once sat. The color difference is stark, a path well worn around it from the footsteps of children once chasing one another. Andi isn't staring at the worn wood on the perimeter, though. Her gaze snags at the center, where the cracks between the hardwood boards are darker than the other places.

I know what she's looking at.

I know why she's shaking.

She brings her hand to her mouth as a tear falls down her cheek, and she walks across the foyer to the living room entryway, then turns around to stare at the dining room again.

Her gaze jerks back to the basement door.

She bolts to it as if she needs to see the scratches again.

"We sat this chair under the knob every time she came

over after the court decided to take away her rights," Andi says, sounding almost out of breath. "Every time she… When she swore she was off the drugs and back on her meds. When she would yell that she just wanted to spend time with me, and when I wouldn't go, when Dad and Tina would scream and fight with her, my mother would yell down to the basement—"

Whore. Stupid little cunt. You think you're better than me. You're too good to see your own mother. I'm doing this for you, and you can't speak to me? I kicked him out for you. You made me like this.

Why don't you love me anymore?

One day, you'll regret not having spent time with your mother.

I remember every fucking word.

Andi darts to the kitchen.

She goes around the bar and stares at the indention in the countertop again, her fingernail picking at the tear in the linoleum-covered block. "I was alone here when this happened," she says. "I don't remember why. I just remember answering the door. I remember her telling me that it was time to go with her, that the voice said it was time for us to leave this place. She said she was better, and we could be together without pain."

Bile rises in my throat.

"I didn't know she had a knife," Andi goes on. "I didn't know she meant *away* away." She grabs the linoleum and peels it back. "I managed to get away from her as she came at me, and the force of her blow struck the counter so hard that…" Andi sniffs back her tears and shakes her head at the ceiling.

Her gaze snags on the hole in the wall, and she stretches toward it.

"This is where she punched the wall when Dad refused to let her take me for the weekend. God, she was so fucking high. I was only thirteen. He was terrified she would do something… Mrs. Lawry called the cops, but they were fucking useless. They were *always* fucking useless."

She looks twice at the dining room.

I can barely keep up with her as she stretches into it again.

In this room, I see her pain coming to a head. It isn't just the memory of pain and fighting. It's fury and regret and suffering. It slides into her eyes as she stands on the dark spot in the middle of the floor and then paces across the foyer to the edge of the staircase.

"I was right here," she says through a strained voice. "I was right here when she…"

Emotion rises in every short breath.

It's in her heaving chest, her slumping shoulders.

"I was right here," she says loudly. "I was shouting back and telling her I was going to college whether she liked it or not. And she told me… she told me if I left her, it was confirmation that I never loved her, and there would be nothing left for her here. She blamed me. She told me I was the reason no one ever loved her again. That I had taken everything away from her the moment I was born. She said she was done. Tired. And I thought… I thought she was bluffing just like every other time. I told her to do it. I told her I never wanted to see her again. *I thought she was bluffing.* I thought she was lying. She'd threatened it so many times before that I just… I thought… And then she dragged that fucking knife across her wrists, and I…"

Her voice drifts as the tears catch up with her, as her breaths refuse to catch. Her entire body shudders and tenses —

Andi grabs a leftover lamp from the floor and hurls it across the foyer with a blood-curdling scream.

The lamp shatters onto the spot in the dining room where her mother had died. I jump back into the kitchen and walk through it to the living room, only to find that it's no safer there than where I was previously standing.

Andi shouts.

"—couldn't save me—none of this—"

She spirals.

"—your fault! *Not mine!* None of this was ever my fault, and yet you made me believe it was!"

She disintegrates and falls.

"—made me believe I didn't deserve protection or love or even *life*—"

Down and down and *down*.

Throwing everything within her at the spot in the dining room where her mother had taken her own life. Screaming at her like she can see her ghost.

"*I was a child!* I was not the reason you couldn't get your shit together. Dad was not the reason—"

It's every word that she ever wanted to say to her. Every word that she's suppressed over the years, thinking that that was the only way to get past it. Every sentence she's had to repeat to herself just to stop the blame once shoved down her throat.

I let her rage.

I let her throw and yell and break.

I let her shriek to the sky, her muscles edging as she releases her rage and pain.

I let her scream those words to the phantom of the person who tried to break her spirit and put the blame for their shitty decisions on her.

Because I know the fucking feeling.

I hold my jaw tight as I watch her, my soul fracturing with hers.

Dammit… it's fucking beautiful.

And maybe that's a pretty fucked up way to look at what's happening, but after years of harboring it, of letting it fester and eat her from the inside, she's breaking free.

I can almost see every rope and chain that had wedged itself tighter and tighter around her soul fall to bits at her feet. She wails and rips and releases everything until she drops to her knees.

Her head sags, her palms press to her thighs, and as the very last drop of rage leaves her, she begins to sob.

I'm standing in the foyer amongst broken porcelain and glass pieces. A silent tear stretches down my cheek as I watch her wipe her bloody hands on her exposed legs. And before she can dab her face, I sink to my knees before her.

I don't care that the shards are cutting through my pants. I'll pick the pieces out just as I have all the other times I've fallen on it.

Without a word, I press my knuckle beneath her chin and lift her to look at me. Her swollen red eyes meet mine, and she chokes as I lean forward to kiss away her tears. She wraps her hands around my wrists and sinks into me with closed eyes, and with every silent, passing second, I feel her breaths begin to even.

I won't let her go.

"I'm sorry," she whispers. "I'm sorry I lost control. Look at this mess—"

I pull back enough to gaze into her eyes. "*Look* at this mess, Andi," I say to her. "Truly look at it, and tell me... tell me it isn't beautiful. Tell me this isn't *absolute* rhapsody."

She stares at me like I've lost my mind, and I sit back so she can fully take in what I see.

"Because it fucking is," I say, my voice thick as I resist my own emotions. "It's fucking *you*. It's everything your body held onto. All the parts of yourself that you thought you could never face. The parts you thought you had to erase just to live above water."

She gags on her fervor and looks around us, and as she

does, a heavy breath enters her lungs. I can see her taking it all in, see her processing my words.

She reaches for my hand and lays her head on my shoulder like she's giving in.

"How do you make me feel safe for this?" she whispers.

I bring her hand to my lips and kiss her fingers before meeting her eyes. "Because I *know*," I manage. "I know, baby."

Her teeth clench hard enough to cause a shudder, and I swipe my thumb over her cheek.

"We're allowed to break free of them, aren't we?" she whispers. "To rip out of their chains and not become who they were?"

Fuck.

My entire being falters at her question. It's the very question I've asked myself for years. The question I never knew how to answer until now.

"Yeah," I breathe, sniffing back my tears. "We don't have to live with the weight of their fuck ups. We're not them."

A full breath enters her lungs. I tilt her head back with my knuckle, and our lips meet in the promise that we'll never be who they were.

Because I swear it.

We'll never be them.

Blue lights flash outside the windows.

My heart drops as the strobes filter inside and bask on the walls. Andi sits back, her eyes wide as we both stare around us.

"Mother *fuck*," I hiss. "Goddamn nosy ass neighbors." I shrug my hoodie off and hand it to Andi as we stand.

Panic is written on Andi's face. "Oh my god—Maddox—" She looks down at her hands, at the blood on her legs—

"Hey—*hey*." I take her face in my palms and make her look up at me. "You're going to tie this around your waist and go in the kitchen to wash your hands," I tell her. "I own this place. We've done nothing wrong. Breaking fucking lamps is nothing compared to the rest of the shit that's happened on this street."

Three knocks sound on the door.

I'm well aware that the cop can see our fuzzy figures through the long windows on either side of the door, and I don't fucking care. All I care about is her and the fact that I know if the cops saw the blood on her, they'd think I had done something to hurt her.

And I would *never* hurt her.

"Police," the cop says, shining his flashlight inside.

"It was probably Mrs. Lawry," Andi says, her jaw gritting. "Fucking Mrs. Lawry. She's always been nosy."

"I got it—*I'm coming!*—" I snap at the door when they knock again. "Probably was her," I agree. "She used to call the cops on me and Reed for noise complaints at least once a month until they basically told her to fuck off."

Andi walks over the broken pieces on the floor and into the kitchen as I reach for the handle. The cop has barely lifted his arm to knock again when I swing open the door, only to be met with a flashlight in my face. I flick the porch light on and lift my hand over my eyes, squinting at the abruptness.

"Whoa—*the fuck*—can you put that down?"

The cop lowers the light, and I blink to get the flash from my vision. I press my fingers to the insides of my eyes, not only to try and correct my sight but to take a deep breath in an attempt to calm my nerves.

"Didn't realize anyone was in this house again," the cop says.

I finally look at him. "What's the issue?" I ask.

The cop appears tired, and I know the stare he's giving me is as scrutinizing as he means it to be. I'm used to it. Had he recognized me, it would have been even more judgmental.

He leans forward to peer around me as if looking for someone else, then sniffs the air.

"If you have a cold, I'd appreciate you getting off my stoop," I say flatly. "You can talk from the grass."

The officer clears his throat, glaring at my comment. "Neighbor called about suspicious activity here," he says. His gaze moves over me, and I note that it lingers on the tattoos on my hands, on the insides of my arms—exposed now that Andi is wearing my hoodie.

"This house has been vacant a few years now. You by yourself?" the cop continues.

"It's not really your business who I'm with," I say.

He examines the floor, the broken glass catching his attention. "Redecorating?" he asks.

A muscle feathers in my jaw. "What kind of suspicious activity are you accusing me of?"

"Said she heard screaming," the cop answers.

I scoff, my mouth curling deviously upward at the corner. "What can I say? My girl gets excited," I say, though the cop doesn't find it as humorous as me.

"And where is she?"

"Carter?"

Andi's voice rings out from a few feet behind me. She's clearing away some of the broken glass from the floor with the broom. However, upon recognizing the cop, she appears in the doorway at my side, a small smile on her face.

The officer's stare softens upon seeing her. "Little Andi Matthews?" he asks, his tongue darting out over his lips as he gives her a once over—eyes staggering a moment too long on her tits.

My fist tightens on the edge of the wood.

I fucking hate this.

"What are you doing here? I didn't realize you were in town," Carter, the cop, says. His smile is wide, and he takes off his hat as if it's the gentlemanly thing to do. Arms open, Carter steps forward to her like he expects a hug.

I shift my stance in front of her, feet planted firmly against any advancement.

I want to tell him to piss off.

"Just for the weekend," she replies, staying far enough away to escape Carter's attempted embrace. "I wanted to see the old place. It's been years for me." Her hand presses to my arm, squeezing me like she realizes how much this exchange is killing me.

"You remember Maddox Keynes? Reed's best friend? He was doing me a favor by letting me in and using some of the old things left behind as batting practice," she says with a laugh.

Carter suspiciously considers her before his eyes move to me. "That true?" he asks.

"Thinking of opening up one of those smash businesses where people pay to go in and break things," I say, and Andi pinches my arm.

I can't help it.

"Thank you for checking, Carter," Andi cuts in. "We're okay, though. Probably be out of here soon."

Carter's gaze darts between us and puts his hat back on, nodding as if he trusts her. "Ms. Matthews," he says. "Mr..." He squints at me.

"Keynes," I reply. "K-E-Y-N-E-S. Since I know you're going to look it up."

And probably come knocking back on the fucking door when you see the other name that comes up with Keynes.

I'm getting tired of hiding, though.

The cop gives me a 'hmph' and then turns his attention back to Andi. "Have a good night. If you need anything..."

"We're fine," Andi says, and thank fuck she presses her hand to my chest so that I don't do anything irrational.

It takes everything in me not to make a smart-ass comment back. Instead, I flip him off when he turns his back on us, and Andi shuts the door before Carter can pivot and see all the obscenities I'm flashing.

"That actually went a lot better than I thought it was going to," she says as her back hits the door.

"Yeah. Lucky the shit bag likes your tits," I say with a jerk of my chin. "He can fuck off."

Andi smiles. "Sounds like you're jealous."

My palms press into the door over her head. I hover over her and pause a moment to truly look at her—the makeup smeared beneath her eyes, the mess of her hair, the dried blood beneath her fingernails—and I reach to her face to brush that stray hair back into her waves.

"No, do you know what I am, Andi?" I ask, my voice coming out in a rasp. "I'm *tormented* by you. I'm going mad with every second that I'm not allowed to touch or claim you as my soul wants to. I have this unrelenting urge to mark you as mine… I want every person on this shit-eating planet to know you belong to me. And I know that sounds completely crazy, but—"

"I am yours," she says, and I think my heart skips a few beats. "I am, Maddox," she adds, taking my shirt in her closed fists. "*I'm fucking yours.*"

There's a special sort of delirium for what we are, for what our souls have found in one another. The bond that tethers us together should be riddled with unraveling threads threatening to break with every flame licking at our wounds.

And yet, here we are.

Standing in the fire together and daring it to singe that final cord.

Because when she kisses me, I lose my grip on reality.

My hands are on her neck, sliding down her waist, bunching the shirt she's wearing to her stomach. I pull the hem up and over her head, leaving that lacy bra beneath that has her breasts pillowing so perfectly. I have to bend down and wrap my hands beneath her ass so that I can have her around my waist. Her breasts hit my mouth as she crashes into the door, and I groan at the spillage wrapped around my face.

She could fucking suffocate me, and I'd come back as a ghost to thank her.

To hell with the glass on the floor.

I carry her to the stairs and set her on the creaking boards. Her hands are in my hair and pushing me lower. I can't get her pants off fast enough. A desperation flows through me. I need to taste her. Fuck her.

Andi unbuttons the front hook of her bra and throws it to the ground as I get her pants off. The instant she's exposed to me, I run my thumb over the long scar on her hip. She flinches at my touch. Our eyes meet, and I lean forward to kiss her, the embrace threaded with my vow.

"Never again," I whisper.

Her fingers drag in my hair when we part, and she swipes her thumb over the old scar cutting through my brow.

"Never," she says, and I know her promise isn't about her own scar.

It prompts the fluttering in my stomach to rise to a new level. A tingling stretches up my spine and out over my arms, and I hug her into my arms again to begin kissing down her throat, her collar, down to her breasts—already riddled with bruises from my bites.

I latch onto her nipple and suck it into my mouth, rolling my tongue ring around its stiff peak. Her head hits the step behind her, my name slipping off her tongue when my fingers find her entrance.

I just need a taste, and then I want her bouncing on my aching dick.

One taste.

But fuck, her pussy is addicting.

She grinds her cunt against my tongue and cries out, her grip so tight in my hair that I wince at the delicious agony. The pain sends chills over my skin. Every hair on my neck and arms rises with that tug and whimper.

I move back up to her lips and kiss her hard before grabbing her by the hands and pulling her to her feet. She doesn't ask any questions as I turn us and sit on a higher step, and without hesitation, she settles herself on my lap.

I punch the wall and groan when she slides easily onto me.

The steps cutting into my back are a pain.

However, for this view? This view is worth it.

I grab her hips as she starts a rhythm, rocking and riding every inch of me. Her nails are digging into my chest, her tits… fucking hell, her tits… I forcefully slap her ass, making it wiggle on my lap, and her skin turns the most beautiful scarlet shade. Again. *Again.* Causing her to moan and sink her nails deeper into me. Those little half-moons are exactly what I want cutting through my skin, and when she does break through, I suck in a sharp breath of air.

I'm already on the verge of release. Her walls are tightening. Her mouth sags. And as she begins to tremble at the very edge, I pull her face down to mine and kiss her.

Her body jerks and tenses as she comes around my dick, as the pleasure rocks her down to her core. She cries out into my mouth, and as the sound works its way into the marrow of my bones, I release inside her.

She collapses in my arms, her cheek lying against my collar. Another groan escapes me as the last of my cum leaves me, and even though we're both satiated, we don't move. I rake my hands from her bare ass up her sides and her spine until reaching her face, and when I do, she lifts her head only enough to look at me. There's a faint smile on her lips, and I can't help when one rises on mine.

Something about taking her in the foyer of a place that was once my sanctuary and her hell is strangely cathartic. I don't know why. Perhaps it's that little bit of mania my inner demon once clung to when the lights went out. Or maybe it's the ravenous angel sitting on my shoulder that can't seem to get enough of both danger and the reprieve that follows.

"We should probably get back," I say, knowing how late it is.

"We should," she agrees. "There's one thing I want first."

"What?"

Andi steps off of me, and as she does, gravity slowly pulls the milky white of my cum out of her swollen pussy and onto her thigh.

Fuck that.

I reach between her thighs and catch it with my thumb, then push it back inside her.

"What are you doing?" she asks, though she doesn't swat me away.

"We can't be wasting this, beautiful," I explain.

Andi snorts. "Don't think you're getting a kid out of me after just a few days. I *am* on birth control."

I grin up at her. "Nothing now. Doesn't mean my soldiers can't have fun trying."

"Oh my god, Maddox." Laughter leaves her, and she starts down the steps away from me.

I don't know what she's up to, and honestly, I don't care.

She reaches across the foyer and grabs the broom by the door, then sweeps away some of the glass so we can both walk without putting our shoes on. On her tiptoes, she takes my sweatshirt and lays it on the floor in front of the ornate floor-length mirror.

I feel myself squinting at her in confusion.

I'm standing by the staircase, waiting for her to tell me

what she wants when she sits on the ground and motions me to join her. I sink to my ass behind her as she grabs her phone from the pocket of her pants—which are thrown on the ground nearby. She settles sideways between my legs and brings up the camera on her phone, and that's when I finally realize she's trying to take a photo of us.

I wrap my arms around her, my chin sitting on her bare shoulder, and together, we look at what we are in the mirror.

Fuck, she's stunning like this.

I move my forearm across her tits and slowly clasp my right hand over her face, letting the skull tattoo line up with her features as she grips my forearm tight. Leaning around just enough that the moonlight coming through the high window catches my eyes, I whisper in her ear, "Snap the photo."

She still has the phone in her hand as I move my arm down her stomach. My fingers slide over her bare pussy, and she shifts so that her legs are spread wide, bent knees toward the ceiling, and bare feet pressed to the floor. Her bottom lip sags behind my hand, a low moan sounding from within her.

"You like this view?" I ask.

She nods. "I love this view."

"What about…" I move my hand down and wrap it around her perfect little throat, and her eyes flutter in response.

She snaps another photo.

My legs tighten around her hips, and I brush my finger over her already sensitive clit. She shudders delightfully against me, causing me to wrap my arms around her waist and hug her close.

"I think my madness has found a home in yours," I say as I look at us.

"I think you're right," she whispers.

Her eyes meet mine when she turns her head, and I can't

stop myself from capturing her lips again. Soft yet somehow passionate, the words are a promise entwining our fractured souls together.

A feeling settles in my abdomen with the confirmation—one that I haven't felt in a long time and never this strongly. It's restless and euphoric and terrifying all at once.

However, with her…

With her, it's fucking worth it.

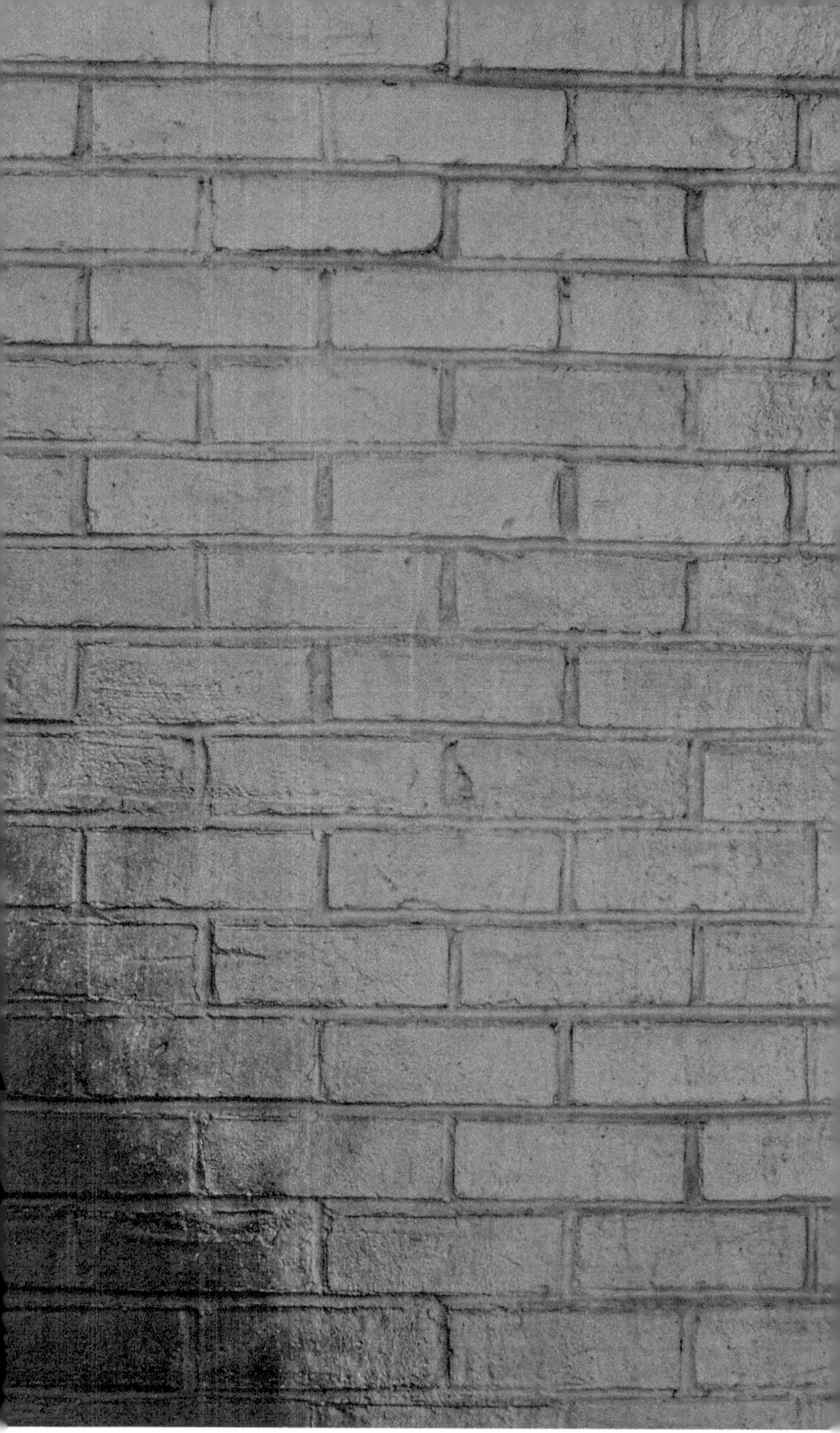

CHAPTER FIFTEEN
ANDI

Somehow, we make it back home without the cop coming back to the house or following us. And once we arrive home and park in the garage, we stay in the truck a while longer, making out like teenagers in the front seat with my legs straddling his lap.

I can't get enough of him.

He's riddled his way into my bones. I crave him in every way. But most especially in lazy moments like this one, when he's holding my face in his fingertips and memorizing the lines of my face. When there's nothing more than the noise of our steady, elongated breaths. When the seconds seem to pass to the beats of our hearts.

"Does it scare you?" I ask as we settle in the silence.

"What?" he asks.

"Anything," I reply. "The world. Playing onstage. Death."

Maddox curls his finger in my hair, eyes softly drifting over me. "The only thing that terrifies me right now is losing you," he whispers. "In any capacity. Whether it's your brother, Adam, or even going back on tour. Anything that takes me from moments like this."

"Why does that scare you?" I ask.

"Because losing you might be the thing that unravels me." I lay my head on his chest and linger against him, my ear to his heart, and for a few more minutes, we soak in our secret bliss.

The morning is a frenzy.

Maddox and I are surviving on a mere few hours of sleep. It's all I can do to throw on sweatpants and a long-sleeved shirt before heading downstairs when I smell the aroma of coffee drifting upstairs.

However, as my feet hit the kitchen threshold, I pause.

Maddox is pacing outside on the deck, phone to his ear.

I study him for a beat. Something about the way he's pacing makes my insides squirm.

"What... What's going on?" I ask my dad. "Is he okay?"

Dad sighs heavily and exchanges a glance with Tina. "Just that council moron trying to stir things up," Dad says.

My heart skips.

"What do you mean?" I ask.

But my phone rings before I can ask more. I frown at it, noting that it's Cynda on the line.

"That'll be your update," my dad says.

"You're probably right—Hey, Cyn," I answer as I slip out the back door.

Maddox glances over his shoulder at me, and I can see the frustration in his eyes. I want to go to him and tell him it's okay. That the people around him will take care of it.

"Hey, so, did you hear?" Cynda says on the phone.

"I actually just walked downstairs for coffee and saw Mads outside. What's going on?" I ask, looping around toward the side of the house.

"That creep from the protests has been slandering Mads all morning on socials," Cynda says. "We'd usually ignore it, but the accusations don't exactly paint the prettiest picture."

"What are they saying?" I ask.

"The guy posted the mugshots of Mads's father, along with redacted police reports of the girls his father was convicted of raping," Cynda says. "The names of the women and even his father's name were blacked out. It's like the asshole is teasing it. At least it hasn't made any headlines."

What. The. *Fuck.*

I nearly fall to my knees.

"What does that have to do with Mads?" I ask. "People can't blame him for his father being an evil fucking bastard."

"Well, he's also saying that Mads has been in and out of jail his entire life—"

For fighting people who keep comparing him to his father, I want to say.

"—That he's an abuser, and that the record company is paying girls off who threaten to talk—"

"Maybe you guys shouldn't have tried to pay Adam off," I mutter.

"—He goes on to say on one comment that the girl Mads is seeing right now has been begging this guy to help her escape him."

White lights flash behind my eyes.

"The fuck—that's... that's *bullshit*—"

I catch myself before I spill everything.

"*Mads isn't his father*," I snap through clenched teeth. "What is the response on the boards?"

"Most people are ignoring him," she replies. "The response from anyone entertaining him is for the guy to fuck off and leave Mads to his privacy. They're telling him he's a jealous troll, and they don't care about what Mads's dead father ever did. Some are expressing solitude and telling their own stories of being judged for what their parents did, going on to say that it doesn't define a person."

At least there's that.

My nostrils flare with emotion. I wrap my hand around my waist and grip my skin tight enough that I wince.

"I thought Heartless was taking care of this," I manage.

"And we are," Cynda says. "This one... This one seems determined."

I'm going to puke.

Maddox.

"What do you need from me?" I ask as a burning sensation swells in my sinuses. "What can I do?"

"I'm sending you legal's number, along with Erin's from Relations. She'll be at the concert today, so you may see her pop in and out backstage. Our team is combing through socials for anything that might have slipped. You don't need to do anything extra or worry about it. We're handling it. I just wanted to give you a heads-up on what's going on. And if you see anything that they might need to know, you'll have their numbers."

My insides twist. "What do you mean?"

"I mean... Anyone suspicious. Activity that could get back to the press and come off as unsavory. That kind of thing," she replies.

"*Unsavory?*" I want to throw my phone. "Are you saying you believe this creep?"

"No, Andi," Cynda says. "I just mean to be on high alert for anyone who might try to get him into a situation he can't get out of."

"Spotting anyone suspicious might be a problem. Tomorrow is Halloween," I say.

"Well, at least all bases will be covered," she says. "Anyway. I think we'll have this swept under the rug by tomorrow."

I glance up to find Maddox bent over his knees, and my heart feels like it's on fire.

"For his sake, I hope you do," I say.

"How is he?" Cynda asks.

"Not great, Cyn."

Maddox's body jerks like he's dry-heaving, and bile rises

in my throat.

"Hey—I have to go. Text me those numbers."

I hang up before Cynda can reply and dart across the deck toward him.

Shit.

Shit. Shit. Shit.

God, this is all my fault.

Maddox heaves again as I reach him, though nothing evacuates from his insides. "Hey—" I press my hand to his arm, the other around his wrist. He's clammy and stiff. His hair falls over his face as he drops his head.

As if he's afraid to let me see him in whatever state he's in.

My jaw quakes at the sight.

I want to hold him.

I want to tell him I'll fix it.

I want to fix it.

I sink to my knees in front of him, not caring if my family looks out the window and sees us. To hell with Reed or anyone who might give us any shit.

I can't let him be alone in this.

"Maddox?" I manage.

He doesn't look at me. His gaze is wholly fixated on the ground. I reach for his arm. However, he sinks into a crouch before I can touch him. His arms wrap around his knees, his forehead falls against his forearm, and I feel my resolve crack when I see his body jerk.

"Maddox?"

Grief wraps around my insides as I stare at him, and I realize it's not the first time I've seen him like this. The stance reminds me of the young boy I'd once sat beside on the back steps so many years ago.

The full moon is staring at us. He's waiting for Reed to come home from piano lessons, and behind us, Tina and my dad are finishing dinner. I can see the fresh cigar mark on his hand that looks like the cigarette burn on my side. I remember wondering if he'd earned his scar for talking back as I had.

And just beneath his shaggy brown hair, I see a freshly bloodied lip.

He's shivering, and I don't know whether it's from the chilly air or the burn. I don't know what to say or how to get him to talk to me—if he even wants to.

"Dad or asshole kids?" I ask about the bloody lip, hoping the simplicity will help.

"Asshole kids," he replies.

"And the burn?" I ask.

Maddox squirms. "Punishment for hitting the asshole kids," he says.

I sink down on the step beside him and sigh. Reed had a dentist appointment earlier, which I know means Maddox walked home alone instead of Tina taking him home.

I look over my shoulder to find Tina feeding Koen some of the ravioli she's made. "Haven't been inside yet?" I ask Maddox, knowing that if he had, Tina would have had a bag of peas pressed to his face by now.

He shakes his head, sorrowful green eyes glancing my way. "Why are you hiding?" he asks me.

I glance up at the full moon. "My Walkman died," I answer, holding up the cassette player. "I snuck around the side through my window. I can't deal with Tina when she's dancing in the kitchen."

A quiet huff of amusement leaves him, a smile slipping onto his lips, and our eyes meet.

"Do you want an ice pack?" I ask. "I can sneak it out when I grab the batteries from the freezer. You can play video games in my room if you want. You don't have to wait alone."

Maddox considers me for a beat, and finally, he nods.

The memory burns my nose. God, that was so long ago.

We're both still running from our ghosts.

"Maddox, please look at me," I beg. I reach for his

forearms and squeeze. "Please."

The seconds feel like centuries. Eventually, he shifts. He picks his head up, and my entire body falters when his gaze meets mine.

His eyes are pink and puffy, his skin pale—almost green with anxiety. There's a tear rolling down his cheek, collecting in his beard as he sniffs.

"Fuck," he mutters as his knees hit the ground. "Fucking *fuck*." He braces his hands on his knees, and I can see how badly he's shaking, how much he's holding back.

Just like on those back steps.

I don't want to tell him it's okay because that would be a lie.

Nothing about this is okay.

I can't promise his team will fix it because I don't know that they can.

I don't know how to stop Adam or keep Maddox safe. And I *want* to. I want to shield him from all of this. I want to mend what's been done.

I don't mean to fix you.

My jaw clenches as I remember his words.

Maybe I don't need to fix this. Maybe I can…

I wrap my hands around his cheeks and tug his chin so that he's looking at me. Our eyes meet. I feel my chest caving with emotion as the silent words press between us. The sorrow and the endless apologies.

And as he wraps his hand around my wrist, I stifle the sob I so desperately need to release.

"Break," I whisper. "I'll pick up the pieces."

Maddox clenches his jaw, his head moving the tiniest bit, and he looks at the sky as if he can't believe I just said that to him.

"Fuck you, Andi," he breathes, and I know it's his attempt at humor. I can see the smile in his eyes, see the tears starting to pour over his cheeks, and I can't take it anymore.

I rise on my knees and wrap my arms around him. He embraces me with as much strength as he has in him, his strong arms weighted around my body.

And I feel him breaking in my grasp.

It's so quiet. Even still, I know he is. His tears land in the crook of my neck, his body quaking against mine. I hold him tighter, hoping I'm enough to get him through this fracture.

I want to be.

I want to be everything that he's ever been for me.

Memories of him coming to the house with new scars from his father's abuse and the fights with the other kids flash behind my eyes. Every black eye, bloody lip, and broken nose. Every burn and welt from the strike of a belt.

Maddox never stopped fighting back. He never broke, no matter how hard things became. He sat at the dinner table with us almost every night and smiled, conversed, and even laughed with the family that took him in.

And I realize in that instant how much his fight affected me.

There was a time when I gave in to my mother taking me for the weekend, when I would tolerate her drug-addled boyfriends staring at me from the next room with their dicks out because I didn't know any better. And while none of them ever touched me, I still thought sitting quietly on the couch was what I was supposed to do. I still thought I had to take her neglect because she was my parent, and I should respect her no matter what.

She never deserved my compliance.

She never deserved my hope that one day, things might change. Especially as I grew older, on the days when she came begging my father for another chance, claiming she was clean and just wanted to spend time with her daughter.

Maddox always reminded me that I didn't have to take it

sitting down, even if he never knew that his mere presence was enough. That the look in his determined eyes was enough.

I clench Maddox harder as the realization pours through me.

It's a few more minutes before I feel him steadily breathing. He hesitantly pulls away, our hands lingering together as if we don't want to part.

And as we gaze at one another with swollen eyes, I only want to kiss him.

I want to promise him that we'll be okay, no matter what.

Maddox swallows. "I don't know how much longer I can go on pretending that you're not *my fucking world*," he says breathlessly. "I need you," he whispers.

I draw a sharp breath, jaw tight at his words. "I need you, too," I manage.

The sliding door opens behind us before either of us can move.

Reed bolts out in nothing more than his sweatpants.

"Hey—Hey, Mom just woke me up. What's going on?" he asks, eyes darting between us. "Why do you two look like someone died? Did someone fucking die?"

Maddox and I rise to our feet, the thought of revealing what we are now amiss.

"It's Adam," I say as I wipe my face.

A muscle feathers in Reed's jaw. "What about him?"

"He's been talking shit about Maddox all night," I say. "Posting his dad's mugshots to Young Decay boards. Slandering his name—"

"I thought they were taking care of this," Reed interjects.

"My boss says they're working on it," I reply. "They have legal down here now. We just…" I turn to Maddox, our little breakdown still in the back of my mind as I try to be professional.

"You've done nothing wrong," I say, and it feels forced.

It feels like a lie that you tell to children.

"You keep playing," I go on. "Don't worry about it. They'll fix it. I swear, Mads."

I want to hold him again.

Reed presses his hands to his hips. "We could get rid of him," he suggests. "They'd help cover that up, too."

The notion makes Maddox smile the tiniest bit. "Yeah, they'd cover it up for you. Their golden boy."

"Damn right," Reed says. "Come on. Don't let this shit get in your head. Friday night show. We can't have the middle slump."

"We might have the middle night fuck up," Maddox mutters.

"Yeah? So fucking what," Reed says. "What—he's going to tell people your dad was a piece of shit rapist who died from the cancer he deserved? Let him. You're nothing like him."

"People don't know that," Maddox argues.

"But *we* know that," Reed says, nodding to me. "And I'll stand on that fucking stage and tell anyone who defines a person by their parents to fuck off and get the hell out of my church. I don't want those kinds of close-minded people hearing our music. They don't deserve to listen to the chords and lyrics you've busted your ass creating all these years."

Maddox cracks his knuckles and stares at the ground as Reed talks. I can see the anguish swimming in his eyes, the want to let it go.

"Your terms," I say, and his gaze lifts to mine. "When you're ready, Mads. Whether it's tomorrow, a decade from now, or never. No one gets to take that from you. We'll make sure of it."

"Fuck that guy," Reed adds. "He doesn't get to take away who you are."

Maddox chews on the inside of his mouth for a beat. "Fuck

that guy," he finally says.

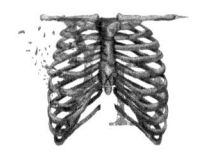

Between sound checks, legal coming over to the house to talk to Maddox, and before show rituals, I don't get a moment alone with Maddox for the entire afternoon. There are too many eyes on us, too many ways for us to cause an unneeded frenzy.

Maddox was so busy going over special effects and the set list upon arriving at the venue that I'd hung back in the seats with my computer and edited a few photos, along with videoing Cynda in during practice so she could see them.

And when they finally hit the stage, all thoughts of Adam, legal, and any other worry in the world are entirely forgotten.

Up until yesterday, I had forgotten what it was like to watch my brother perform.

How he steps in front of the crowd and makes commanding it look easy definitely isn't. Though, he's always had that talent. I don't know where he got it from. Perhaps our dad.

Somehow, Reed gains energy through the audience. He only stays in one place for a few bars. He's constantly moving around the stage, jumping up and down with the crowd, playing the guitar, leaping on the speakers or the railings, or even climbing the platform to jam with Bonnie.

And through all of that, he never loses his voice.

Seeing Maddox and Reed's dreams come to fruition after they were just two teens with long hair, head banging in the garage all those years ago is surreal. I'll never get used to seeing my little brother onstage and hearing thousands of voices chant his name.

I try to keep up with him running for a while. However, the best photos I get of him are when he spots me hanging back, and his response is to grin sideways or stick his tongue out at me.

Except for the one time he takes my camera out of my hands, brings it onstage, and then proceeds to point at me and exclaims to the entire crown, "Hey, this is my sister!"

At least the picture he takes of the crowd is a good one.

I get more photos of Maddox and Reed when they interact with each other. It's so hard getting a read on Maddox. Nevertheless, I know my brother can tell everything he's thinking—mask or no mask.

Every time I meet Maddox's eyes, my heart does a little dance.

Reed stays onstage to talk to the crowd and play an acoustic bit so the rest of the band can take a few minutes off for water. He sits on the floor with his ankles crossed, the acoustic guitar in his lap, and everyone in the room pulls their phones out with flashlights on.

My own phone buzzes as I pull it out to join in. I expect it to be Cynda. However, the message across my screen makes my thighs tighten with anticipation.

Meet me in the back hallway between sets, Maddox texts me.

I glance at where he's standing in the shadows, but he isn't looking my way. He has his phone out, his back turned as he takes a drink of water.

I'll be waiting, I text him back.

He sends me the name of the last song on the setlist before the break. Before I can reply again, he's back on stage and picking up his bass.

For the next twenty minutes, I keep sneaking glances at

Maddox, and at least half the time, I find his eyes on me.

Yet, even with the suspense building within me for whatever he has planned, Reed somehow gets my full attention back on the music—to the point that I nearly miss my chance to run back in time to meet Maddox.

The music is a hum backstage. The lights are dulled. I spot James heading my way. He jerks his chin toward a darkened hallway past the dressing rooms with a sign pointing to the emergency exit door.

My palms sweat as I reach the hallway and lean against the black brick. I hear the crowd scream, the music lull, and my heart picks up pace.

I don't know what to do as I wait.

I have enough awareness to set my camera on a nearby box.

"Hey, James—"

Maddox.

My stomach drops, breaths already short.

"—This hallway is closed."

James doesn't respond.

My heart leaps into my throat. I can see Maddox's shadow on the floor. It's all I can do to keep my composure and not run into his arms.

Yet, when Maddox rounds the corner, I'm paralyzed by his stare.

His eyes are sinfully dark. I can practically see the adrenaline rushing through him. He's set on whatever idea that's running through his head.

Maddox looks over me like he's starving. Desperate. No words leave his lips as he advances. He pushes the mask down around his neck. I try to find my breath, my words, yet it's all I can do to swallow.

At arm's length, he grabs me by the front of my throat and pulls me into his embrace so hard and fast that I don't have time to catch my breath. His lips ravenously crash upon mine. My back hits the wall—

Maddox *devours* me.

He traps me between him and the brick, and wastes no time before pushing my shirt up, damn anyone that might try to get past his bodyguard and discover us.

And I realize something as he kisses me.

Maddox Keynes owns me.

Mind. Body. Soul. And every little darkened crevice in between.

We're the mayhem of what it looks like when two broken entities find one another amongst the fragments everyone else has left behind. We're the pieces no one else knew what to do with, the ones discarded in the corners of poorly swept abandoned spaces.

We're messy and chaotic, and *god*… I can't get enough of this beautifully fucked up thing that we are.

Jesus, that *grip*.

He kisses me like he hasn't seen me for weeks, months, *centuries*. Like the hour he was just onstage was another lifetime before.

His fingers easily find my warm center, and his smile lifts against my mouth.

"Hey, beautiful," he says in a hoarse rasp.

He consumes my voice with his lips back on mine before I can respond. I fiddle with his belt buckle, desperate to have him inside me. He sucks a sharp breath as I finally succeed and wrap my hand around what I can of his full length, and the groan that leaves him has me grinning triumphantly.

"Fuck, Andi," he hisses. He reaches for my arms, places them around his neck, and grabs my ass to haul me onto his waist. I gasp against his lips at the tickle of his dick so near my entrance. Teasing me. Making me whimper in anticipation.

And when he thrusts inside me, I have to remind myself not to cry out.

I'm still getting used to him. Even after every time he's been inside me this week, his size still catches me off-guard. My moan drowns in his mouth. He only gives me a few seconds to orient myself, and when he knows I'm ready, he's all in.

His motions are rough and relentless, the eager pace making me tremble and whine. Mads harshly presses his hand over my lips, the slight ache sending insatiable chills over my arms. My cries are muffled behind his calloused fingers, each thrust sending me further and further into a state of hazy bliss that I can't control.

My thighs and ass are already bruising from his motions—the brick wall accentuating that pain.

And it feels fucking incredible.

Maddox replaces his hand with his lips, and it limps me. I need him closer. I need to draw out every second that we have behind this corner, every second that he should be taking a break. I want his dick still wet with my release when he walks back on that stage.

As if he can sense that need, Maddox plunges deep. Deeper than before. As deep as he can drive his cock within me. I suck air through my teeth at the unabating fill, my face burying into his neck and legs squirming up into my ribs to accommodate his greed. He pauses briefly, and I feel my bottom lip quiver when he curses against my cheek.

"You make me want to miss the rest of this gig just so I can stay here," he groans in a hushed whisper. "Dammit, Andi."

Each following plunge inside me is deliberate. Languid. With each long, desperate stroke, his dick brushes against the sensitive spot inside me, causing me to practically mewl with restlessness.

"Shh…" he utters.

"I can't," I manage. "I need… Shit, I'm going to come."

"Don't you fucking dare," he says.

"—three minutes!" I hear someone call out.

We both freeze at the sound of someone letting everyone know to be back in position for the show to go on.

"—the fuck is Mads?" Zeb says, and I know they're leaving the dressing room. "He must be taking a long shit."

"Probably smoking out back," Reed replies.

Maddox smiles against my throat as he resumes his prolonged, filling motions. His lips land fleetingly on my skin, his hand moving from beneath my thigh, and he reaches for something in his pocket.

A pick.

"Bite this," he says.

I inhale a short breath as he places the thick pick between my teeth, and that smile lingers beneath his beard.

"Don't lose it," he adds.

I nod, my teeth gritting hard around that piece of plastic, and as I feel the glisten rise in my eyes from denying my release, he rails inside me again. It's deep, satiating, and positively unlike anything I thought possible.

I swear I'm leaving teeth marks on this fucking plastic.

He curses into the crook of my neck. I can feel his hands getting tighter and tighter, and with every squeeze, I drown further. I'm on my last edge. I need to scream. My orgasm swells. It feels as if my entire body will implode. I can't breathe. A tear stretches down my cheek. I shut my eyes tight and fist his jacket so hard I can't even feel my hands. I strain to keep my composure together, yet it's too much—

My orgasm topples over. It sends me clenching my entire body around Maddox, squeezing and crying and nearly fainting as it pours over me. I'm shaking and withering in his arms. Maddox slams inside me three more times, and on the third, I sob at the feeling of him coming inside me.

"Two minutes!"

Maddox groans into my neck, and I sink my head against the wall. He takes a second to kiss my collar, my neck, my jaw, and when he reaches my mouth, a deep chuckle sounds from him. He leans forward and takes the pick out of my teeth with his own, the smile rising in his eyes.

"I couldn't wait," he says after stuffing it in his pocket. "Not after…" He pauses to catch his breath, his words trailing as he slides out of me.

My feet hit the ground, my heart fluttering at the way he's watching us come apart. I have to hold onto his arm as he helps me straighten my clothes.

I can't feel my legs.

Maddox takes a step back to adjust himself and bring his pants back up once I'm presentable. He pulls his mask up and fluffs his hair, giving it that freshly-fucked look he somehow keeps without much effort. I gulp when his eyes lift to mine, and then, he flicks that damn pick beneath my chin in a playful manner.

"What do you want to do after the show?" he asks.

I don't know.

I'm pretty sure he just fucked me into next week.

I don't even know if I'm still alive and breathing.

"Ah… That? Again?" I suggest.

He chuckles. "I mean, before we get to that. There's no party after. Legal thought it best to lay low tonight. We're going to hang out with the opening band instead. What do you think?"

I feel myself soften at the notion. "That sounds nice."

"ONE MINUTE!"

"Mads!" Avie is shouting for him this time. "Goddamn it. Where is he? *Mads!* Let's go!"

Maddox glances back toward where everyone is waiting on him just in time to see James peek his head around the corner. The bodyguard clears his throat and jerks his head toward the stage. However, Maddox holds up one finger to him.

He crosses the space between us once more and kisses me through the mask.

It's somehow increasingly sexy to kiss him like this, with the fabric between us. It makes my heart flutter as if that fabric is just another thing keeping us apart and telling us we can't be anything more than friends.

Screw that.

He lingers over me momentarily when we part, and those slivers of green on his blown, wild eyes cause my knees to weaken.

"I want that tonight," I manage.

A wickedness rises in his pupils. "This?" he asks, pointing to the mask.

I swallow the dryness in my mouth and nod. "Yes."

He huffs amusedly and leans in to kiss me through it once more. "I'll see you after, beautiful," he says when we part.

I stay back to catch my breath, staring at him as he walks back down the hallway. He glances back over his shoulder one more time when he hits the corner and says, "Don't lose my soldiers."

I burst out laughing.

The three fingers he holds up with that last look sends my breath jagged, and I sign it back.

Because I know it's only been a few days, but it's true.

Oh, goddamn it, Maddox Keynes.

CHAPTER SIXTEEN
ANDI

After the show, Young Decay signs autographs out back for a little longer than usual since they aren't heading out anywhere. I try to get a few photos of them conversing with fans, of Maddox handing the setlist to the girl sitting on the sidewalk, barely able to keep her eyes open as she waits just to get a glimpse of them. I try to get the photos and selfies people take, the tattoos of signatures, and the band emblem on their bodies.

Someone even hands Maddox a Jack Skellington plush. No one can see the grin on his face, but I know it's there. It glimmers in the green of his bright eyes when he takes the plush and nudges Reed in the side.

"Hey—check this out," Maddox says to Reed.

"Ah, no fucking way," Reed says upon seeing it, his grin wide enough for the both of them. "Do you know how much this guy loves this movie?" he asks the fan.

She laughs. "We heard the radio interview the other day," she says. "Tonight was the only night we could get tickets, so we knew we had to get this. We were hoping it might remind you guys of how much all of us love you. Nothing someone says about who you might be will change that."

My stomach is an empty pit.

"Ah…" Maddox scratches the back of his neck nervously.

"I mean—shit, I shouldn't have said anything," the girl says quickly. "I just mean to say that we don't care what your dad—" She pauses and looks around them, noticing a few others have stopped talking to listen in. "I just wanted you to know that we love you."

A quiet chuckle sounds from Maddox as he signs the record she's given him. "Guy is a prick," he says, and I can't believe he's steady enough to make light of this. "Doesn't know how to leave people to make their own choices."

Reed backs up and wraps his long arm over Maddox's shoulder, a playful grin on his face. "Some people want to bring down what they don't understand," he says. "Just like the protestors out front. We embrace the demons they shun. Life's too short to live with that kind of hatred. Our Mads here can talk about who he is when he's ready. Fuck those guys."

The fans around them laugh. "Fuck those guys," a few echo back.

I want to hug my brother.

Maddox and I sneak away from the group when everyone goes outside for the full moon. Reed is so wrapped up chatting with their guitarist that getting away from him isn't too hard.

And once we're back in the confines of my room, Maddox's promise for *that* again is fulfilled beyond belief.

Only this time, he leaves the mask on, the hood of his open jacket up, so that all I'm looking at above me is his tattooed body and his shadowed, wild eyes.

I don't know how I'm ever supposed to look at a skull mask the same again, how I'm supposed to see him on stage and not think of the way he's staring down at me with every languid thrust—one hand over my mouth and the other on my hip. I'm buried beneath him, my legs latched around his waist.

My wrists are bound to the headboard with climbing rope that we found in the garage.

His dick brushes my spot with every drive. I'm already tightening around his length for the second time, my pussy pulsing with his every motion. I want to squirm and cry, to tell him that I don't know how much longer I can hold out.

He shifts his grasp from my mouth and rakes his thumb across my cheek, the other squeezing my tit. I latch onto his arm with my free hand, nearly whimpering as my orgasm begins to crest.

"Maddox," I whine. "Please."

"Shh…" He leans down and drags his covered nose against my cheek, the heat from his body making me tremble. "You're going to come for me, beautiful. Over and over. You'll come every time you feel yourself on the edge. Just know that every time you do, I'll find another way to rake more out of this body."

"I don't know if I can," I hiss through my teeth. "I don't know how many more times—"

"You can, and you will," he tells me. "You're so ready to take more of me."

He draws out my release with his hand pressing against my throat. I barely have time to finish coming down before he flips me over onto my stomach, forces my bound hands behind my back, and slams inside me from behind.

Every inch of my skin erupts in goosebumps. White lights dance behind my eyes. I'm trapped beneath his rapacity and strength, utterly left to his mercy, and I realize it's everything I've ever wanted.

Spit dribbles down my ass. I feel him swipe his finger in it before slipping that very digit into my ass. I groan into the sheet, knees hiking beneath me as I stretch my spine and arch my back.

Pleasure seems like too weak of a word for what I feel

when I'm with him. For the way he reaps it out of me and knows exactly how much I can truly take. I trust him more than I've ever trusted anyone—a feat I didn't think anyone was patient enough to earn from me.

And by the time he finally comes, I'm sore in places I didn't know someone could be.

My cheek is on the pillow. I'm wasted on his dick. His taste. His touch. Maddox squeezes my ass for a final lazy thrust as if he's making sure his cum is buried deep inside me, unties my wrists, and when he pulls out, I hear him groan in an exhausted manner.

"That's fucking stunning," I hear him hiss.

"What?" I manage, feeling empty without him.

"What we do to each other," he says. "I love it."

I sit up just enough to wrap my hand behind his head and bring his face to mine, not caring that the mask is still on his face as I kiss him.

The only thing that makes this night better is the lazy shower we take after. I've never had someone wash my hair, let alone my body. However, Maddox does. He holds me steady on my wobbly legs and takes deliberate care of every space, leaving kisses behind in the wake of the warm water.

The tap runs to drown out the sound of our voices as he cradles me in the bottom of the tub. I can't help staring at the man who's been standing in front of me for so many years, now ogling at the man he's become.

"One more night," I say as we sit there.

Maddox rests his forehead against my temple. "You make it sound like that's all we have," he replies softly.

"Tell me we have more," I nearly plead.

He huffs an amused breath, his lips pressing to my cheek. "I'm never going another day without you," he says. "You're mine, beautiful."

His arms hug me a little tighter. I can hear his heartbeat

against my ear. It's so steady and patient, and I know mine is the same.

"Did you get any update from your boss tonight?" he asks after a few minutes.

I stare at the white porcelain around us. "Nothing," I reply. "That girl at the concert… Are you okay? You handled it better than I would have."

"Yeah," he says. "It kind of kicked me on my ass, to be honest."

I smile up at him. "How so?"

Maddox adjusts himself a little, the water sloshing around us. "I started wearing the mask so people wouldn't know who I was and, more importantly, so that my father wouldn't get wind of any kind of success the band had when he was released from jail. I knew he would have tried to be Father of the Fucking Year, asked for money, or thought he could shadow on what we had made. I didn't want to think of the kind of stunts he might have pulled with the excuse, 'My son is the bassist for Young Decay,' because I know the bastard would have used my name. And now that he's gone…" Maddox sighs heavily and toys with my fingers for a beat.

"I love that fucking mask," he goes on. "I love that it gives me the escape onstage. I love that the fans go insane over it, and it leaves that mystery. And I don't want that to change. But…"

His words drift, and I squeeze his hands.

"Fuck, I don't know," he admits defeatedly. He looks at me and lets his head slump back against the lip of the tub. "Tell me what I should do."

He's cute like this.

"I can't tell you what to do," I say. "It's your decision."

"Yeah, I know, but your opinion might help," he says.

My smile widens, though not because the situation is in any way amusing.

Only because he's adorable in this new, vulnerable state.

"What if you do nothing," I say as I sit up.

Maddox's stare narrows. "What do you mean?"

"I mean… What if you do nothing?" I repeat with a shrug. "You shouldn't have to reveal yourself because you feel the pressure. How you look at it can change, though. You don't have to keep yourself in his prison if you're ready to be free of it. Keep the mask. But wear it for the reason you just told me, not because you're afraid of what might happen if you take it off."

He clenches his teeth, his gaze skirting over my naked body again until it lands on my hip, where the clear, waterproof bandage is still in place. He reaches out and slides his thumb over it.

"You think I'm afraid?" he asks as his eyes rise to mine.

A faint smile flickers on my lips. "Maddox Keynes… You're as afraid of your shadow as I am of mine." I lean down and kiss him softly. "It's cute, though."

His mouth lifts into a smile that causes my entire body to wither. He wraps his hand beneath my jaw, fingers threading into the roots of my hair. And when he kisses me, goosebumps erupt over my skin, which has nothing to do with how cold the water is getting.

"As long as you think it's cute," he says when we part.

I chuckle against his lips. "We're all afraid of something. It's up to us whether we let it get in the way of something we truly want."

"What do you think I want?" he asks.

I toy with his beard as I consider the question. "I think you want someone to tell you everything will be okay. That the world won't stop turning if you take his weight off your shoulders."

A muscle flinches in his jaw. "And you? What do you want?"

I think my heart has somehow melted into him.

"I just want you," I admit. "Maddox Keynes. Mads Tourning. I don't care which mask you wear. So long as the name I get to call you at the end of the day is 'Mine.'"

He swallows, his eyes narrowing negligibly, and he squeezes me tighter. A shadow of that same fear flickers in his gaze when it searches over me. I wait for him to come back with an amusing comment. Yet, he sighs so heavily that his chest raises me, and we fall together.

"Done," he swears.

My hair is still damp when he leaves me passed out in the cool sheets. I don't wake for a few hours, though when I do, my stomach is grumbling.

The water and banana he had me eat after the shower wasn't enough.

I put on clothes, sneak out of my room and into the house, then head down the hallway past the upstairs bedrooms toward the staircase. My gaze catches on a light coming from the bathroom, and I go to inspect it just in case it's one of my brothers.

It's Reed.

I have to pause with wide eyes upon finding him.

"*Reed!*"

He has the bottle of green hair dye in his hands, and he's trying his hardest. Even still, it's *everywhere*.

"Oh my god, Reed," I exclaim as I grab towels from the closet. "Tina is going to kill you."

Reed grins sideways at me. "She loves me too much for that."

I laugh at him, the innocence in his big blue eyes. "This— why didn't you wake me up? I told you I would help."

"Didn't want to wake you," he shrugs.

"I mean, we could blame this on Kamden and get away with it, but—" I throw the towels on the floor. "Give me this and sit on the toilet—and then search how to get green hair dye off of walls."

Reed obeys with the biggest smile, his tall, lanky body still so awkward as he moves to the toilet and sits backward. I wrap a towel around his shoulders and in his lap, and he already has his phone out, trying to find how to clean the mess.

"You realize you needed to bleach your hair first, right? Like, this is going to be a tint of green. Not neon," I tell him.

"I have spray, too," he says. "This was just the base coat."

I smile at him through the mirror and shake my head. "You are going to make the best Joker tonight. If only we could find your Harley Quinn. Or Batman. "

Reed scoffs. "Me? Find someone? You're speaking fantasies. Especially with the band. It's hard to meet anyone that isn't just with me in the hopes they'll get their picture taken."

"So maybe someone who's already used to that," I suggest.

Reed frowns at me. "Yeah, okay."

"But also, I hope they're the grumpiest of grumps."

A quiet chuckle leaves him. "Yeah, yeah," he agrees. "What about you?"

"What about me?"

"When are you going to find someone?" he asks. "I thought maybe you had already by the way you've been this week."

I pause for a second. "What do you mean?"

Reed shrugs. "You seem happier, is all," he says, and I feel my brows narrow.

"How so?" I ask.

"Usually, when you smile, I can see the ghosts behind your eyes," he explains. "The last few days, they haven't been there."

"Wow, those new meds must be working," I say, and Reed

laughs.

"No, I mean it," he says.

"Maybe I mean it," I say as our eyes meet. "Go ahead. Laugh. Sometimes, those meds are all that keep me from digging my own grave."

His smile softens. "Andi…"

I sigh heavily and drop the brush. "Ask it then," I tell him.

"Have you met someone?"

"Ah…" I start painting his hair again. "Something like that."

"Serious?"

"I don't know," I admit. "Feels like it could be, yeah. We haven't talked about it."

"Do I know them?"

Just your best friend.

"How would you know them? Maybe it's someone from work," I answer.

"Maybe I should know them, then," he says.

"Why? So you can rough them up?"

"Yes," he replies like it's obvious.

I shake my head at him, thinking of Maddox. "When I find out what it is, I'll tell you his name."

"So, it is a guy," he says, pretending as if he's writing it down. "Clue number one. Got it. What color is his hair? Can I get a last name?"

I see he has my Instagram pulled up, and I shove him slightly. "Stop looking through my followers," I tell him. "Mr. Hands." I almost roll my eyes at him.

"Hey, speaking of hands, I need you to do me a favor at sound check," he says.

"No," I say without asking what it is.

"Come on. I need you to video me wrapping my hands around the mic while we practice."

I nearly slap the back of his head. "You are a *child*," I say.

"People will love it," he replies.

"Get Bonnie to do it," I tell him. "Maybe you should be practicing your crowd dive instead of what your hands are doing."

He grins. "I don't need to practice that," he says. "It's adrenaline-fueled. I barely even notice I'm doing it anymore."

"Do you do that every night?" I ask.

"Not always on the same song. I like changing it up so fans don't see the same show every night. We had a festival a few months back. I got to climb the light scaffolding."

"Yes, I saw the photos," I say, remembering how terrifying it had looked.

"Does it scare you?" he asks.

"The scaffolding picture? Yes."

"No, I mean when I jump into the crowd, and you're standing right there."

I slow my paint strokes. "Yeah," I admit. "Yeah, because my first instinct is to make sure you're okay. It's like watching you jump into those ball pits as a kid."

"See, I've had good training," he replies.

I purse my lips at him, and he smirks at me through the mirror.

"Have I told you how much I'm glad you're home?" he asks.

I meet his gaze, noting the sincerity in his eyes. "I'm glad I came home, too."

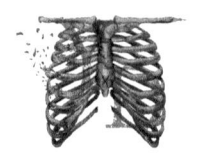

***

We all sleep in until after noon.

When I finally go downstairs, I find Tina sorting

Halloween candy to leave outside in little bags on the stoop. She appears frazzled, and I chuckle at her.

"You're not going to be home, but you have to make sure the neighborhood kids are taken care of," I say teasingly to her.

Tina smiles sweetly. "I hate to miss it, but we haven't seen Reed perform in years. I still don't know what to wear," she says, an obvious fluster in her voice.

"Reed won't care," I say. "He just wants you guys there."

She looks back at the last few bags she's putting together and holds up the full-size candy bars. "Color coordinate or random?" she asks.

"Random," I reply.

Tina goes back to sorting. I make myself a cup of coffee and sip it in silence as she finishes, my phone out on the counter to scroll through social media for a few minutes.

When I'm on my second cup, thoughts of the other night at the old house, the words that had run through my mind as I walked around that space. I'd thought of so many things to say to Tina, and now, standing before her, I feel like a child again.

I shift in my seat and hug the mug to me, feeling myself tense.

I have to get this out.

She needs to know.

"Hey, I wanted to talk to you about something," I say, and I don't know why I'm so nervous.

"What is it?" Tina asks, still sorting.

"I just… I wanted to apologize," I say as I feel my heart thud in my ears.

Tina stops fidgeting and finally looks at me. "For what?"

I clench my jaw, fighting back the emotion I don't want to spill. "For the chaos you and your boys had to endure because of me. Through all of those years." My voice is sticking, breaths coming in too short. "If my mother hadn't been around, they would never have been exposed to—"

"Whoa." Tina comes around the bar and grabs my hands. "No, Andi. You never have to apologize for that. That was never your fault."

"No, I know— I mean, I know that now," I force out. "It's taken me a while to realize it, but I still wanted… I wanted you to know that I am sorry. For everything. And I want to thank you."

Tina frowns, her eyes glistening. "For what?"

"For treating me like I was yours," I manage as a tear slips down my cheek. "You could have told Dad to kick me out so that your boys never had to endure any part of my mother, but you didn't. You helped, and I never… I never thanked you for that. And I'm so sorry you had to deal with it."

I'm a puddle as I look into her eyes again, as I feel my jaw quake with the last sentence.

"And I'm sorry that I never… I'm sorry I never called you 'mom,'" I say. "Because you deserved it. You deserved better than me calling you your name all these years. You were always my mom."

Tears spill from Tina's eyes, and she throws her arms around me.

She hugs me for a long few minutes, long enough that I spend my tears. When I nearly feel myself coming back to normal, when I feel her stop shaking, Tina pulls back and brings the candy bowl closer.

I choke on a laugh but take a Twix from the bowl anyway.

"Thank you," I say.

"You never have to apologize to me for anything, Andi," she says as she wipes her face. "What brought this on? Is it just being back here? Is that why you haven't been home?"

I wipe my face harshly and take a deep breath. "I drove by the old house the other day," I answer. "It brought back a few things I hadn't dealt with."

Tina sinks into the chair beside me. "Gosh, I haven't been over there since we sold it," she says. "Randall has. He occasionally takes Mrs. Lawry dinners when he's helping out the food bank. But I…" She sighs heavily. "I think I tried to put it behind me as much as you have," she adds as she takes my hand again. "I'm sorry. I didn't realize that was why you weren't coming home."

"It's not the only reason," I say.

Tina stares at me. "It's that boy that you brought home for Thanksgiving a few years ago, isn't it? I knew he wasn't a good one. He felt… slimy."

I can't help it when I brush my hand over my cheek, the memory of the other night filling me with dread. "A little worse than slimy," I mutter. "He's the one trying to expose Maddox."

Tina's brows raise. "That guy? He's the one on the council trying to take Maddox's safety away from him?"

Anger slides over her face, the very mention of someone hurting one of her boys putting her in 'mama bear' mode within a blink.

"What did Maddox ever do to him?" Tina asks. "Why would he want to hurt him?"

"It's my fault," I admit. "All of it. If I hadn't brought Adam home that Thanksgiving, if he'd never met Maddox, none of this would have happened. The other night at the bar, Adam recognized Maddox. They were protesting the concerts before, but once Adam realized who Maddox was, it just… It ignited the entire thing."

"None of this is on you," Tina says. "Adam is probably angry that he let you slip away."

Kamden and Koen come around the corner then, both of them groaning and appearing as if they've been run over by trucks in their sleep. I'm grateful for the smile it puts on my lips, and Tina shakes her head at her sons.

"Mom, we're starving," Koen says. "What do you have to eat?"

Tina glances back at me. "It doesn't matter how old they get. They're still children when they come home for the weekend," she says as she stands again. She squeezes my hand one more time, and with one look at her, I'm glad I said something.

"Are you hungry, Andi?" Tina asks.

I slide off of my own stool. "I'm okay. I need to check and see if Maddox needs me to do anything to help him get ready for tonight. I helped Reed with his hair last night, so—"

"What did he do to his beautiful hair?" Tina asks.

I smirk. "Oh… well… it's just green."

"Green?!"

A chuckle leaves me. "Don't worry. I cleaned up the bathroom."

Tina sighs in relief. "Oh, thank you," she says. "I don't care about the color. I was more concerned about the countertops."

As I laugh, I reach for the second cup of coffee I had made for myself. "I'm taking this to Maddox," I say before leaving through the sliding door.

The smell of birch and falling leaves fills my nose as I step out into the cool midday of Halloween. A deep, crisp breath fills my lungs when I look around at the changing leaves that have fallen overnight on the deck. I kick one and smile at the ground upon reaching the pool house door, though I don't bother knocking before going inside.

I've barely closed the door when I realize Maddox is standing behind the corner of the couch, hands in the pockets of his sweatpants and watching me as if he'd been waiting on me there.

I eye the way he's staring. "What?" I ask.

"You were smiling the entire walk over," he says.

"No, I wasn't," I say quickly.

His lips quirk up at the corners. "You were," he argues. "Did something happen, or are you just excited to see me?"

I sit the cup on the counter and give him a dull stare. "Don't do this," I say, though it's hard not to smile at him.

"Do what?"

"Turn me into one of those giddy girls."

His brows raise. "Giddy girls?" He slides his arms around my waist when he reaches me, causing my entire body to feel like he's lit it on fire. His lips land fleetingly on mine, and he hums a quiet noise of satisfaction. "I like my sad girl," he says. "But that's purely for the satisfaction of knowing that when you smile, it's because of me."

I slink my arms around his neck. "How very possessive of you."

"Tell me you hate it," he asks, staring at my lips.

"Don't ever stop."

My eyes lift to his, and as my heart seems to burst out of my chest, he kisses me in the slowest, most tantalizing way I've ever been kissed.

I *love* the way he kisses me.

It's engulfing and obsessive.

It leaves no room for doubts or questions of whether what we are is real.

He's all in, damn the consequences.

He grins against my lips when we part. "Morning, beautiful," he says before kissing the tip of my nose.

"Hi," I manage.

"You're very… something, today," he says, his eyes narrowing slightly.

"Had a good week," I reply.

His smile somehow broadens. "I was thinking last night —"

"Well, that's a dangerous statement," I mutter.

He pinches my ass in response, chuckling. "I was thinking last night about all the things I want to do to you after this week," he goes on. "I stayed up after I left you and looked at week-long getaways for us to the middle of the desert just so I don't have to worry about anyone hearing your screams."

I resist a smirk. "I think that's the most romantic thing anyone has ever said to me," I tell him.

A huff of amusement leaves him, and he leans down to skim his nose against my cheek and down to my jaw. "I want you spread eagle and tied across the bed," he says, his voice low. "I want you gagged and blind to my plans. I want your body wholly responsive to me and my touch. I crave every tear and whimper and cry you're capable of, and when I've taken you all the way to the edge of your limit, to the point when your safe word sits on the tip of your tongue and you think you can't take anymore… You'll come in ways you never thought possible. All of this… all of this, and *so much more*. Do you think you can handle that, beautiful?"

I'm nearly salivating at his promises.

"Handcuffs?" I ask.

He smiles. "If you want handcuffs, I'll give you handcuffs."

"More ropes? Floggers? Edible panties?"

A chuckle rolls out of him. "You're so desperate, baby."

I am.

I am fucking desperate.

I'm desperate for how safe he makes me feel, for the way he treats the darkest parts of me. I'm desperate for the care he takes and his challenge, for the shared respect and obsession we have for one another.

"You have no idea," I manage.

He takes a jagged breath, his fingers raking through my hair, and the soft way he smiles debilitates me. "Our break starts in a few weeks. I can make it happen if you can."

He's serious.

"I have vacation days saved up," I say. "Are we really talking about this?"

His nose nudges mine. My heart flutters in response, and I grab his shirt to stay balanced when he kisses me.

"I mean to keep you as long as you'll have me, Andersyn Matthews," he whispers once we part.

"Why?" I ask.

"Because I like the way our broken pieces fit, even if they were never meant to."

So do I.

I kiss him again, and as I do, I feel the aching warmth in my heart spread through my extremities. It's deliberate and soft, his tongue sweeping longingly against mine in a way that isn't entirely lustful but rather threaded in promises to one another.

When we part, I take another deep breath, forehead against his, my fingers twisting in his beard.

Maddox frowns at my fingers. "Why are your hands green?" he asks.

"Shit, they're going to be green for a week," I say, stepping back. "I found Reed trying to dye his hair after we went to bed, so I helped him. Speaking of which, we have to get you ready, too."

"What do you mean?" he asks.

"You have—" I tap twice on my phone screen "—four hours until the concert. I'm doing Reed's makeup there in the dressing room, but it might be easier to braid your hair here, so it's done."

"Braiding my hair?" he questions, brows raised.

"I mean, yeah. You said you're wearing the Bane mask. Have you tried it on? We might have to braid your beard, too."

Maddox juts his chin out and scratches beneath his messy chestnut hair. "Sounds like a lot of prep. I thought I was going to get to take my time with you before."

I snort. "Let's get you sorted, and we'll see."

Maddox grabs the costume and the mask from the bedroom. I take one look at it and know he'll have to have his beard braided as well, so I sit on the back of the couch and have him sit in front of me so that I can work.

"I think you can do this with your pussy in my mouth, too," he says with his back turned to me.

"Why, are you hungry?" I taunt him.

"*Starving*," he groans.

I can tell he's grinning, and I laugh. "If you think I would be able to do anything except pull your hair while you're doing that, you overestimate my willpower against you. Besides. Reed is upstairs and will probably burst through that door at any moment."

He acts like he wants to sulk but turns on a scary movie instead.

It doesn't take me more than a few minutes to finish pulling back his hair in a French braid. He's massaging my calf and foot in a manner that causes me to take longer than it should have.

After a lingering kiss, I shove him toward the bedroom to change his clothes, as he hasn't tried it on yet.

"What are you going to be tonight?" he says from the bedroom.

"I have a Sally dress that I'm going to wear," I tell him. "I wonder if Bonnie dyed her hair already or if she's waiting for me. I—"

Maddox comes out of the bedroom with the Bane mask on and the vest, and I grab onto the counter to stay upright. He has the camel-color long wool jacket as well, and as he slides it on and adjusts the lapels, I feel every ounce of feminism leave my body.

Mother fuck, how am I supposed to breathe tonight?

I can't speak. I can't look anywhere except his body because I know if I look into his eyes, I will lose my mind.

I tuck my arms around my chest, elbow bending as I start biting my thumbnail.

"Andi?"

My eyes widen. I stiffen. His voice is muffled, somehow raspier behind it.

I have to swallow when my eyes lift. "Hm?"

"What do you think? Does it work?"

Jesus mother fucking, goddamn cheese, crackers, and holy shit balls.

"I think… I think if you don't rail me like a dirty fucking whore over the back of this couch or by my throat against a window this very second, we're going to have a problem."

His brow lifts, and I gulp.

"Please," I add.

The way his eyes rake over me makes me shift, makes me well aware of every little movement, breath, and blink. I want to know what he's thinking, what he's about to do to me.

Without a word, Maddox steps deliberately in front of the armchair to his left and picks up the back of the coat as he sits in it. I don't know that I care that I just told him we couldn't do this because Reed was sure to come through the door at any moment. If this was how Reed found out we were together, then so be it.

The aura surrounding Maddox as he stares at me has me not knowing what to do with myself. I'm not entirely sure I'm still breathing. Maybe I died the moment he came out of that room, and this is just my corpse living out the fantasy I'd been enamored with before.

His hands slide down to the ends of the chair arms, and he grips the padding with spread fingers.

"Crawl to me, beautiful."

My knees hit the floor as if the ground was swept from beneath my feet.

A satisfied gleam lifts into his darkened eyes. I can see the outline of his dick already, as if the sight of me dropping to my knees has him going as mad for me as I am for him.

I want him in my mouth. I want him to hold me over his knees and break me like the actual character.

If he broke my back in this outfit, I'd thank him for it.

"Yo—are you—oh, *shit*."

Reed.

Reed swings through the door and stops a foot from the door, the biggest grin I've ever seen on his face as he notices Maddox in his costume.

He doesn't even see me on the floor, crawling in front of the television.

Maddox shifts narrowly in his seat as if he's just watching the movie.

"Damn, Mads," Reed goes on. "That's insane."

I pretend like I'm picking up something from the floor. However, there's nothing down here.

Maddox kicks over a box of Skittles as he stands up, and I hit my head on the coffee table.

"Ow—fuck—" I sit back on my knees as Maddox takes the mask off, and Reed frowns at me.

"Ow," I say again, rubbing my head. "Dammit, that hurt."

"What are you doing in here?" Reed asks.

"Dammit. What does it look like?" I ask as I bend back over to pick up the candy. "I was braiding Maddox's hair," I say.

"Oh. Nice job. It looks fucking awesome," Reed says, apparently stoked about their concert. "Tonight is going to be epic."

"Fuck yeah," Maddox agrees.

"James is out front already," Reed goes on. "Want to change, and then we'll head over?"

"Yeah, sounds good."

Reed's gaze moves to me as I stand. "You hitching a ride with us?"

"I actually still have a lot of things to do before I go over there," I tell him. "I still need to shower and do makeup. And make sure Dad knows where to go tonight. Tina acted really excited this morning. I'll be there in an hour or so."

"Sweet. We have to do my makeup," he replies. "You have to make me look scarier than him," he says with a nod to Maddox.

I smirk. "I'll do my best."

CHAPTER SEVENTEEN
ANDI

I'm still hard from the sight of you on your hands and knees, Maddox texts me as I'm driving on the way to the venue. *Think you can do that for me later?*

Keep that outfit on, and I'll lick your fucking boots.

I honestly don't know if I'm exaggerating.

Cynda texted me just after Maddox and Reed left. Legal was able to pull all of the comments down about Maddox overnight. They served Adam a cease and desist order that very morning, stating that while he had every legal right to post about Maddox's father, the slander against Maddox himself was grounds for a lawsuit because it put him in danger.

I hope Erin, our relations manager, is there telling Maddox the good news.

I pull into the venue parking lot a few minutes later and park around back, where James had instructed me to park the day before. There's a small protest happening outside the front of the building that immediately makes me nauseous. I don't bother going near it to see what it's about because I know it's probably a group of fanatics against not only Young Decay, but also Halloween in general.

James is standing at the emergency exit door when I make it across the lot.

"Hi, James," I say to him.

James nods and clears his throat, causing me to pause at his side.

"Parents here tonight?" he says as if the question is enough.

I frown. "They are."

He stares pointedly at me, and I realize why he's being grumpy.

The memory of Maddox fucking me against the wall the night before enters my mind.

"Oh. *Oh*. Um. Did you tell him?" I ask, referring to Maddox.

James smirks. "I tried."

A laugh escapes me. "I'll mention it again. Did Erin show up?"

"She just left," James replies.

I blow out an audible breath, and James's smile lifts to his dark eyes.

"Big weight off," he says.

"Let's hope Adam isn't stupid enough to do it anyway," I say as I cross my fingers.

James chuckles. "Don't tell your brother that. He had Avie bring energy drinks into the dressing room for him to shake up and fizz in celebration."

"Oh god," I mutter before pushing past him toward the dressing room.

The band is in a frenzy.

When I open the door, I'm immediately splattered with fizz from the drink Reed has just popped open. I gasp and halt in my tracks, throwing my hands over my face in the hopes that none of it gets on my Halloween makeup.

"Reed!"

"Oh shit—sorry, sis!" Reed grabs a towel and tries to help me blot the liquid off my dress. "Did you hear?"

I laugh, my gaze moving across the room to Maddox, who is leaning against the vanity and laughing quietly, his head shaking at his bandmates' display. Zeb goes over and roughs him up by the shoulders, trying to get him to get up and celebrate with them, though the bassist just stuffs his hands back in his pockets.

I exhale some of my fear when our eyes meet.

"I did," I say.

Bonnie throws her arms in the air upon seeing me, and I dodge her hands because she has red hair dye all over them.

"Whoa—my hands are already green from this idiot," I say, pointing toward Reed.

"Air hug," Bonnie says. She holds her arms up, and I laugh when I wrap my arms around her.

"Thank fuck we don't have to worry about that asshat anymore," Bonnie says as I release her. "Thought we were going to have to have a group seance to banish him tonight."

"Happy Halloween," I say.

"You look hot, by the way," Bonnie adds. "I love the Sally makeup."

I shrug and look at the stitches I've drawn to extend my red lips, across my forehead and through my eyebrow, along with two across my throat. The makeup around my eyes is heavier than I usually wear, though it's perfect for the Sally look.

"I found an extra eyeliner and thought, what the hell," I reply.

"Looks amazing. I love you. *Hey!*—" Bonnie darts over to Reed and bends backward so that he can pour the energy drink into her mouth, and as she does, I finally make my way over to Maddox.

Maddox's eyes drag a little longer over me, and I exhale a uneven breath under his surprised stare.

"Congratulations," I tell him as I lean on the counter beside him. "Looks like the demons won this round."

"For now," he says, and I know why he's hesitant about celebrating.

He crosses his arms over his chest and examines me up and down again, causing me to look away before I do something rash.

"I heard we were under a 'no walls' rule tonight," I say as cryptically as possible.

Maddox scoffs. "I heard the same." His eyes lock on mine, and he raises a brow. "After, though."

I wish I could kiss him.

Because I want to bite that smirk off his lips.

I suck my bottom lip between my teeth, practically feeling my eyes dilate upon him. "After, though."

I can see the darkened smirk in his eyes when he gazes at me, and before anyone can notice us, he lays his hand atop mine and squeezes it.

"Hey, Andi—" Reed calls from the door. "Can you do my makeup?"

My head swivels in his direction, Maddox and I's hands parting. "And turn you into the Joker? Yes. I can do that," I say as I push off the counter.

Our family arrives an hour before the set start—just in time to say a quick 'hello' before the band starts their rituals. Tina brings bags of candy for each of them. They stay to chat for a while, and by the time they're ready to leave, the opening act is less than fifteen minutes from going on.

I know I should leave, too.

I wish I could have one minute with Maddox to see how he's feeling, what he's thinking after the news of Adam being stifled. Even so, I know it'll have to wait.

Work first.

As we part ways and I head out into the pit, I see Maddox backstage beginning his before-show walking rounds. I get my camera ready and check the settings, even snapping a few pictures of the mass of people in costumes in the front row.

Someone screams behind me and points toward the wings. I swing my lens to the stage, finding Maddox with the Bane mask on and standing in the shadows between the curtains. Another person yells, "Bane!" as loud as they can, and a few others follow.

"I bet it's Mads," one fan says.

"Definitely Mads," another agrees. "He always hangs out in the wings before the show."

My phone buzzes, and I reach into my pocket to find that Maddox is texting me.

I couldn't tell you back there, but you look fucking amazing, he says.

I clench my teeth to stop from grinning too widely. *I thought you might like the added touch.*

You know how much I love Sally.

It's the scars, isn't it? I tease. *The stitches?*

The legs, he says.

I chuckle at the screen, my gaze darting up to find that he's disappeared.

I love how you smile at the phone when you're texting me, he says, and I draw my lip behind my teeth, shaking my head because I can't find him anymore.

Where are you?

Walking.

The lights go down.

The crowd erupts, and I know I only have a few seconds to prepare for the opening band. I feel security walk up behind me, though they're closer than I like.

You're going to kill it tonight, I text Maddox. *I'll see you after.*

"What about now?"

The question comes in a hushed rasp from the person behind me.

My heart skips.

Maddox.

It's so dark that I can hardly see him. Yet I know it's him. *I know.* I can smell the woodsy scent of his beard oil. The strobes start up, and I'm granted a look at him in flickered glimpses. He's wearing a long black jacket over the Bane vest, and the jacket's hood is pulled over his head.

Though…

My eyes widen, my entire body caving at…

He isn't wearing his mask.

My heart drops.

"*Maddox?*" I whisper in disbelief. "What are you—"

Panic grips me.

He's out in front of the entire theater—with no mask—and even though he has his hood up, the Bane mask is in his left hand.

People just saw him wearing it.

"Maddox, *what are you doing?*" I ask.

"This." He wraps his hand around my face, and I don't have a second to think before his lips are on mine.

The kiss sinks me. It's as deep and obsessive as every other kiss has been. And when he slows down enough to release my mouth, I'm left dumbfounded and staring at him.

"What…" I can hardly breathe, let alone speak. "Maddox, your mask—"

"Maybe I can do nothing," he whispers. "And maybe 'nothing' means I don't have to fear this."

A few people in the crowd are whistling at us, obvious they can't tell who we are. The strobe lights continue to flicker. The opening act is standing in the shadows waiting for their beat drop.

He presses his forehead to mine, eyes closing. "My terms," he says. "With you."

My heart swells ten times its normal size.

Maddox kisses me again, and this time, I don't hesitate. I don't hold back any part of me that the previous embrace had snagged on. I know he can feel the smile on my lips, though I wonder if he knows just how fast my pulse is racing right now.

His forehead braces against mine for another moment when we part. I see his smile, hear his soft, nervous chuckle, and I laugh in the same way as emotion burns behind my nose.

He's out front. No mask.

His choice.

Maddox kisses my forehead and hands me the Bane mask to put on him for the show. I wish I could stop grinning, yet I can't.

When he bends down, I carefully place it over his head and face. That same sensation I'd felt in the pool house floods me. Warm pools over my neck and chest, spreading down to my center.

His hood falls back, and some of the people around us gasp.

"Oh, shit—Was that—"

"Fucking *Mads!*"

"Mads Tourning!"

I can see the smile in Maddox's eyes. He takes the jacket that was just over him and places it around me, pulling the hood up because he knows I'm going to need it after that display.

The opening act is coming onto the stage, and Maddox brushes his thumb against my cheek one more time.

"See you after," he says.

My heart does a giddy dance as I watch him turn toward the crowd, flash the horns with his arms in the air to the sound of the fans around us going insane, and then jump onto the stage at the corner where James is waiting to haul him up—and probably scold him. James gives me a tired expression. However, there's nothing I could have done.

Once Maddox is out of sight, I clasp my chest and exhale an audible breath as the adrenaline of what just happened seizes me.

I can't keep the ridiculous smile off of my face the entire set. I have to escape into the curtains between bands because of the people trying to talk to me. I don't see Maddox again, not until he's seen making his rounds back and forth on the other side of the stage.

Fans shout when they see him again and again. I chuckle. I know he's doing it to settle his nerves, but he's such a tease about it.

Smoke billows over the drum platform when the lights go down. I see the rest of my family watching from the side, Tina jumping up and down as the band gets their entrance going. Strobes set off. Tonight, they have horror film laughter tracks bouncing from corner to corner, some rising in crescendos until they take over the entire room.

The noise sends goosebumps rolling down my spine.

Bonnie appears behind her drum set. Her first few beats send the crowd into a frenzy. The Poison Ivy makeup, hair, and costume looks as though it were made for her. She's embodying the villain tonight, no question.

Zeb and Maddox step onstage to a staggering whirl of screams, and as sexy as they are, I know the screams are just getting started. I know the moment Reed steps out looking like the Joker, people will lose their shit.

Or their minds. Whichever comes first.

Reed takes tonight to sing the first verse of one of their more popular songs off stage, and I laugh. He's always been dramatic.

The band, the shows… it takes his love for theatrics to new levels.

I couldn't be more proud of him.

The audience goes *insane* when he finally hits the stage, and Reed turns into the performer he was always meant to be.

I can hardly keep up with him.

Reed is in the middle of a chorus a few songs later when I see him look twice to his left, and there's emotion behind my eyes as he runs to the edge of the stage and grabs Tina's hand.

She protests and tries to fight him, though Reed is too contagious, too strong, and he hauls her into the middle of the stage to a roar of applause.

"Everyone say hi to my mom!" Reed tells the crowd.

They do.

Every single person in the room shouts, "Hi, mom!"

Tina laughs and jumps a few times when Reed sings a few lines. James beckons her to the edge again, and Reed gives her a hug before she has to go back.

There's no full intermission tonight. They take a few breaks throughout the entire show, allowing the performers they've hired for the night to take over the stage when they do. Reed stays out to do a few acoustic songs on the piano and chat with the audience—going as far as bringing Koen and Kamden on the stage with him.

I make a mental note to tell him what a horrible idea that was once this is over.

Kamden will use the photo to get laid for the next ten years.

I have to give it to the band… when they said they wanted their last night to blow peoples minds, they fucking did it.

My phone buzzes when they're nearly done.

I frown at seeing Cynda's name on the screen and hit 'ignore.'

Last two songs, I text her. *Will call when they're about to wrap up.*

Cynda sends back a thumbs-up emoji as the last song starts up.

Orange inflatable pumpkins fall from the ceiling. The strobes go crazy. I snap a few photos of Reed as the flares rain down from the rafters over the front of the stage, then try to grab some of the rest of the band with the smoke and different colors.

And as they go into the bridge, I feel my phone vibrating again.

I glance up at Maddox to find him watching me, and I flash him three fingers and point to the back. He signs the same, and I take the opportunity to dart out of the walk and head backstage so that hopefully I can be back in time to grab a few shots of them at the very end.

When I pass by James, I hold up my phone and point to the emergency exit at the back. "Is it okay for me to use that door to go out and take this?" I ask.

He nods. "Area is clear. You're all good."

The chilled air hits my face when I push through the door and onto the back stoop. The wind brushes the hood off of my hair. I can still hear the drums from inside, though everything else is muffled. I know I'll be yelling at Cynda when I get her on the phone.

The hair on the back of my neck stands, though I don't know if it's from the chill or from the fact that it's creepy as hell back here alone.

I swear I hear footsteps.

I turn around, phone to my ear. A frown slips onto my face when I don't see anything.

"Just your fucking imagination, Andi," I mutter to myself.

"Hey, girl," Cynda says on the other line when she answers.

"Hey—What's up?" I ask her.

"I just wanted to check to see how things were going," she says. "There's a photo on social media going pretty viral right now that I'd love to hear more about."

My entire face furls. "What? One of mine?"

"No, but you're in it," she says. "Check your messages."

I put her on speaker and slide over to my messages, and when I pull up the photo, my knees almost give out.

It's a shitty photo. The person who took it got lucky enough to grab it when the strobe lights were highlighting us from behind.

It's Maddox. Kissing me.

There are no discerning features on his face, at least. Just the hood over his head. However, it's clear that the girl is me with the 'press' lanyard and camera in my hand.

"Mother fuck—"

Cynda sighs heavily. "Upper management has already called. They want to know how many other bands you've been sleeping with on assignment—"

"I've never done that before," I argue.

"Yeah, well, luckily I was able to convince him that even if you were sleeping with all of them, you are still a damn good photographer and do your fucking job like a professional," Cynda says. "Either way, they want you in on Monday to chat."

"What did Decay's manager have to say?" I ask.

"He said Mads slipped out of his sight and that he hasn't seen you act unprofessional all week," she answers. "Seems like he likes you."

"It's a temporary assignment," I argue.

"Doesn't seem like it's about this one particular band. All upper wants to know is if you're doing this with every band, and if you're taking any photos off the books that might compromise one of their clients."

"You've got to be shitting me," I snap.

Cynda sighs. "We'll take care of it, Andi," she assures me. "Go back inside. I just wanted to call you and give you a head's up before someone ambushed you after the show."

My heart is in my throat. "Thank you," I tell her. "I'll call you tomorrow to get details on Monday."

"Have fun tonight," Cynda says, and she hangs up before I can reply.

I press my hands into the railing and take a deep breath. My insides are twisting to the point I feel like I might puke.

Shit.

Shit. Shit. Shit.

God, we're fucked. So fucking fucked.

We have to tell Reed before he gets his phone after the show. I need to tell my dad, Tina.

Footsteps brush over the gravel nearby. I hear the crowd in a roar. The show must be over. I don't even look at the person coming my way. I don't care. I don't know what to do—

Cold steel presses to my side.

Breath wholly escapes me.

"Do you think you can put yourself back together once I open up these stitches, *Sally?*"

I cringe, my teeth grinding. I know the voice.

Somewhere deep inside me, I start to panic. Even still, I try to stay cool despite the tears already welling in my eyes.

No one will hear me scream.

Not with the music, the crowd shouting, the jubilation happening just feet behind me.

"You were always the worst when it came to pick-up lines," I manage as my chin hits my shoulder.

Adam is wearing that stupid Myers mask again. I force a laugh.

"Do you think that mask makes you look scarier? Or were you just too coward to show up here without it?"

He jerks me closer, the tip of the knife pressing into my

side. I stifle the yelp I so desperately need to release when it pierces my skin. My entire body shudders.

He takes my hair and jerks my head back. "Scream like you want to," he says. "No one will hear it."

I'll never give you the satisfaction of it.

I jab my elbow into his gut, making him grunt and double over. He lets go of my hair. I seize the opportunity and whip around to strike him across the side of the face with my camera. He yells, completely releasing his grip on me this time, and I dash toward the steps. My camera crashes to the ground—

Adam's strides catch me.

He grabs my hair and throws me into the iron railing. My head strikes the cold steel, and I fall.

I tumble down the hard steps. I tumble and tumble and fall into a damp puddle, and for a second, I'm stunned.

It feels like a lightning strike cutting down my spine. I cry out from the pain, from the fear suddenly gripping me. The noise that comes from me sounds as if someone has my bones in their hands and is ripping them out of my body. I can't see. Everything is double. My head throbs in a pound so agonizing that nausea swells in my throat. I drag my knees up, ripping my stockings in an attempt to stand.

I have to get away.

I can't let him take me.

I try to scream again, yet it comes out as a groan and cry.

My nails break on the cement when I brace my hands beneath me. I manage to rise my chest off the asphalt—

His boot lands on my back, and I falter beneath it.

I hate the sobbing wail that leaves me.

I hate the helplessness of this pain.

He won't take me, too.

For a blink, I'm back at the old house. A hand is on my wrist and pulling me out of the door. I fight back and scream.

No one hears me.

"Stop!" I cry out to Adam, shoving the memory away. "Leave me alone. Why are you doin—*No! Get off*—"

His knee is on my thigh to lock me down. I twist and squirm and scream. Panic swells, throwing adrenaline into the veins and muscles that want to fail me. He tries to grab my arms. I swat at every turn. My motions are frantic. Breath refuses to catch. I'm swatting and slapping and kicking and screaming for anyone—*anyone*—to hear me.

His entire weight is on my thighs. He's speaking, though I don't know what he's saying.

I don't *care* what he's saying.

The knife presses against my neck, and I still.

"Stop fucking moving," he warns.

There's gravel on my face mixing with the tears.

"*What do you want?*" I manage.

"You think I didn't see that photo from tonight?" Adam asks. "I always knew you were fucking him. He doesn't deserve you. He never has. He's no good for you."

He shoves my face into the ground and moves his knee onto my elbow. My arms are trapped behind my back. I writhe and kick. He has my hands.

I feel him wrapping something thin around my arms, and the absolute wails leaving me don't sound like they belong to a person.

Zip ties tighten on my wrists.

"And you think tying me up and taking me away somehow makes you better?!" I yell.

"I'll do what I have to to save you from him," Adam says.

Maddox.

Maddox.

As if saying his name enough times might make him appear.

Adam's weight moves off me. I start to scramble my feet,

but he grabs me by the hair and my bound wrists. He hauls me to my feet as if I'm an animal he's just tied up for slaughter. My back arches to his will.

"Walk, Andi," Adam growls. "I want to know just how wet this scuffle made you."

Ice water seems to pour over me. I squirm as much as my body will allow. "*Don't you fucking touch me—*"

The sharpest pain I've ever felt slices through my side. I gasp. My eyes bulge. The pain stuns me. And before I can stop myself, my knees give out. I try to make my body move, try to push away the agony and scream out again.

I can't let him take me.
I can't let him take me.

Adam throws me over his shoulder.

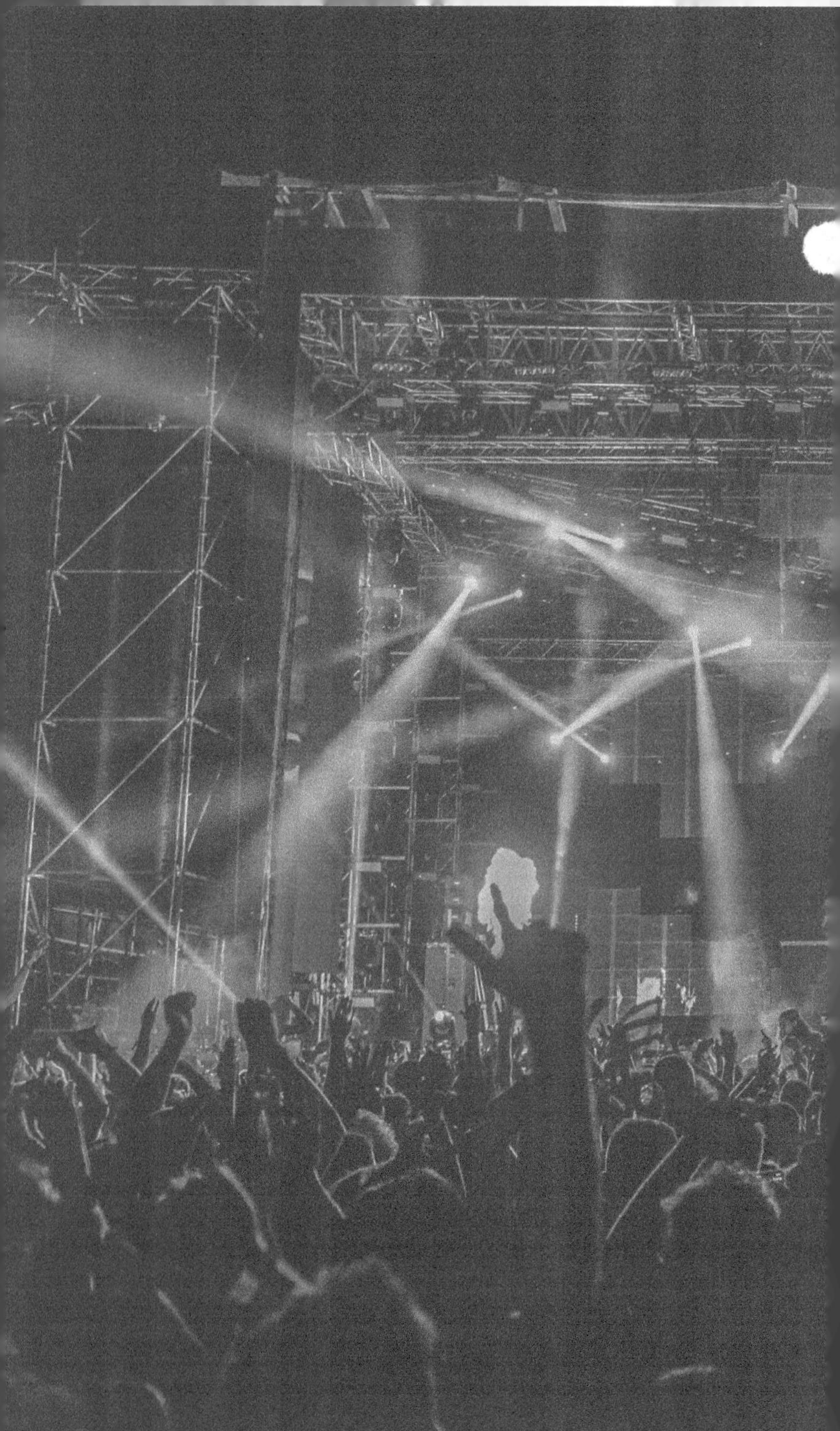

CHAPTER EIGHTEEN
MADDOX

Taking bows after this show feels like we've just ended an era.

The crowd is going insane. I've never heard screams like this.

The four of us grab one another and take a bow, grinning because there's nothing like this feeling—the fucking elation and pride of playing three shows back to back in your hometown for fans that have driven across the country and followed us for months now.

I had already changed out of the Bane mask and into my normal mask before our bows. I had to get that damn thing off of me. It was not made for extended wear beneath stage lights.

Bonnie tugs me down in front of her and undoes the braid in my hair, making everyone yell when she drags her hands in it and shakes the messy waves in a ragging manner. Arms in the air, she jumps up and down beside me, her now red hair glimmering in the stage light.

I flip the hair out of my face as she runs to the edge of the stage and starts tossing her broken drumsticks out into the crowd, Zeb does the same with his spare guitar picks.

And as they do that, Reed engulfs me in a hug that sends us both off balance.

"Fucking amazing, man," I say to him.

"No, *you're* fucking amazing," Reed argues.

I glance toward the curtains as we hug again and find Reed's family in the shadows. I see our manager. The DJ. James. A few other familiar faces.

I don't see Andi.

It makes my eyes narrow.

She would be here. I *know* she would be here.

It's too big of a moment for her to miss.

Reed separates from me and heads back to the stage, jumping down into the walk between the stage and audience barrier where Andi had hung out all night. Our manager runs onstage to throw him a sharpie, and while everyone is distracted, I take the opportunity to dart off.

I'll come back.

I just want to know where she is.

Reed's family tackles me with hugs and jumps and excitement. Tina kisses me on the cheek.

I want to enjoy it.

I want to hug them back with as much enthusiasm as they're giving me. I want to soak in their adrenaline, but mine has taken on a monster of its own.

"What's wrong, Maddox?" Tina says. She can tell I'm distracted.

"I'm just—I'm trying to find Andi," I say. "Have you seen her?"

"Ah…" Tina and Randall look between each other. "No. Not since she was down in the pit," Randall asks. "Does she have something you need?"

"She's… Yeah," I answer. "Something like that."

I clap Kamden on the arm and stop into the dressing room in the hopes that she's waiting in there. When I don't see her, I toss the Bane mask on the table and head out to circle the stage again.

Even after another run around, I still don't see Andi.

"Hey—" I trot up to James, who's making sure Reed gets off without being tackled. "Hey, did you see Andi back here?" I ask him.

"Yeah." He nods toward the back exit. "She was taking a phone call out back."

"Oh. Okay. Did anyone go out with her?" I ask.

"It was just a couple of minutes ago," James said. "Do you want me to go check?"

I glance out at the stage and shake my head when I see Reed is still out there signing a few autographs and chatting with fans, the houselights on now.

"No," I tell him. "No, I'll go get her."

Something doesn't feel right in the pit of my stomach. I don't know why. I don't know if it's because I didn't immediately find her or if it's something else.

I open and close my fist as I make my way to the door, hoping that when I open it, I'll find her on the phone and she'll smile back at me.

My hands hit the door. I say her name as it opens—
She isn't there.

The back steps are empty.

In the distance, I hear a few cars starting up, people leaving the venue. I start to walk down the platform, yet my foot knocks into something.

The sound of metal scrapes the concrete. I look down, and my stomach drops.

Andi's camera is broken on the ground.
Shit.

I can't even bring myself to pick it up. Without thinking twice, I press my phone to my ear and dial James's number. And when I look toward the steps, I see her phone smashed.

There's blood on the asphalt.

Fear spikes my heart rate. My head is on a swivel as I

search the lot, panic threading through every nerve. I'm already so hyped on adrenaline that the fright makes me feel as if I'm about to implode.

"Andi!" I shout into the darkness.

James still hasn't answered.

"Andi!"

Pick up. Pick up.

"Yeah?" James answers.

"I need you," I say.

"Something wrong?" James asks.

"I don't… I don't…" I can't think straight. I gasp as my breaths run too short. Too panicked. "It's Andi. She isn't—"

My eyes snag on a beige SUV on the other side of the back lot parked by the exit road. There's a man placing a woman from his shoulder into the back seat. I squint against the dim street light that's over the car. The man pauses outside the door. It looks as though he's struggling with her.

A flash of purple slides from beneath the hood over the woman's hair.

Purple hair.

"Mother fu—"

The phone drops. I jump over the banister down to the ground, and I bolt.

Andi.

"ANDI!"

I can see her kicking, hear the guy shouting. The distinct noise of a slap cuts the chilled air, and I see his hand swing back.

"ANDI!"

Her head whips up from the back seat. I can't make out the expression on her face, but I hear the panic in her voice, see her hair falling over her features.

"MADDOX!"

"ANDI!"

The guy looks back over his shoulder and shoves her inside. She starts to jump out. The door slams in her face, and he practically dives into the front.

I reach him as he cranks up the car. I throw myself into the open window without thinking and drag the bastard out of the driver's seat. His Myers mask falls off when we both topple to the ground.

I can't feel my body as Adam stares back at me.

"I'll fucking kill you—"

Adam scrambles to his feet. I'm faster. I hear Andi screaming and kicking on the back door, though I don't try to get her out.

She's safer in there than out here.

I lunge at Adam and slam him into the driver side door. He says something, but I don't hear it. White hot rage has me blind, numb, and nearly fucking deaf to everything except her.

Something sharp drives into my side.

Fuck.

I stumble back and grab my side, the familiar feeling of steel in my skin making me curse and stagger.

"Maddox!"

Andi shouting my name is enough fuel to keep me going.

The knife clatters on the asphalt when I grab it from my side. Adam stares at me with wide eyes. His lips are moving. I wonder if he's giving an excuse for this or if he's insulting me in some way.

I don't fucking care.

Adam runs at me. His arms wrap around my waist and send me flying into the cement. He's on top of me. His fist swings into my face—

"GET OFF!"

Reed.

Reed grabs Adam and throws him off me. I get to my feet

fast. I can't let Reed get involved. If anyone is taking the fall for anything, it's me. I'm the the one with the history in this family. Not Reed. Reed is too good.

I pick Reed up by his jacket and shove him off of Adam.

"Get Andi!" I tell him, grabbing my side and pushing through the pain. "I'll handle this."

Reed shakes his head as if he knows why I'm shouting at him. "No—"

I grab him by his ripped t-shirt. "Get your fucking sister," I snap in his face. "If anyone is going down for this, it's me. Now, *go*."

I don't give Reed a chance to argue. I propel him behind me and pull my hood over my head as I see people are coming around for autographs.

Adam has rolled onto his stomach. He's rising on his hands and knees. I'm fucking shaking as I look at this miserable excuse for a human.

My boot lands in his stomach, the kicking blow sending Adam flailing again.

His groans sound like nails on a chalkboard.

"What were you going to do—*kidnap her?*" I ask, circling his mewling figure.

Adam presses up on his hands and spits out blood. I kick him again and send him on his back. He curls up in a ball, wincing at the pain.

Good.

"After everything you already put her through, you thought she deserved this, too?" I sink to one knee and grab him up with my fists so I can see the fear in his eyes.

"Maddox! *Knife!*"

Andi's voice makes me blink, and when I do, Adam shifts.

He swings his arm, his knife hiding in his hand where I can't see it. It slices my knee. Screams sound around us. I fall back and try to shake off the pain.

Adam grapples his way up before I can get my bearings.

He swings the knife again, and I see it. I see the moment I know my life is done. The gleam of the silver heading toward my throat to end me.

Andi screams my name.

I catch Adam's wrist and twist it backward, stopping the knife a breath away from my face. It clatters to the ground with his yelp, and my fist meets his face.

Adam falls onto his back, and I think I black out.

One punch after the other, I lay into him. I punch him until it isn't just blood splattering back. It's bone and matter and teeth and tissue. I rail into him long after I know he's done, long after I see his eyes fade and feel his fight drain.

Long after I stop hearing the screams of my name and pleas to stop.

I. *Can't.*

The very image of Andi's hip fills my mind, the fear in her eyes when he dragged her down that alley, the noise of her screaming as he tried to take her away from me before, the look in her eyes when her mother used to try and take her away.

He tried to take her away from me.

"Maddox!"

Hers is the only voice I hear, and it's the only voice that can get me to pause, and when I do, I finally realize it's over.

The bastard lays lifeless in front of me.

Somehow, I rise to my feet. Somehow, I step off of him. I spit the blood from my own mouth onto his corpse, and then —

Noise rushes into my ears.

People are *screaming*.

I feel hands on mine, though I don't know whose they are. The person moves me off of Adam's body and closer to the SUV. My eyes lift, and when they do, I feel a tear mix with the blood already running down my face.

Andi pulls out of Reed's grasp, bolts across the asphalt, and thrusts herself into my arms. Sobs and incomprehensible words leave her that I barely catch.

It's all I can do to hold her.

The world is a haze around us. I can't breathe. Can't think. Blue lights dance in the distance. People continue to scream.

I don't fucking care about any of it.

I pull back just enough to see her, and I brace my palms on her cheeks. Tears streak down her face. She's trying to sniff back her sobs, trying to hold herself together, and through all of it, all I can think is just how much my heart felt like it had been ripped out of my chest when I saw that camera broken on the ground.

"He was going to take me," she manages. "I tried to get away from him. I didn't take my spray out. I tried kicking and yelling, but—"

Her wide eyes dart to the body on the ground behind us. "Maddox—"

I tug her face to mine again. "Hey. *Hey*—look at me. Andi, *look at me*."

I pull my mask down. I don't give two shits if anyone else sees my face.

She's the only thing in my fucking world right now.

"He's gone," I say, my voice breathless when our eyes meet. "He's never going to hurt you again. He's never going to fucking *look* at you again. I told you… I promised you, beautiful. I promised you."

My forehead presses to hers. There are tears in my own eyes that I don't attempt to suppress. Because she's broken in front of me, and while I'm trying to hold onto the pieces for us both, I know the cracks are too much.

A sob chokes from her, and before either of us can think about the rest of the people surrounding us, I kiss her.

I kiss her with my entire soul.

Damn any consequences that might be awaiting us when we part.

She's everything.

"You've got to be fucking kidding me."

Someone shoves me away from her, and I register as I stumble that it's Reed coming between us.

Goddammit.

"Reed, wait—"

Reed barges into me again, advancing and ignoring his sister's pleas. The sharp pain of the stab wound in my side grapples my entire body. Jaw twitching, I straighten and glare in Reed's direction, shoving the agony to the back of my mind as my gaze meets the stark blue of his wild eyes.

"How long have you been fucking my sister?" Reed asks, and I see his fist closing.

I don't back down. Not even when Reed grabs my jacket and pushes me back.

"It's more than that," I finally say.

"Yeah?" Reed scoffs. "You've been trying to get in her pants since we were teens, and you're telling me it isn't just your dick finally getting what its always wanted?"

I stand my ground this time when he starts to push. "I said *it's more than that*," I say through my teeth.

"Reed, *stop*," Andi begs. "This is stupid—"

"Stay out of it," Reed tells her. His attention turns back to me. "How long?" Reed asks.

"This week," I answer.

Reed laughs a sardonic laugh that I've heard him use before. When he's pissed and in disbelief. When he's about to throttle the person talking back to him.

"This week." He chews his mouth for a beat. "Fucking this week—I thought you were my friend—*my best friend*."

"Why does this have to change anything?" I ask.

"Because you made a promise!" Reed shouts, his voice elevating as if he's held it in for as long as he can. "You swore. We pinky swore—"

"That promise was ten years ago," I argue.

Police sirens blare around us.

"I trusted you," Reed yells. "God, I trusted you for years. And after everything we've been through, you betray me. You lie to me. You put her—*You put her before the band*. Before *us*—"

"Because I'm in love with her!" I yell.

There's a beat of silence between us. Rage spreads from Reed's eyes and moves over his shoulders into the rest of him.

And with an elongated shout as his warning, Reed runs at me.

He tackles me at the waist and throws us both on the ground. His fist strikes my cheekbone, throwing my head back into the pavement. God, he punches like a mother fucker. *Fuck.* I wrap my legs around him as he gets in another punch, this time on my jaw. I spit the blood out and thrust my hands toward his face, trying to push him off of me.

"Reed, this is ridiculous—"

"Swear you'll never touch her again!"

"Fuck you," I manage.

Andi's shouting both of our names. Blue lights cascade over us.

Reed doesn't seem to notice.

He's pulling my hair and swinging at my face. I finally get my legs up and my feet around his hips enough to roll him on to his back. Reed swings left. Right. Yells echo in the air. I shove his face sideways into the pavement and get my knees on his arms. He's squirming and trying to bite my hand—

"I trusted you! You were family—"

"We are family! You say you trusted me, then fucking trust

me, brother," I yell as I get my hand around his throat. Reed's eyes widen up at me, his hands wrapping around my wrist.

"Never—"

"Trust me when I say I'd rather carve out my own heart than break hers," I continue. "I've loved your sister since we were asshole teenagers running around with mullet haircuts, and I'll love her for as long as she lets me."

Reed stops wriggling. I loosen my grip on him, eyeing my best friend as I release him.

Reed propels me backward off of him, and I catch myself on my wrists. The unrelenting pain in my side makes my entire body shudder. My shirt is soaked with blood.

Even so, I grapple onto whatever adrenaline is left within me.

Because the pain I feel beneath Reed's furious gaze is worse than any wound could ever be.

"You're my family, Reed," I force out. "Shit, after everything that we've been through together? Every night we stayed up when I didn't want to sleep because I couldn't handle my nightmares? Every time you rescued me from home and took me into yours?" My heart is heavy as I watch his eyes soften. "Goddammit, Reed. I just beat the life out of someone for her, and you don't think you can trust me?"

Reed's gaze flickers to the lifeless body just feet away, and then his eyes are back on me.

He still doesn't speak, and I feel my resolve weakening.

"I can't lose you," I say in a thick voice. "But I can't lose her either."

It's a plea.

An outright *beg* for him to understand.

Maybe not for him to approve, because I know I've hurt him. I know it's a wound I'll have to mend with time.

Noise becomes an echo around us as I wait for him to speak.

To say anything.

Hands wrap around my arms and pull them behind my back. I'm brought to my knees, and I know the blue lights that had been closing in on us are finally there.

Andi and Bonnie are screaming. People around us are shouting. I don't know what they're saying.

I'm still waiting for Reed to speak.

Cold handcuffs enclose around my wrists. I'm hauled to my feet.

"Reed…"

Reed's gaze moves from me to over my shoulder, and he rises in a frantic motion.

"No—Wait. It was self-defense," he starts to tell the cop arresting me.

"We'll find that out," the man replies.

There are fans running in from the parking lot to see what the commotion is all about. I can hear them shouting and screaming at the calamity happening in front of them.

And I'm breaking with every ignore from Reed.

"Reed," I try again.

Andi appears in front of me, her hands on my face despite the police trying to pull her off. She leans forward and kisses me, and my heart swells at the taste of her.

"We'll come get you," she swears. "We'll meet you there. I won't leave you. This wasn't your fault—"

"I love you," I tell her.

It's just loud enough that she can hear me, and she swallows as a tear falls down her face.

"Go to the hospital," I continue before she can reply.

Because I don't care if she's ready to say it.

I love her, and no matter what happens right now, I need her to know it.

"Go. You're hurt. Get checked out," I nearly beg.

"What about you? You've been stabbed, Maddox."

"I'll be fine," I say.

The cop is pulling me away.

She grabs my face and kisses me again, her tears mixing with mine, and when she pulls back, I hear her whisper, "I love you."

And I think I could die right now and be perfectly okay with it.

Reed appears at my side.

"Hang on," Reed yells. "Wait—*you can't take him!* It was self-defense. The creep was trying to rape and kidnap my sister—" I don't hear what the cop says. He passes me off to another cop as a paramedic ushers Andi to an ambulance. The medic wraps a blanket over her shoulders. The woman holding my wrists says something about the hospital for myself..

I barely hear her.

Andi is safe.

Reed stops running after us and finally meets my eyes.

"I trust you," he says.

It's the last thing I hear before the cop hoists me up into the arms of a paramedic, and then clamors inside the ambulance after me.

EPILOGUE
MADDOX

It's been a little over a year since I was stuffed into the back of an ambulance and interrogated for murdering Andi's ex-boyfriend.

With as many witnesses as there were around us at the concert, I got off on self-defense. The cops dismissed the charges after only a week—the amount of time it took them to interview everyone who came forward to tell them how they'd seen the asshole dragging Andi in the parking lot and beating her. Initially, they thought I'd done it because Adam had been the one trying to expose me.

However, the number of witnesses was hard to refute. Not to mention the camera on the corner of the building in the back that showed everything.

Andi and the band visited me every day in jail, and every morning, I could hear the slew of fans outside chanting for my release.

Since the story hit news outlets, our popularity has skyrocketed. Concert tickets are selling out faster than before—I guess the notion that I'd murdered a man in defense of the woman I'm in love with spoke volumes.

"Stop fidgeting," Reed says beside me. "You're making me nervous."

"If I knew how, I would," I reply.

Because I can't. I'm all jitters and nerves. I haven't seen

Andi since September.

It's just three days from Christmas. Zeb and Bonnie took separate planes to see their families in New York and Hawaii.

We have the next ten days off until a New Year's show at the hometown stadium.

She flew into New York in September when she had a few days off. However, that's the last I've seen her other than our video dates. As much as I want her on the tour, we decided—along with management—that it was best to keep the band separate from what we are.

And what we are is fucking amazing.

She's the first person I talk to when I wake up and the last voice I hear before I fall asleep. I still look at her every day and wonder how I got so lucky to have her.

Reed is still adjusting, though he's getting better with it.

His main stipulation was not to make out in front of him, which we were happy to oblige with.

Andi still has her job with Heartless. Upper management suspended her with pay for a month while the press settled down. We stayed at the Matthews's for a few more weeks, hiding securely from media until Heartless felt it safe enough for Young Decay to go back on tour.

We'd had to go to her supervisors together with our relationship. Our plea was enough for them to trust Andi again, and she was placed back on photographing the local indie gigs that she enjoys.

I crack my knuckles as I stare at the terminal hallway in anticipation of her coming down at any moment. I debate walking around the airport again.

The nerves are too much.

I should have taken another gummy.

Stuffing my hands in my pockets, I glance over to the video Reed is watching on his phone, and when I realize what it is, I shove him in his side.

"What?" Reed asks.

"The fuck are you watching that again for?" I ask, jerking my chin to the video.

A grin slides onto Reed's lips. "It's nice seeing your face in proper lighting," he says, and I scoff.

I eye him sideways before glancing down at the video. "Let me see it," I say with a curl of my fingers.

Reed backs away. "What—why?"

"Because I haven't watched it, yet," I admit.

Reed's brows raise. "You haven't watched… Fuck." He takes out one of his earbuds and hands it to me, then holds the phone between us so I can see the video.

It's a podcast interview we did once I was in the clear with legal, and the madness had died down some. The record company left it entirely up to me whether I wanted to do the show, mask or no mask. Everyone had obviously seen the mugshot already, yet something about having the mask off in the studio was strangely foreign.

"—here with Young Decay, and, I think this is an exclusive—the real Mads Tourning, everyone," the podcast host, Amanda, says, her face all grins as she looks me over. "No mask today."

Reed and Zeb clap me on the shoulder and shake me. The podcaster claps her hands. Bonnie makes a celebratory noise.

"How does it feel without it?" Amanda asks.

I huff and nervously scratch my beard. "I feel fucking naked," I admit, much to their amusement.

"Now, just to clarify, we did not request this," Amanda says. "We have not put any pressure whatsoever on him to come on without it. But we're very, very excited to actually see you in the flesh. Though, I have to say. I love your mask."

I hold it up from my pocket. "I can put it on," I say.

Reed and Zeb reach over one another and try to grab it out of my hands, though I dodge them easily.

"I mean, if you're tired of seeing my face already—"

"No, no." Amanda chuckles. "I don't think any of us will tire of seeing this face." She clears her throat and suggestively raises her brows, making the rest of us laugh as she taps her cards on the table. "So, tour. You're wrapping up the international leg tonight here in London. Now, these dates were pushed back a few months. How does it feel being back on the road?"

"It's insane," Bonnie answers. "International shows are always a wild vibe."

"You were in Europe before a few years back, weren't you?" Amanda asks.

I tune out the next minute or so of the interview. I was so nervous about it, thinking she would focus on the trial or ask a lot of questions about that night. However, Amanda had been great. She didn't make any more comments about my being sans mask—even if I ended up putting it back on when we left the studio.

"Ah, fuck," Reed grunts when he looks up.

The sound of his disapproval makes me frown and pull the earbud out of my ear. "What's up?" I ask as he pulls his beanie down further as if it will hide his eyes.

Reed jerks his chin toward a woman exiting the terminal, a gaggle of photographers and fans swarming around her as she pauses to sign a few autographs.

I almost laugh. I know her.

"You're still pissed about her?" I ask him. "It was one interview."

Reed chews the inside of his mouth, his stark blue eyes never leaving the actress. "One interview is enough."

I grin at his annoyance. "Who knew one comment would have your panties in a fucking twist."

"How are you not pissed about it?" Reed asks.

"I have better things to be in a knot about," I reply. "And she said she liked me."

"Yeah." Reed scoffs, a pout on his lips. "She didn't say *you* looked like the emo member of a boy band."

I snort. "I mean…" My brows raise as I step back and look him over—the skinny black pants, hoodie, and shaggy hair sticking out from beneath the beanie.

Reed pushes me sideways, and I laugh as I grab my stomach.

"Who fucking cares what she thinks?" I ask him. "Maybe you should invite her to a concert. Show her you're the furthest thing from some pop star."

"Yeah, maybe."

"Fuck her senseless after," I suggest.

Reed's eyes shift my way before he's glaring at her again, and this time, the actress's gaze lifts to find him staring at her. It's a short exchange, barely more than a blink, and yet I swear I see her eyes roll when she turns away from us.

Reed gapes at me in disbelief. "Did you see that?"

I try to hold my lips together. I try to keep my amusement in check.

Regardless, he's so bent out of shape about this girl that I burst into laughter before I can stop myself.

Reed flips me off, looking utterly annoyed about his own frustrations.

"Suck my dick, Mads," Reed grunts.

I double over and catch myself on my knees as I try to contain my hysterics. Even still, I haven't laughed this hard in a long time, and for some reason, I can't hold it in.

"Now, that is a noise I don't hear often enough."

My heart skips at the sound of Andi's voice. It sobers me slightly, and I wipe the tears from my eyes as I finally straighten and look down the walk where I heard her voice.

My entire body caves upon seeing her. She has her hair pulled up, her freshly cut bangs down, and she's wearing one of my hoodies, ripped leggings, and Vans. Our eyes meet, and I feel myself falter beneath her gleaming stare.

I didn't know love could feel like this.

I didn't know that it could consume me, yet still feel as if I need her more. I didn't know anything could be this achingly blissful.

My tongue darts over my lips, and I press my hands to my knees again, the restless ache of being so close to touching her causing my breaths to shorten.

I can't keep the stupid fucking grin off my lips.

"I'm about to make out with your sister," I tell Reed. "I'm giving you the courtesy of a heads up."

Reed groans. "Yeah, fine. Go get her," he concedes.

Andi drops her bag and darts across the space, an almost skip in her steps that makes me laugh.

I need her in my arms.

Now.

"I'll just be simmering in my loneliness," Reed calls out.

Andi reaches my open arms and jumps into them. It sends us staggering off balance, and I catch us with a spin. Her headphones are blaring a song that makes me smile more than a second before.

Fuck, she still smells like that orange body wash—even though she's been on a six-hour plane ride.

When her feet hit the ground and we're stable, I grin at her briefly before grasping her neck with both hands and kissing her.

I've fucking missed kissing her.

Our kiss is deliberate and haunting. It's as obsessive as we are with one another.

I don't think I'll stop kissing her this week.

We only part when neither of us can breathe, when it's becoming so much that if we continue, we'll end up in the family bathroom while Reed keeps an annoyed lookout.

The smile she gives me when we part is just as addicting.

Her forehead leans against mine as we slow, fingers in my beard.

"This is still so weird," she says about my not wearing the mask.

"Yeah?" I kiss her again. "It's weird for me, too."

"Hey—can we go get something to eat?" Reed calls out to us.

We ignore him.

I take Andi's left hand in mine and turn it to where I can see the inside of her ring finger, and the butterflies swarm inside me when I see the tattoo there.

We may not be married, yet that didn't stop us from having 'til Death' tattooed on the inside of our left ring fingers.

Yet, the tattoo I love most is the anatomical heart on my chest with her hand wrapped around it.

It's the deal we made when I told her I wanted my handprint tattooed on her throat, and while that placement didn't work out, my handprint is on her hip instead.

A compromise I was happily willing to settle for.

I lean in and kiss her forehead, prompting her to smile at me again.

"Hey, beautiful," I whisper.

"I booked us a hotel after Christmas until New Year's," she says. "And I brought a few surprises," she adds, a wicked glint in her eyes.

"Oh, yeah?" I wrap my arm around her shoulders. "What did you bring us?"

"Something red. Possibly lace. Maybe leather." Her brows raise, and I have to kiss her again.

"Starving brother over here," Reed calls out.

Andi gives him a sideways glare. "You are ridiculous. Do you know that?"

Reed beams and holds out his arms. "I don't get a hug?" he

asks.

Andi shakes her head and hauls away from me.

And as she embraces her brother in a tight hug, I press my hands into my pockets. My finger hits the cold, circular band that's been burning a hole in these jeans for what feels like months, even if Reed and I only found it yesterday after a few weeks of searching.

God, I hope she likes it.

Reed gives me a poignant stare over Andi's shoulder, brows raising like he wants me to get down on one knee right there.

I answer with the slightest shift of my head.

Not here.

Not in public like this.

I'll ask her later when we're alone and spent, and I can celebrate with her in a way that doesn't include a long cab ride home and cameras threatening to swarm around us.

Andi faces me again, and I inhale the deepest breath I've taken in a while.

Music may be my savior, but she's my fucking keeper.

Fuck everything that says she shouldn't be.

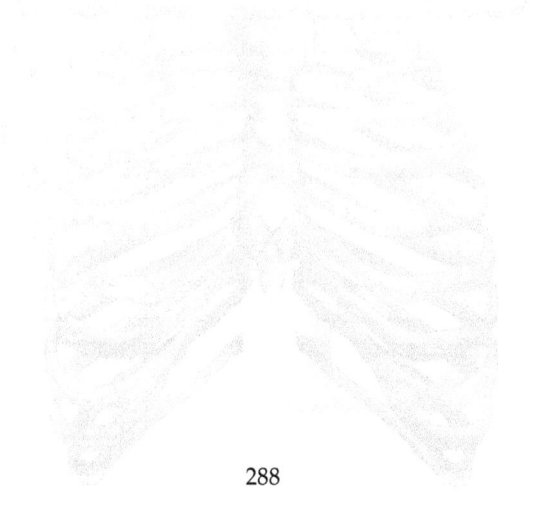

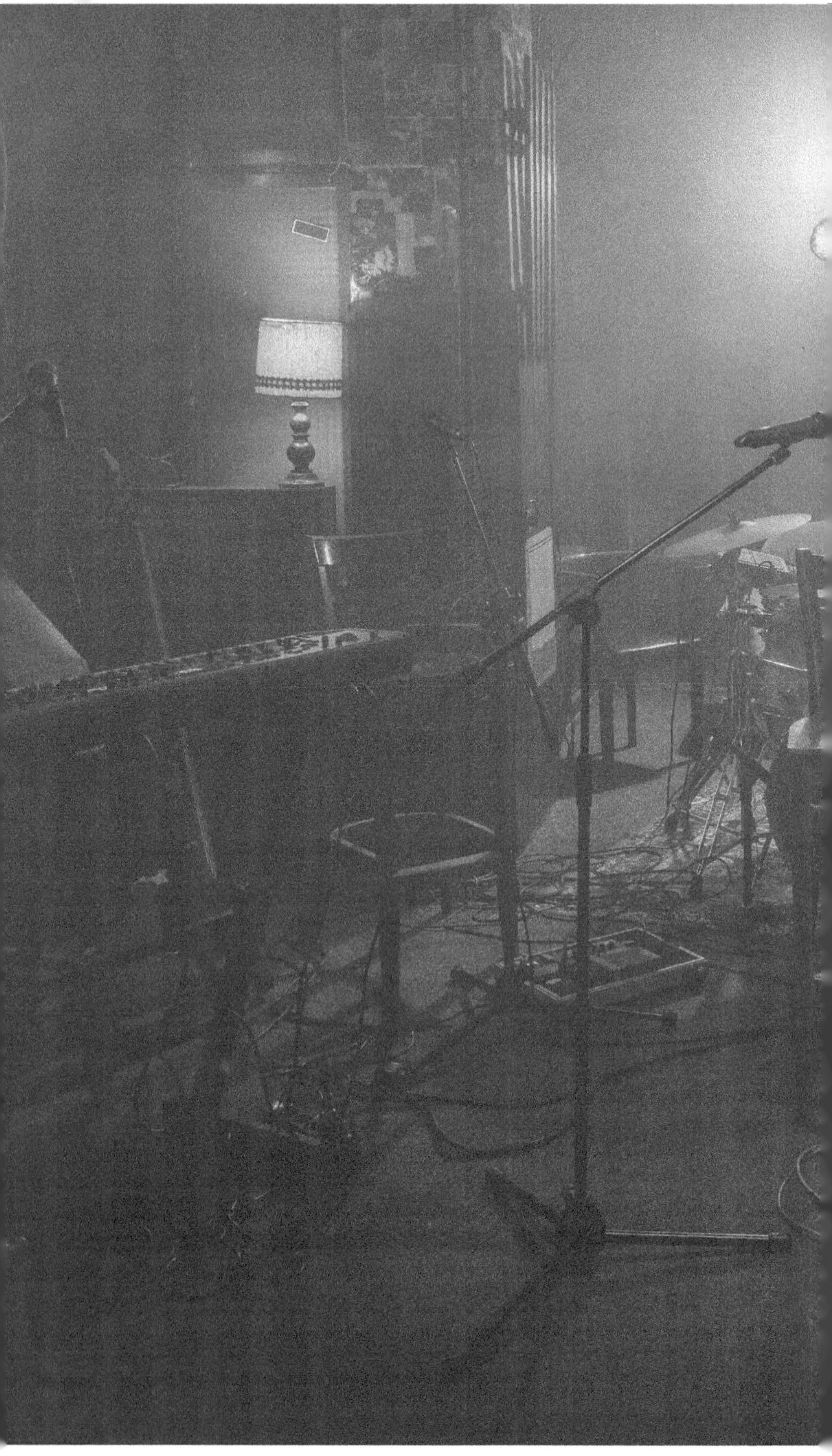

Acknowledgments

So, this was as much a surprise to me as it was to you.

I never meant to write this story, and for some reason, those seem to be the stories I cling to the most. Maddox and Andi now hold a part of me that I didn't know I needed held.

I hope you loved them as much as I do.

I have a few amazing people to thank personally, including Kay, Alexis, and Emily for always being on board to read anything I throw at them, and especially Emily for being so amazing and editing this one for me. Thank you to Kay for being a genius and coming up with band names when I was on the struggle bus—and Hallie for helping us choose which one to go with!

To my family for being amazing with support as always, I love you all.

To all the ARC readers, influencers, and more who read this book and spread love for it, THANK YOU! I will say it again and again, I cannot do this without you.

And to anyone I missed, just know how much I appreciate and love you all.

Rock on, bitches.

Oh, and Reed is up next with his story.

He's very excited.

Other Works by
Jack Whitney

Dead Moons Rising
Book One in the Honest Scrolls Series

Flames of Promise
Book Two in the Honest Scrolls Series

The Gathering
An Honest Scrolls Novella

Betrayal of Kings
Book Three in the Honest Scrolls series
Coming January 2024

Sweet Girl
A Cupid Novella

Finding You
A Sweet Girl Novel

Ballad of Nightmares
Book One in the Nightmares Duology

Hymn of Shadows
Book Two in the Nightmares Duology
Coming Fall 2024

Anyone And You
An autumn erotica novella

Break The Glass
A Blood Mary inspired novella

MADNESS
A Young Decay Novel

CHAOS
A Young Decay Novel
Coming Summer 2024

About The Author

Jack Whitney is an adult dark fantasy and romance author out of North Carolina, US.
You can usually find her playing in dark and strange worlds. Her characters are always in charge.
She is fueled by coffee, whiskey, and shadow daydreams. If you're reading her books, they probably came with a warning label.

Welcome to the Nightmare of Ravens.

Jack also feels very weird about writing bios because she's not sure what you want to know.
She is almost always stalking social media and procrastinating, so if you would like to find her to ask more questions, please feel free.
@Jack.Whitney.Writer

Milton Keynes UK
Ingram Content Group UK Ltd.
UKHW020828051224
3433UKWH00045B/572

9 798985 508895